*For Joe – who first convinced me that words really
can have power – then proved it with a late-night
lamppost run. I owe you, old man.*

1

The key chittered around the lock, tapping out an erratic beat that echoed down the stairwell. He cursed under his breath, wrapped his right hand around his left to steady it and tried again. Finally got the key in the lock, heard the click, hissed as he turned the door handle and a flash of pain lanced up his arm. Shouldered his way into the flat and kicked the door shut behind him, taking a moment to make sure it was securely locked. Threading the chain only took three attempts.

He stood in the dark and fought to slow his breath, stop the sour tingle of adrenalin that made it feel as though his lungs were on fire and his heart was about to explode from his chest. Forced himself to pause, listen to the quiet. The ticking of a cooling radiator; the faint, almost comforting swish of traffic from the main road. Tried to soak it in, let it calm him, stop the trembling that hit him like aftershocks from a quake. The bag in his hand suddenly felt intolerably heavy, and he dropped it onto the small chest of drawers that sat below the coat rack. He stared at it, felt the rage begin to snarl and unfurl in the back of his mind again. That sudden, insatiable need – no, *hunger* – to lash out, act. Take revenge.

He remembered the voice. Smug, arrogant, cultured. The world was his, everyone in it merely there to do his bidding. *I think you'll find this very, ah, interesting. Very educational. Smile! I'm about to make your dream come true.*

Bastard. Fucking bastard.

He walked towards the bathroom, a stumbling lurch on legs that felt heavy and alien, partly from the spent adrenalin, partly from the effort of the kicks he'd delivered. He hadn't meant to, he told himself as he remembered the meaty thud of his foot connecting with yielding muscle and fat; his victim lying on the floor, belching a hacking grunt as the need to breathe and the agony it caused waged a war in his shattered torso. He felt his stomach lurch and he staggered for the toilet, his wretch a silent scream as ropey, burning bile splashed into the bowl.

Standing slowly, he turned to the sink. A face he didn't recognise looked back at him from the mirror. Eyes sunken into dark pits, glittering with a feverish, manic look that made his stomach give another sickening turn. Skin grey and sallow, the colour of old concrete blocks left out in the rain too long. His hair stood up in jagged spikes, like an experiment in Eighties backcombing that had gone tragically wrong. His cheekbones, which were always prominent, threatened to burst through his skin. To test the theory, he pulled his face into what should have been a smile, producing only an empty leer that exposed teeth streaked with blood from the bites he had sunk into his bottom lip. Otherwise, his face was untouched, showing no trace of what had happened. He felt a savage stab of pride at that. His attack had been so sudden, ferocious and, yes, out of character, that the bastard hadn't even been able to land a blow on him. He knew he should feel shame about that. Wondered what it said about him that he didn't.

The least of his problems.

He stripped stiffly, his clothes a sweaty, fetid bundle on the floor, then stepped into the shower. Turned it up as hot as he could bear and stuck his head under the showerhead, hoping the hissing static of the water would drown out the sound of his blows raining down, the pathetic, mewling pleas to "stop, just stop, please, I was wrong, I know I was wrong". It didn't work.

The soap stung his bruised and cut knuckles, cold agony against the heat of the water. He lashed out, driving his fist against the tiles, a monstrous bolt of pain raging up from his hand all the way to his shoulder. He drove his fist forward again, smears of blood standing out against the sterile white of the tiles.

When he couldn't stand to be under the water any longer he shut the shower off and stepped out, avoiding the mirror as he reached for a towel. Scooped up his clothes and carried them to the bedroom, picking out the flash drive from his jeans pocket. He turned it around in his fingers. It was a small piece of black and grey plastic, about half the size of a pack of chewing gum. An everyday item – he must have a dozen of them himself, filled with stories and research and pictures. But he knew the truth about this one. It may have looked like just another flash drive, but it wasn't.

It was a bomb. An armed one. And when it went off, it would destroy the lives of everyone around it.

He headed for the living room, stopping in the hall to pick up the bag, which contained a laptop, and then detouring via the kitchen. Sat down on the couch, laying the bag on the coffee table in front of him along with a glass, joining a bottle of Jameson that was already there. He was tightening his hand around the neck to unscrew the bottle when he stopped, considered. Juggled the bottle to his other hand and twisted with his right hand instead. Better. No pain, just the awkwardness of unfamiliarity.

He closed his eyes for a second, remembering what had happened all those months ago: another night of violence and pain. He could still feel Diane Pearson's foot stomping down on his hand, the sound of his bones snapping and grinding together. He lifted his left hand and looked at it now. The scars were almost healed, the bones knitted together with the help of surgery and steel pins. But the pain lingered deep in his bones, a gnawing ache that no whisky or painkiller could reach. He flexed his fingers slowly, then tightened his hand into a fist as hard as he could, slow waves of pins and needles washing from the tips of his fingers and up his wrist to his elbow. Trapped nerves due to the break and the way his arm had twisted when his hand had been stamped on; the doctors had said he was lucky not to have any loss of sensation or motor control.

He snorted at that. Lucky. Right.

He poured a large measure into the glass, paused then topped it up. Lifted the glass to his lips, close enough to feel the fumes nip at his eyes, when he heard the voice. The voice he always heard. The voice he hated. The voice he wanted to silence forever.

Don't fall into the bottle, it whispered.

"Go fuck yourself," he said aloud, downing half the glass in one acidic gulp.

He topped up the glass then sat back, considering the bag in front of him and the flash drive in his hand. It felt hot, heavy. Should he look at it again? *Could* he? Or should he just destroy it, forget he'd ever seen it? But if he did that, how would he know that it was one of a kind? That his victim had been telling the truth and what was on it existed there and only there? His mind turned it over and over again; whirling and sparking like a Catherine wheel. He swallowed more whisky then made a decision. There was nothing else for it, he would have to look at it again, see what else he could find, if anything.

He just hoped he could be forgiven for doing it.

He was reaching for the laptop bag when the buzzer went, making him start. His head jerked towards the living room door, eyes wide, as if he could see the answers to his questions through the door.

Had he come for a rematch? To retrieve his property? Sent his pals to even the odds? Didn't matter, the answer would be the same.

Downing the last of the whisky in a gulp, he grabbed the bottle by the neck as though it was a club and headed for the door. He imagined swinging the bottle at the first head that appeared as he opened the door. Felt a tickle of revulsion at the back of his throat as he realised he was eager to find out what sound it would make as it shattered over his victim's skull. He lifted the wall-mounted security phone, pressed the button that activated the CCTV camera. He stopped dead, the whisky curdling and giving an oily

4

roll in his stomach as shock and panic shot through him in a stuttering electric current.

She stood framed in the small, black-and-white screen, glancing nervously about. Her arms were crossed over her chest tightly as she rocked from side to side. When she looked straight at the camera, he was sure he saw the glint of tears on her cheeks.

Fucking bastard. He had told her. Everything. His final revenge. And now she was here. For what? To confront him? To take the flash drive? To ask him what the hell he had been thinking? Arrest him?

He pressed the talk button with a shaking finger, struggled to keep his voice neutral. His lips were numb, his tongue a dead slug in his mouth.

"Susie? It's late. What's…"

"Doug, I, ah… Look, I'm sorry it's late, but can I come up please? I really need to talk to you." Her voice was little more than a whisper, fragile and roughened by tears. His panic bled away, replaced by a dread that leached the warmth from his body.

"Sure," he said, buzzing the lock release. "Come on up."

He heard the main door to the tenement creak open then bang shut. Turned and dived back into the living room, grabbing the bag and stuffing it behind the sofa. He glanced at the flash drive, thought about hiding it, decided it was pointless. That was why she was here. She knew about that. When she knocked on the front door, he forced his breathing to return to normal, to ignore the hammering of his heart. Struggled to think of some first words, found there was nothing he could say but the obvious.

"Susie, I'm so sor…" he started as he swung the door open.

She didn't so much walk into the flat but fall into it, grasping for him as she did. Wrapped her arms around him, buried her head into his chest and sobbed. Doug felt as though the room was spinning around him. Too much was happening too quickly. Why was she here? What did she know? Who had told her? He blinked, bit down on his lip and tried to concentrate as he returned her rough hug, ignoring the pain in his hand and arm as he held her close and let her cry against him.

He felt the sobbing ease, her arms loosening and pushing him away. She took a half-step back, looked at him hard, something halfway between anger and apology in her grey-green eyes. He saw her jaw tighten, knew only too well that it meant she was chewing on unpleasant words.

"Sorry," she said, wiping a pale hand across her eyes. "It's just that, well…" She paused, the words she was grasping for as elusive as smoke. "Sorry," she said again, her voice hardening as she fought to project the illusion of control. Typical cop trick. Command every situation. "Look, I know it's late, if this is a bad time? If Rebecca…?" She let the sentence linger in the air, made a show of looking over his shoulder and back into the flat.

He gave his head an abrupt shake. "Becky's not here," he said. "Look, Susie, what's…?"

She held up a hand as she moved past him, heading for the living room. He tried to get in front of her, double-check he hadn't missed anything, but it was impossible. When Susie set her mind on something, it was easier just to get out of the way. She sat on the sofa he'd stuffed the laptop behind, hunched forward, arms hanging between her knees. Doug could see that the flash drive was directly in her line of sight; he felt a cold sting of shame as a memory darted across his mind.

Hair tousled, cheeks flushed. The thin sheen of sweat on her naked skin. The sheet a twist of white cotton, pulled down below her stomach, revealing…

He blinked, forced the image back and sat down opposite her, the coffee table a barrier between them, the bomb sitting unexploded in no-man's-land.

She looked up at him, a small, rueful smile twitching at her lips as she nodded to the whisky bottle. "Got a glass?"

What the fuck? He wanted to grab her, scream into her face, ask her what was going on. Was this a game? A trap? Get him to tell her what he knew first? Instead, he gestured to the glass sitting in front of her, the one he had been using only a moment ago.

"Use that one, I've got another one here," he said, reaching down for the glass that sat abandoned on the carpet. He couldn't remember leaving it there, remembered only waking in the chair with a start at 4am the morning before, heart hammering, the same nightmare he'd been having for months seared into his thoughts.

She nodded, pulled the bottle and glass to her. Poured a measure that was at least a quad and drained half the glass. She took a moment to consider it as the colour rose in her cheeks and her eyes shimmered with fresh tears. When she spoke, her voice was flat and dead, as cold as graveyard dirt.

"He's dead," she said. "Third Degree called me about half an hour ago, wanted me to hear before… well, before you know…"

Doug felt the room give a lurch. "What?" he said, his own voice little more than a cracked whisper. "Who? Who's dead? Susie, what the hell is going on?"

She fixed him with a look he had never seen before. Cold, broken; rage and heartbreak flitting across her eyes like a fast-moving weather front. "Paul Redmonds," she said finally, nodding slowly as if confirming it to herself. "You remember him? Best known for shagging a stupid young detective at a Christmas party in Glasgow?" Her voice hardened, eyes locking with his. "You should remember that story at least, Doug. After all, it's how we met."

Doug sat in his chair, pinned. He couldn't talk, fought to breathe. Panic and terror raged inside him, churning like the sea in a hurricane.

Paul Redmonds. Former Assistant Chief Superintendent Paul Redmonds. Recently retired, now under investigation for alleged links to one of Edinburgh's biggest gangsters. Paul Redmonds, the married man who had been the focus of the gossip columns a few years ago when he had a one-night stand with a young DS at the police Christmas party in Glasgow. Hadn't taken long for Doug to be put on the story and find the details and who the DS was – she was sitting across from him now. Not the best way to start a friendship, but somehow it had worked for them. Most of the time.

Paul Redmonds, who Doug had seen only an hour before, lying in front of him, begging him to stop as he drove kick after kick after kick into his guts.

Paul Redmonds, whose stolen laptop was wedged less than a foot behind Susie's back.

Paul Redmonds. The man Doug McGregor had just killed.

2

The generator chugged and spluttered, the sound abrupt and harsh in the streetlight-stained hush of the early morning before dawn, the spotlights it powered dimming and brightening in time with the grunts of the engine. In the centre of the spotlights, the SOCOs' tent covered most of Paul Redmonds' driveway, the officers' shadows playing across the surface of the tent like circus mimes as they went about their work, dancing around the silhouette of a car.

DCI Jason "Third Degree" Burns stood at the foot of the driveway, watching them as the tent rippled in the gentle breeze. He thought about the car as he glanced down at the heap of rubble that was once a low dividing wall between Redmonds' driveway and his neighbour's property. It was a high-end BMW, less than a year old, low and aggressive and sleek, all sweeping lines and fluid curves that gave the impression of speed and grace. At least it had been, before tonight. Now the car told a different story. An uglier one. The front wing that had hit the wall was a frozen sneer of metal, the raw steel standing out against what remained of the gloss-black paint that surrounded it, one headlight hanging down over the front bumper like an eyeball dangling by a single nerve.

Burns looked up from the rubble and surveyed the wider scene beyond the police tape that cordoned off most of Lomond Road. Saw the familiar twitch of curtains at what should have been an hour of rest. The houses were semi-detached sandstone and granite villas barricaded behind neatly clipped hedges. Mature trees whispered in the breeze, their leaves shimmering like slivers of copper in the dull amber glow of the streetlights. It was a long time since he'd been in Trinity. It was typical of Edinburgh's more well-heeled suburbs: tasteful, reserved, a study in the quiet affluence that the city did so well. It wasn't the most expensive part of the city, but still, it wasn't bad on a former copper's wages.

And that was part of the problem, wasn't it?

The rumours had started six months ago, shortly after a raid on a townhouse in the New Town revealed it to be a high-class brothel frequented by some of Edinburgh's most well-kent faces. The raid had been a textbook operation; after an anonymous tip-off, the property had been placed under surveillance, the proper suspicions confirmed and the warrants secured. Job done, and the press team was more than happy to use the story to show off Police Scotland's ruthless efficiency and enviable crime detection skills, especially after some of the other headlines they had been forced to deal with recently.

Unfortunately, the happy ending was soured slightly when one of the brothel's clients was dragged from the arms of his companion with a light frosting of white powder around his nose and a freezer bag full of class-A drugs in his holdall. It got worse when one of the officers attending recognised the client in question as the former Assistant Chief Super on the old Lothian and Borders Police who took early retirement and a tidy lump sum when the eight regional forces combined into Police Scotland. The order came down quickly from on high, no doubt Redmonds' ex-wife – herself a former Assistant Chief Super and, from what Burns recalled from one brief meeting, a real ice queen – calling in a favour with the Chief Constable. The media team could release the story about the raid, but under no circumstances was Redmonds' presence to be mentioned or even alluded to. So far, so routine. After all, it wasn't the first time that a former copper's involvement in an embarrassing case was quietly forgotten – it was almost expected, favours called in and favours due, police officers looking after each other, even after the warrant cards had been handed in.

But then the questions started. Mostly from that smug little shite Doug McGregor, who seemed to have a talent for knowing what you didn't want him to. Instead of doing what most papers and news sites would do these days and just regurgitating the press release about the raid, McGregor actually acted like a journalist and went digging. It didn't take him long to trace the brothel back to the operations of one of Edinburgh's biggest and most feared hardmen, Dessie Banks. Banks had been a nightmare looming over Edinburgh for years, with long, skeletal fingers that stretched into murder, prostitution, protection rackets, loan sharking and a dozen other illegal activities. Burns had seen the wreckage he had left strewn in his wake, the ruined lives and the shattered families, and he wanted Banks, badly. So badly, he had even agreed to take the promotion to DCI as it would give him more freedom to assign workloads and make sure the Banks investigation didn't die a quiet death.

But despite all that, he'd never been able to get a proper glimpse behind the curtain and into Banks' world. Until the brothel raid. McGregor had established the link with Banks; and Redmonds, who'd never exactly been a poster boy for Police Scotland, was found there with a fat wad of cash. Coincidence? Or something more?

Burns had started looking for potential links between the two. There wasn't much to find at first, but there were enough rumours that Banks had a few officers on the payroll to keep him digging.

And then there was the call tonight. It had come in at 3.47am, routed to the Gayfield Square CID hub from the main call-handling centre out at Bilston in Midlothian. Redmonds' neighbour – a small, harassed-looking woman with too-pale skin and huge, glittering dark eyes – had been woken by the sound of Redmonds' car hitting the dividing wall. She'd rushed to check if he was okay then spotted the blood trailing from the car to the house, and the bloody smear arced across the front door like a perverted rainbow.

"I just couldn't go in," she had said in a small, trembling voice as she shook her head slowly, dark eyes unblinking. "All that blood." She had looked up at Burns then, panicked. "I just couldn't. So I phoned you. But if I'd gone in, could I have helped him?"

Burns reassured her that she had done the right thing by staying away from the house and just calling the police. And it was the right thing to do. Never entering a potentially dangerous situation was rule number one; the fight or flight response whittled down to police mantra. That didn't mean he had to like it though.

The officers who had been dispatched to the scene found Redmonds in the living room, lying in a widening pool of his own blood. While the cause of death had yet to be established, from the state of the body it was obvious he had been subjected to a severe beating before he had staggered home to die.

But who, Burns thought, had beaten him so brutally? And why? And if it was somehow linked to Dessie Banks, why had he let him go after the initial attack? Why not just kill him and dump the body quietly?

Burns sighed as he rummaged in his pockets and produced a packet of cigarettes. He pulled one from the packet then started to strip it slowly, dumping small clots of tobacco into his mouth and starting to chew. Once the duty Detective Sergeant learned who the probable victim was, he had called Burns. It was, on the face of it, the sensible thing to do – notify a senior officer about a case that would no doubt get very public very quickly – but it was also a royal pain in the bollocks for Burns. Now that he was attached to the case, the shit would flow straight down from the high heidyins to him. Which is why he had called Drummond to tell her what had happened and what was likely coming next. He may not like her links to that shite McGregor, but she was one of his officers, with the makings of a good detective, and he wanted to prepare her for the shitstorm that was undoubtedly coming her way.

3

The shakes started the moment he swung the door shut on Susie: great, crashing spasms that wracked Doug's body and made it almost impossible to stand. He closed his eyes and leaned against the front door, fighting back the tears that tore at his eyelids, white-hot and demanding to be unleashed. He wanted to scream out, knew that if he started, he would never stop.

Redmonds. Dead. The thought was a shriek in his mind, a clarion call to every nightmare and scuttling fear, sending them swarming across his thoughts, a screaming static of terror.

Redmonds. Dead. And he had killed him. He imagined what would happen when Susie found out, what she would think when she realised she had sat with her former lover's killer and asked him for support and help. And what about his parents? His boss, Walter? His friend, Hal?

Jesus, and Becky. When she found out, it would destroy her. And her career.

Fuck.

He saw the trial, standing in the dock, all the people he had failed staring at him from the public gallery, felt their anger and hatred and disappointment. Heard the judge sentence him to twenty-five years in a tone that was at once sanctimonious and bored, felt the security guards' rough hands on him as he was led away, heard the clang of the cell door as it swung shut. It sounded like Redmonds' screams for mercy.

He took a deep breath, bit down on his lip again, hard enough to reopen the wound from earlier in the night. Forced himself to push down the panic. To remember what had set this nightmare in motion.

Think, Doug. For fuck's sake. Think.

His phone had started buzzing just before 1am, startling him from the drunken half-doze he had fallen into on the couch. He had flailed for it in a confused panic, wondering who it could be calling him at this time of night, knowing that no good news ever came in the small hours.

Didn't know then how right he was.

The screen showed a number he didn't know, but he hit *Answer* anyway.

"Hello?"

A brief pause on the line. And then a voice he didn't recognise.

"McGregor? Is that Douglas McGregor?" Cultured, controlled. The hard glint of cold fury only slightly thawed by the subtle drawl that told Doug whoever he was speaking to had been drinking.

"Doug," he corrected. "It's Doug. Who's this?"

Another pause. The sound of swallowing and a soft gasp. Whisky, Doug thought. Whoever was calling him was drinking whisky.

"We've not spoken before, McGregor," the voice said, whisky unable to blunt the contempt this time. "But you've been sticking your nose into my business for far too fucking long. But that's going to end. Tonight. Understood?"

Doug smiled, reached for his own glass. "I'm sorry, didn't realise I had a new editor at the *Tribune* to tell me what stories I can and can't cover. Care to tell me your name, or is this going to be one of those anonymous rants I love so much?"

"We have a mutual acquaintance, McGregor. Though I'm guessing I know her better than you do. This is Paul Redmonds."

Doug's hand paused, the glass frozen halfway to his lips.

I know her better than you do.

He swallowed the fury down, took a breath, adopted a neutral tone.

"Mr Redmonds. Can't imagine why you'd be calling me at this hour. As I understand it, your evenings are usually more exciting than this. Care to comment?"

"Smart-arse wee prick," Redmonds spat. "Don't be cute, McGregor. I know you've been asking around about me, trying to put me at the scene of a recent brothel sting, trying to drag my name through the shit. I don't know who's been talking to you, but I've got a few ideas. Not that it matters. It ends. Now. Clear?"

"Not really," Doug said, swallowing the whisky in a gulp. It didn't burn as much as the rage churning in his guts. "Though since you've been good enough to call me and save me the effort of tracking you down, perhaps you'd like to comment on claims that you were lifted during the recent raid on the Falcon's Rest in Morningside, and given a free pass by former colleagues in order to save your ex-wife, who happens to sit on the Police Scotland board, the embarrassment of being linked to you for all the wrong reasons… again?"

Quiet at the other end of the line, almost long enough for Doug to think Redmonds had hung up on him. He was just about to end the call and hit *Redial* when he heard a sound that sent something cold scuttling down his spine. Redmonds was laughing. A slow, humourless hacking sound filled with sneering arrogance.

"You're a cocky wee bastard, aren't you?" he said as the laughter trickled away, dirty water gurgling down a drain. "But don't worry about that. We'll sort that out soon enough. You want a statement from me? Fine. But not on the phone. In person. Portobello, Edinburgh end, near the five-a-side pitches. Half an hour. If you've got the balls for it."

"It's not about balls, Redmonds," Doug said. "It's brains. Why should I meet you in a secluded location in the dead of night? What do you think I am, stupid? Or keen to get my head kicked in by an ex-copper with a grudge?"

Redmonds sighed patiently. "I'm not going to hurt you, McGregor. We're just going to talk. And I'm going to make your dream come true. Trust me on that. The Pitz. Thirty minutes. It'll change your life."

And then he had cut the call, leaving Doug sitting in a silence that was too loud to bear, his mind filled with questions. He should call Becky or someone, tell them what had happened. Let them be the voice of reason, talk him out of it.

He looked at the phone in his hand for a long moment. Then he went and got his car keys.

• • •

Portobello sits on the east coast, just on the border where Edinburgh gives way to East Lothian. It's a former fishing village, like its nearest neighbour, Musselburgh, where Doug lived. Unlike Musselburgh, Portobello also has a promenade that faces out to the Forth and across to Fife. Doug remembered being brought here with his parents as a kid, the cheap arcades filled with old slot machines and the usual array of rigged games. Not that he cared, he badgered his parents for change to play the games anyway, remembered an old *Star Wars* game that always drew crowds of kids who wanted to be Luke Skywalker, even if it was only for a minute or two. There was a playpark further up the promenade as well, a big one with slides and swings and a roundabout that Doug always wanted to try but never got the chance.

"That's where the girl was grabbed from," his mother had told him when he asked for what felt like the millionth time to be allowed to go and play. "That's where the bad man took her from. That's why you mustn't play there. It's tainted." It was only years later that Doug found out what his mum had meant. The playpark was where the serial killer and paedophile Robert Black snatched a five-year-old girl called Caroline Hogg.

The promenade had been refurbished over the years, an attempt made to rebrand it as "Edinburgh's Riviera". With the Edinburgh weather being what it was, Doug didn't think the French tourist board had much to worry about any time soon.

It only took ten minutes to drive to the five-a-side pitches Redmonds had spoken of. They were at the far end of the town heading back towards Edinburgh, tucked away down a narrow side street. He slid the car slowly to a halt, saw an achingly stylish BMW parked just ahead, the immaculate paintwork glistening in the streetlights. It was the only other car that was occupied.

He killed the engine, sat considering. It wasn't too late. He could start the car up again, take off, forget all this. It made more sense than meeting a potentially bent ex-cop in the dead of night with no witnesses.

But…

I'm going to make your dream come true, he had said.

Doug sighed. Took the key and got out of the car before he could change his mind. As he walked he flexed his hand slowly, trying to ease the pins and needles that were crawling up his arm, the price to be paid for holding his arm straight and gripping the steering wheel. But he was lucky. The doctors had told him so.

The interior light of the BMW came on as he approached, Redmonds unfolding himself from the car. He couldn't see him clearly in the gloom, but Doug knew the face well enough. Thick, dark hair, brown eyes that seemed black in the half-light. A nose that had been reset at least once, full lips with a small scar tracing a silvery line from his mouth and gently down the chin. He was a couple of inches taller than Doug and a lot wider everywhere else, especially around the gut. Retirement and scandal, it seemed, agreed with him.

"McGregor," he spat, taking a step forward and making Doug stop suddenly. "Glad you had the bollocks to show up."

"Look, Redmonds," Doug said, trying to sound calmer and more assertive than he felt, "can we just cut the shit and get on with this please? It's late, I've got stories to write…"

"Ah, yes, stories." Redmonds smiled, showing off dental work too perfect to be natural. "You are quite the storyteller, aren't you

McGregor? The work you did on Richard Buchan, and then that whole business with the Gulf War vet last year – what was his name?"

The roar of the gun. Blood and brains exploding from his temple in a crimson and grey torrent...

"Pearson," Doug said flatly. "Gavin Pearson."

"Yes, that was it. You do like your stories, don't you? Well, I've got one to tell you as well, though you may not like the ending."

"Look, if that's a threat…"

Redmonds grated out another mirthless laugh, smiled as he held up a hand. "No, no. You misunderstand me, McGregor. I don't give a shit who you've been speaking to about me, or what they've been saying. But if it makes you feel any better, I was at the Falcon's Rest that night. And you're not going to write a word about it."

It was Doug's turn to laugh. "And why's that? You going to deny we ever had this meeting? Say I made it all up? I'm not a muck-raking tabloid hack, you know Redmonds. I do have some credibility in this game."

Redmonds nodded. When he spoke, his voice oozed with a smug arrogance that made Doug want to scream. "Oh, I know that, McGregor. I did a little checking of my own. And I owe you some thanks, it would appear. For the way you looked after Susie and didn't print the story about our, ah…" – he leered at Doug, exposing those too-white teeth – "night together."

Doug took a step forward before he knew he was going to and Redmonds raised his hand again. "No need for that, McGregor, I'm trying to say I owe you. And I always pay my debts. So I'm going to make you a happy man. And then you're going to forget all about me."

Doug snorted. "Blackmail? You brought me here" – he gestured around the street, the blackened windows of the flats staring down at them – "to try and blackmail me? Well, thanks for nothing. But don't worry, the *Tribune*'s a family paper, the subs won't let me describe you as a 'fucking dickhead' when I write this up."

Redmonds' face twitched in a smile. "You don't understand," he said slowly, turning his chest away from Doug and reaching back into the open window of the BMW, moving in the slightly deliberate, over-exaggerated way that spoke of drinking earlier in the evening. Doug froze, expecting him to turn around with a weapon. Felt confusion when he saw Redmonds pull a slim laptop from a bag and place it on the roof of the car.

He beckoned to Doug. "Come on, McGregor," he said, pulling a small flash drive from his pocket, "I think you'll find this very, ah, interesting. Very educational. Smile! I'm about to make your dream come true."

Doug stepped forward warily, bunching his prickling hand into a fist. If Redmonds was going to try something, he wanted to be ready. Or as ready as he could be.

Redmonds hit the space bar on the laptop and the screen flared to life, almost blinding in the gloom of the street. He plugged the flash drive in and accessed it, smiling at Doug. "You see, McGregor," he said, nodding towards the screen, the smell of whisky heavy on his breath, "I promised I'd make your dream come true."

Doug glanced from Redmonds back at the screen, rooted to the spot. He felt as though he had been wired up to the mains and Redmonds had thrown the switch. The screen of the laptop seemed to pulse in front of him, what he was seeing burning into his mind. He looked back to Redmonds, his face a stark relief of light from the laptop and the shadows of the night.

Hair tousled, cheeks flushed. The thin sheen of sweat on her naked skin. The sheet a twist of white cotton, pulled down below her stomach, revealing...

Redmonds nodded slowly, glanced at the laptop. "Now do you see why you're not going to write a word about me, McGregor? Because if you do, this..." – he jutted his jaw at the laptop – "goes online. Now that would be a story, wouldn't it?"

Doug screwed his eyes shut, trying to think. Flexed his hand, felt the pain crawl up his wrist. Thoughts and memories crowded into his mind. Diane Pearson stamping on his hand, the pure savage glee in her face as she attacked him; of his boss being assassinated right in front of him in a spray of blood and shattered internal organs; of the betrayal by Harvey Robertson, the man he had thought of as a second father.

"So, Douglas, do we have a deal?"

Doug snapped his eyes open, saw Redmonds smiling down at him, smugly arrogant in his victory. And for an instant Doug saw another face, one that had worn the same look.

...Harvey...

He lashed out suddenly, catching Redmonds with a right hook to the temple that sent him staggering backwards, then lunged forward and hit him with a hard left, the agony exploding in his hand and racing up his arm as he felt Redmonds' cheek give under the force of the blow. Redmonds crashed to the ground, air and expletives forced out of him on impact. Doug snatched for the flash drive and turned to run as Redmonds got to his knees, lunging forward to stop him as he hawked back and spat blood and phlegm on the street in a viscous wad.

"You little FUCK!" he barked, still trying to catch his breath, the veneer of civility ripped away by the shock of violence. "I'll fucking end you for this. You and that fucking hoor, I swear I..."

Doug whirled round and, taking a step forward, kicked out at Redmonds as hard as he could, catching him in the face. He felt teeth splinter and snap against his shoe, Redmonds' head jerking back at an angle it was never meant to, the shock shuddering up Doug's leg.

And suddenly everything he was trying to suppress boiled out of him in a poisonous, fetid torrent. Doug closed in on Redmonds, mouth contorted in a silent scream, the tears and terror too big to come out. He kicked at him again, heard breath explode from his lungs in a gagging, choking cough, forcing him onto his back, trapped between Doug and the BMW. The image from the laptop rose up in Doug's mind and he stamped down on Redmonds.

"You twisted fuck," he snarled, the tears now hot and burning on his cheeks. "Fucking twisted CUNT!" He stamped down again and again, feeling muscles part and bones grind together under his foot. Felt his bile and hatred flare black and burning as his foot hit soft, yielding gut. Redmonds' cries for mercy – "Stop, just stop, please, I was wrong, I know I was wrong" – were discordant screeches in his ears, fuelling the rage that engulfed him. He stamped down again, losing his footing as he bounced off Redmonds' shoulder and staggered back, heaving for breath.

Doug looked up and took in what he had done, his lungs raw furnaces, senses slowly returning as the rage cooled. Saw not a monster but a small, broken man lying in front of him, ink-black blood oozing from his ruined face and glinting in the streetlights. He stepped forward, over the wreck of Redmonds, felt a guilty sting of relief as he heard him moan softly on the pavement. He scooped up the laptop in shaking hands, zipping it back into its bag then backed away slowly. Glanced around the street, no lights suddenly flaring on, no panicked shouts to "Call the polis, some guy's just kilt a man."

He got into his car, fumbled the key into the ignition and started it up, the sound like the Devil's roar in the charged aftermath of violence. He backed out of the sidestreet, barely suppressing the urge just to floor it and drive as fast as he could. Bore down on the steering wheel, ignoring the pain in his hand as he did so.

It was the least he deserved after this.

Doug made it back to the flat, managed to get in and changed before Susie had arrived to tell him that Redmonds was dead. She had stuck around for about an hour, the whisky slowly taking the edge off her shock, but going over and over the rumours and gossip about her that would resurface when Redmonds' death became public.

His death. At Doug's hands.

Doug shook his head. He was breathing when he had left him. And, from what Susie had said, he had been found at home, not in Portobello. So he had lived at least for a while.

Doug staggered to the living room. Pulled the laptop bag out from behind the sofa and laid it on the table beside the flash drive. This was what a man had died for. *What I killed him for*, he thought, and shuddered.

But he couldn't accept that. Yet. Yes, he had lost it. Beaten Redmonds badly. But killed him? He couldn't believe that. Wouldn't. Not yet anyway. It may only have been a guilty man's delusion but…

…but…

Doug picked up his mobile. It was a call he didn't want to make. But it was the only one he could.

Guilty or not. He had to know.

4

Rebecca Summers, one of Police Scotland's senior communications officers, glanced up at the clock on her office wall as her mobile began to ring, smiled slightly in spite of the indecent hour it showed. 5.17am. More than an hour since Burns had called to tell her about Paul Redmonds, the inevitable media feeding frenzy that was about to break on them and the possible backlash on Susie Drummond, who was not only a colleague but an old friend of hers. Rebecca had tried Susie after putting the phone down on Burns, wasn't totally surprised when the call went straight to voicemail.

5.17am. Before the Pearson mess last year, she would have bet on this call coming less than ten minutes after she had heard the news herself. But the Pearson case had left its mark on everyone. She picked up the phone, surprised that the thought of just declining the call flashed across her mind, then hit *Answer* anyway.

"Morning, Doug," she said. "I'm guessing you're not calling to tell me you've booked that weekend away you're always promising me?"

A brief pause on the line. This was new too. Being able to faze him, throw him off track. She wasn't sure she liked it.

"Ah, no, no, it's not. Sorry. Listen, Becky, I'm sorry to call so early, but Susie's just left and I'm guessing you've heard about Paul Redmonds by now..."

Susie's just left. So that explained the hour's delay. "And you thought you could get an early quote from me, get the jump on the press statement and a quick splash for the *Tribune*? Talk about making a girl feel special."

"No, it's not that, Becky. Just… ah, something that Susie said doesn't make sense to me. I, ah, I just wanted to see if there was anything you could tell me – see if I could help, is all."

Rebecca's eyes crept back to the clock. Too early for him to be drinking, surely. Still drunk from the night before? Or from a late few with Susie?

It had started at about the same time as he began rehab for the injuries to his hand – the quick nip after work, offering her wine and pouring himself a Jameson when he was cooking dinner. "Just a small one to take the edge off," he told her, holding up his wounded hand and flexing it stiffly for effect. But the moaning as he slept, the tossing and turning, his sweat stale and heavy with the scent of booze… it all told a different story. She hadn't asked him about it directly, thought he would come to her when he was ready. Wasn't so sure now.

"Doug," – she swallowed, picked her words carefully – "you okay? It's just that you sound a bit… ah, addled?"

A harsh bark down the phone, polite laughter made coarse by its forced use. "Me? Nah. Sorry, Becky, just been a long night. Didn't sleep well with the hand. And then Susie turned up at the door and, well, you know."

"Yeah, I guess I do," she said. But it was something else. There was a strain in his voice, a tension that she had only heard once before. The night he was driving to confront a killer. She shuddered slightly.

"Look, Doug, I'm not sure there's much I can tell you yet. On the record, I'll confirm to you that the body of a forty-nine-year-old male was found at his home in the Trinity area in the early hours of this morning. The identity is being withheld until next of kin have been informed which should" – she made a quick calculation in her head – "be in the next thirty minutes."

Rebecca paused, considered for a moment then plunged on. "Off the record, the press statement I'm working on now will confirm that the body is that of former Assistant Chief Superintendent

Paul Redmonds and yes, the death is being treated as suspicious. This is between us, Doug, but someone beat the living shit out of him."

"Has a cause of death been established?" Doug asked, his voice so cold and emotionless that Rebecca almost physically recoiled from the phone.

"No, not yet. Williams is rushing the post-mortem through, we should have preliminary findings in the next hour. Look, Doug, what's this about? What did Susie say that didn't make sense? Has this got something to do with what you're working on – the brothel sting?"

She felt the familiar unease in her stomach as she asked the question. Working in the Police Scotland press team and going out with the most inquisitive, well-connected crime reporter she had ever encountered wasn't the best of ideas, and it made for plenty of stilted silences and awkward conversations. "Call it the thrill of sleeping with the enemy," Doug had joked early in their relationship when the issue came up over a court case against an officer convicted of using excessive force in the apprehension of a drunken student up at Potterrow. They laughed about it at the time. Promised they wouldn't let work get in the way of their relationship or vice versa.

Rebecca was having trouble finding the humour in the joke now.

Doug's voice shook her from her thoughts, that same robotic drone chilling her. What was wrong with him?

"No, it's, ah, it's not that. Thanks, Becky, sorry for bothering you. I'll write it up for the first edition, make sure I double-check everything with the statement you issue on the wires when I do."

"Thanks, Doug. Look, sorry about the weekend away crack. Just a hell of a start to the day, and being somewhere other than here sounds even more appealing today."

Doug gave a bitter, humourless laugh. "You have no idea how true that is," he said.

"I'm going to be busy all morning, and we've got a press conference scheduled here at Fettes for 11am. But do you want to get a coffee and talk after it?"

"Yeah," he said, sounding distracted. "Sounds great. I'll see you at eleven. And Becky, if you hear anything from Williams, I'd really appreciate it if you let me know, okay? It's important."

"Yeah, no problem, Doug, I'll let you know." She knew there was no need, the timer was ticking on his calling her back to check up on her the moment she had mentioned that Williams was fast-tracking the post-mortem.

"Thanks, Becky. I owe you, again."

"And I will collect," she said automatically, finishing the exchange that was quickly becoming a cliché between them. She softened her voice, trying to drop the professional pretence for a second. "Look, Doug, I've got to go. But I'll see you at eleven, okay?

"Will do," he said, and, before she could say anything else, the line went dead. Not that there was anything left to say. Was there?

5

The exhaustion made Mark's eyes burn and his vision blur for an instant, the screen doubling then trebling in front of him. He lifted his glasses and rubbed at his face, hard, trying to wipe away the fatigue and the memory of what he had just done.

The call had come at just after 2am, his annoyance at the interruption to the *Game of Thrones* episode he was watching quickly dissipating as he read the caller ID. He answered quickly, felt the all-too-familiar shiver of tension tangle his guts into a cold, heavy knot. Kept his tone neutral, eyes fixed on the now-muted TV in front of him.

"Hello?"

When the caller spoke, his stomach gave an extra clench. The voice was the same as ever: cool, controlled, utterly commanding. But beneath it, lurking in the raised tone and the faster-than-normal speech, he heard something new, something he had thought the caller incapable of.

Concern.

"I need you to check for breaches," the voice said. "Any unauthorised access or withdrawals, anything at all out of the ordinary. If there is, I need to know about it, understood?"

On the screen, a man was run through with a sword, blood exploding from the wound as he sank to his knees. He paused the image, concentrated on it.

"Understood," Mark said, his jaw tight. "What's the timescale?"

"Most probably in the last twelve hours, but better check the full day just to be sure. I'll call you back in forty minutes. And

Mark," – the voice slowed to its more normal speed, the tone as dark as the blood on the screen – "be thorough."

"Of course," he said, his voice suddenly loud in the silence of the room.

The line went dead and he pulled the phone from his ear, glancing at the clock on the display. Forty minutes was a tight turnaround to check everything, especially if he had to be thorough, but he had no choice. The last thing he wanted was a personal visit from the individual who had just called.

He moved to the spare bedroom, which he had converted into an office, and worked as quickly as he could, ignoring the growing panic as he glanced nervously at the clock on the wall above his desk. Exactly forty minutes later, the phone began to buzz beside him. He answered it, told the caller what he had found, then waited. Heard soft breath on the line as the information was considered.

"And you're sure?" the voice said finally.

"There's no doubt about it," he replied, trying to ignore the small, terrified voice in his mind that screamed, *But you could be wrong. Forty minutes isn't enough time to check everything properly! Is it?*

"Good," the caller said, as though a decision had been made. "I'll be in touch if I need anything else."

Mark threw the phone across the desk when the call ended, wanting it away from him. He leaned back in his chair asking himself again why he had allowed himself to get involved in this. Images of what he had seen flashed across his mind, snippets of horror and terror and fear that he knew would make sleep impossible.

"Why the fuck are you doing this?" he muttered to himself as he slipped his glasses back down and stood up, heading back to the living room.

But the answer was simple; evident in the fifty-inch TV mounted on the wall, the top-of-the-range stereo on the shelving

28

unit, and the Audi Coupé that sat in the garage below the flats. As he flopped back into the couch, he remembered visiting his gran a few years ago, when the MPs' expenses scandal was at its height. She sat in her chair in front of the TV, a small woman with an expansive laugh and white hair stained a jaundiced yellow by a lifetime of smoking.

"Aye," she said, nodding as a politician – wearing the standard issue suit and humble, yet self-important expression that Mark guessed must have taken hours in front of a mirror to perfect – bullshitted his way through an interview, "it's true what they say, the love of money is the root of all evil, right enough. Greedy bastards, the lot o' them."

She had died less than a year later, a heart attack taking her in the middle of Tesco. And, for the first time, he was glad she was gone. He couldn't bear the thought of her knowing he had become one of the greedy bastards she hated so much, tempted by the thought of quick and easy money in return for his expertise and his silence.

Mark's eyes drifted to the TV screen and the frozen image of the silently screaming man, blood dribbling from his mouth and between his fingers as he clutched the sword wound in his chest. He felt something shudder up his back, knew he wouldn't sleep that night.

He watched some more TV, tried to read, to distract himself. But the question remained, insistent in his mind. What was going on? He knew the basic facts, but the picture made no sense to him. What did it mean? Why the late-night check? The urgency and panic? He looked at the clock, grimaced at the time. Thought briefly about phoning in sick and just taking the day off, knew that wasn't a possibility. His caller would find out quickly enough. And they would be displeased. He had seen the aftermath of that displeasure on more than one occasion, the fury written in pumping gouts of blood and yawning, ragged wounds gouged into flesh. For a moment, the thought occurred to him again – the nuclear option he had considered if things ever got too bad. Go to the police. Admit everything. Beg for protection.

But no. No. It would be his death sentence, he knew that. Better just to do as he was asked, take the money and keep quiet.

After all, he had made a deal with the Devil. And there was no way out now.

6

Susie stood in the shower, the water just this side of scalding, inhaling the steam and the smell of soap and shampoo as if it could clean her on the inside as well as the out.

After leaving Doug, she had come back to her flat on Broughton Road, but found the four walls a prison she couldn't bear. So she had slipped on her running gear and headed out, pounding the deserted streets. Usually, the steady rhythm of her feet slapping on the pavement and the burn of her muscles helped to calm and refocus her. But this time she was unable to outrun the thoughts that threatened to overwhelm her, the music blaring in her ears from her iPod unable to drown out the whispering accusations and jibes she remembered all too well.

She had met Redmonds at the old Lothian and Borders CID Christmas party, which was held in a Glasgow hotel so nobody "shit on their own doorstep". Having only recently transferred from Stirling, it wasn't long before Susie found herself alone at the bar, watching the party unfold in front of her as the officers drifted off into tight groups and cliques. Soon enough, Redmonds had sidled up to her and the combination of loneliness and booze made what happened next inevitable.

She felt a burning in her cheeks that was nothing to do with the heat from the shower as the night came back to her in snatches; his hand resting on hers at the bar, his soft, almost embarrassed explanation that his wife had told him it was over and the divorce was just an inevitability. The fumbling that started as soon as the lift doors slid shut, his tongue forcing its way into her mouth, his hands rough on her breasts as the room door swung shut. His insistence about putting a porn movie on in the background as he fucked her, his technique all about trying to get her to give him a blowjob before descending into frantic thrusts and heavy-handed caresses, mercifully building quickly to an orgasm that had him panting like a bull in her ear.

They had ordered a bottle of champagne and Susie had most of it, passing out after they fucked a second time, more at her insistence than his as she tried, and failed, to glean some sliver of pleasure from the evening. She remembered the awkward conversation the next morning, the stilted silence and guilty smiles as he gathered his clothes and slipped from her room back to his own.

The rumours had started almost immediately; that Redmonds had got lucky at the office party with a young officer who hadn't long transferred in to Lothian and Borders. And with the rumours came the innuendos, sneering asides and the practical jokes – including a morning-after pill left on her desk – as her fellow police officers revelled in the chance to let their inner school bully out to play for a little while. The worst of it came from those who knew Redmonds' wife, Alicia, who was also an Assistant Chief Super in Perth at the time. There were hard glances in the bathrooms, conversations that went silent as she passed tables in the canteen at Fettes, the disgusted sniffs at the marriage wrecker who had cost Alicia her happiness. It was, Susie thought, typical. The husband was the unfaithful shithead, but it was the other woman who took the shit.

The situation got worse when she took a call from Doug McGregor, who had just been made the crime reporter at the *Capital Tribune*. She had agreed to meet him at a café on Broughton Road, fully prepared to tell him to go fuck himself then go and hand her notice in. But Doug had surprised her. Instead of pushing her for a comment, he told her he wasn't going to run the story. She had suspected blackmail – that he was going to try and make her his source – but he waved this aside. He wanted an introduction, nothing more.

As time passed, she was forced to admit that Doug was a useful route into the press and a way of getting information from sources that would never speak to the police. The story had died away and, despite the lingering reputation as "the girl who fucked the Super", Susie got on with her job, working some hard cases and doing good work.

Until now.

Now the rumour mill would grind into life again. All the old allegations and smears coming to light. Doug had tried to reassure her that she wouldn't be named: he was the only reporter who knew she had slept with Redmonds and he wasn't about to release her name, and if anyone else did it would only be a footnote in a much bigger and bloodier story. "Sex sells, Susie," he had told her as he topped up her whisky, "but not as much as a nasty cop murder. Trust me, you're not going to be the story in any of this."

But he was wrong, she knew it. She knew what police officers were like. Burns had called to warn her, to give her time to prepare for what she would face in the office. And she *would* face it. She was damned if she would let those bastards see her upset because of a drunken mistake she had made years before.

She stepped from the shower, wiped the steam from the mirror and stared at herself. Forced her eyes to harden, the doubt and the fear retreating into the dark of her pupils. She nodded slightly and wrapped a towel around her. Let them whisper. Let them gossip. Let them play their jokes. This was all they would get in return. DS Susie Drummond. Professional. Controlled. Competent.

And if they had a problem with that, they would see exactly how professional she could be.

7

Doug sat squinting at his laptop, crunching painkillers between his teeth as he flexed his arm and tried to ease the ache that ran from his elbow to the tips of his fingers. It was always worse after sitting at the laptop, arms held at forty-five degrees as he typed.

His eyes drifted to the whisky on the coffee table, poured but untouched. He considered it for a moment, then forced his concentration back to the article he had been working on. After speaking to Becky – a version of her name he suddenly realised only he used – he had started to work up the story as he would any other. Not because he was going to actually send it to his editor, Walter McKay, but more for something to distract him from the torture of waiting to call her back and find out what the pathologist had learned.

He skimmed the copy again, wondering what he was reading – another crime story or his own obituary? Either way it would never run, he could never put the *Tribune* in the position of running copy on a killing that he was either directly responsible for or a key player in.

The thought roused the panic in him again, cold fingers spreading through his guts. He would explain to Becky, Susie and Walter, then hand himself in. Not to Susie – he couldn't, *wouldn't*, do that to her. And not to her prick of a boss, Burns – he wouldn't give him the satisfaction. But Susie had said good things about DC Eddie King recently, found him to be developing into a good detective and, more importantly, someone she could trust.

The man who would be King, he thought bitterly. Wouldn't

do his career any harm, arresting the man who had murdered a former Assistant Chief Superintendent.

Doug reached for the glass, the thoughts of Redmonds' grunt and moans filling his mind. The pleas for mercy, the sneering aside about Susie…

I know her better than you.

He had deserved it, yes, but had he really killed him? He was able to drive himself home. But had he been dying as he drove, the effects from Doug's kicks turning his body into a timebomb?

…timebomb…

He looked at the flash drive on the coffee table, inches from the glass Susie had drained before leaving. What should he do with it? Technically, it was evidence – even, he was forced to admit, motive. And it should be handed in, along with Redmonds' laptop. But could he do that?

He raised the glass to his lips, closed his eyes. Felt the tears threaten again, forced them down. He slammed the glass back onto the table, hard enough for whisky to splash onto his hand, glanced at the clock on the laptop screen. 6.09am, not quite an hour since he had called Becky and tried to get some sense of what was going on.

And why was he doing that? To convince himself he wasn't a killer, or to start constructing an alibi? Not that there was any point: they would trace the call Redmonds made to him soon enough. Whatever way he looked at it, he was…

guilty

…implicated.

Hand shaking, he hit *Redial* and clamped the phone to his ear. The ringing was a drill in his ear, grating, and he felt adrenalin course through him, a freezing, rising terror that wrapped itself around him and started to squeeze. He suddenly felt cold, clammy, his breathing becoming ragged and shallow. It was no use, he was going to lose it, to scream out, explode from the couch, throw the laptop across the room, run for the…

"Doug." Becky's voice was heavy with exhaustion and tight with irritation. "Your watch is running fast again, that's not been an hour yet. What, you couldn't wait to talk to me?"

He took a deep breath, opened his eyes. Roughly pushed the laptop from his knee, surged to his feet, galvanised by the sudden urge to move.

"Becky, sorry, you know what I'm like when I'm on a splash, get carried away. Any word from Williams?"

"Are you okay, Doug?" The tension in Rebecca's voice eased, replaced by confused concern. "You still don't sound yourself. Is your hand really bad tonight?"

He bit back a sudden, almost hysterical compulsion to laugh. Yes, that was it. His hand was the only problem he had right now. Lucky him. Thought instead of Redmonds lying on the street in front of him, felt the laughter die away.

"I'm fine, Becky, really. But I'd be better if you had anything to tell me."

She sighed in exasperation, and Doug knew she was collecting her thoughts. The delay was torture. He stared down at the glass of whisky, hard, thought about knocking it back in one gulp. Maybe it would help. Couldn't hurt. He was starting to lean forward when Rebecca spoke, freezing him.

"Yes, we've heard from Williams, got the preliminaries in. But I'm not sure I should give you anything before the presser at eleven, Doug. The Chief has this strictly embargoed before then – he'd have my arse in a sling if you ran it in the first edition before that."

"Off the record, totally," he said, amazed by the calm, measured tone in his voice. "Purely to prep me. I'll write it up for second, have the drop on the rest of the press pack but won't deviate from your script. It'll just mean we can update the website faster than anyone else."

She sighed again. "You promise me, Doug? This cannot go anywhere before the presser. Clear?"

"Absolutely," he said, the word falling from his mouth like a boulder.

"Okay."

He heard the shuffling of papers on the other end of the line, Becky's voice growing softer and more guarded as she spoke. In a police station, it always paid to talk in whispers.

"As you know, Redmonds was found by the duty Detective Sergeant who was called to the scene in Trinity in the early hours. On entering the property, he found Redmonds in the living room, badly beaten –"

"Did he die from the beating?" Doug interrupted, lips numb, heart pounding. His T-shirt was sticking to his back and he was shivering as though he had just plunged into an ice bath.

"I was getting to that," Rebecca snapped, impatience raw in her voice. "When he first saw the body, Williams initially thought cause of death would be some kind of internal injury. He was a mess, Doug, bruised everywhere. Three cracked ribs, broken jaw and nose, wrist shattered – that was probably a defensive wound, according to Williams."

Doug felt tears start to slip down his cheeks. Jesus, he had killed him. He had really done it. He was a killer, a murderer, a…

"Doug? You still there?"

He pawed angrily at his face with his free hand. "Yeah, sorry Becky, just taking notes. What did you say?"

"I said it was an internal injury that killed him, but not directly resulting from the bare-handed beating he took. Williams didn't spot it until he stripped the body and cleaned him up, but there was a stab wound about an inch above the belly button. Something thin and very sharp, he said. When he opened Redmonds up, he found the chest cavity was filled with blood. Whatever he was stabbed with, it hit his…" – she paused, tone changing as she read from Williams' notes – "ah, inferior vena cava. Caused internal bleeding. That's what killed him."

Doug felt as though all the air had been sucked from the room and he was in a vacuum. His blood roared through his ears, vision doubling as he started to sob. He gulped for air, forced himself to focus. Transferred the phone to his other hand and flexed his left, using the massive bolt of pain to clear his thoughts.

"So," he said slowly, not quite trusting his voice yet, "you're saying that cause of death was stabbing?"

"Yes," Rebecca said patiently. "Seems he was beaten, then stabbed, then drove himself home, bleeding internally. Explains why he crashed into the dividing wall between his house and his neighbours; Williams says that with that level of blood loss, he would have been drifting in and out of consciousness as he drove."

"How long would it have taken for the stab wound to kill him?" Doug asked, feeling like a spectator in his own body.

"Come on, Doug," Rebecca said in a you-know-better tone. "You know how Williams hates to guess. All he could say is that, with wounds like this, the victim can stay conscious for between ten and thirty minutes."

Doug nodded. Found he didn't know what else to say. Fell back on instinct, playing the role he was meant to. "And you're going to be releasing all this at the press conference at eleven?"

"Everything apart from how long between the injury being inflicted and him dying. Body's been formally identified by his ex-wife, Williams' report will be finalised soon. But I mean it, Doug, not a whisper of this makes it into first edition. Clear?"

"Clear," he murmured. He felt as though the volume was being turned down on her now, replaced by the clamouring static of questions in his mind.

"Good. So I'll see you at eleven. And Doug?"

"Yes?"

"You definitely owe me that weekend for this."

He gave a laugh that grated in his ears and finished the call. Held the phone for a moment longer then let it drop to the floor as the sobbing turned into spasms that shook him to his core. He doubled over, chest touching his knees, tears darkening the rug between his feet. He tried to slow his thoughts, stop thinking for just one moment, but found he couldn't.

He wasn't a killer. He hadn't caused Redmonds' death. Someone else had. But who? And why? He had seen Redmonds around two, the call from his neighbour had come in at almost 4am. So a two-hour gap between Doug leaving Redmonds and his death. Where had he gone? Who had he seen in those two hours? And why had he been stabbed?

Doug straightened up slowly, looking at the items on the coffee table. Whisky, the flash drive, Redmonds' laptop in its bag.

He reached for the whisky then brought his own laptop to his knees. Thought. Time. He needed time. He was implicated in this, but he wasn't the killer. Did they know about the flash drive? The laptop? Or was Redmonds killed because of his possible links to Dessie Banks?

He needed to know. And he couldn't find any of that out if he just handed himself in and told Eddie King the whole story. There was still the call from Redmonds' phone to his, but he would deal with that later. For now, he needed answers.

He swallowed the whisky in one gulp, grimacing as it burned his throat. Skimmed the copy one more time then hit *Send*. Felt a momentary twinge of guilt at putting the *Tribune* and Walter in the position he was, brushed it aside. "Prime suspect in murder writes his own splash," he muttered.

Guilt. He could worry about guilt, and the fact that he had just ended his career, later. For now, he needed to know what was going on. And that, he realised with a shiver of disgust, would mean searching the flash drive and Redmonds' laptop for what-ever else they contained. Redmonds' voice in his mind now, heavy with arrogance and hatred: *You're not going to write a word, McGregor. Because if you do, this goes online. Now that would be a story, wouldn't it?*

Pouring another whisky, Doug reached for the laptop bag and got to work.

8

The coffee was strong and black, the slightly bitter aroma curling around his nostrils as he took his first sip and leaned back in his chair. He looked out of the window, a thin patina of rain across the glass making the trees indistinct smears of green below a morning sky that was already smothering the sun and staining the light a dull, industrial grey.

He glanced back at the monitor on the desk in front of him, the first news of the murder already on many of the news websites. But while the mainstream outlets, the BBC, PA, the *Capital Tribune* and the rest of them restricted their coverage to the established facts, "citizen journalists" had already taken to social media, boiling rumour, innuendo and supposition down into 140-character statements of absolute fact. The reports ranged from a drugs feud gone wrong to a gay tryst turning violent when the wife walked in on Redmonds and her husband. He smiled at that, wished he could show it to Redmonds himself and enjoy the bastard's discomfort.

He had always known that involving Redmonds was a mistake. The guiding principle had always been discretion, restraint. But Redmonds had a different agenda. He was flashy, bombastic, overbearing in his desires and his ambitions. But, ultimately, a coward. That much was plain from his reaction to the pressure the reporter McGregor put on him in the wake of the Falcon's Rest raid. And for what? McGregor had nothing. If Redmonds had kept his mouth shut, McGregor would still have nothing. And Redmonds would still be alive. For now, anyway.

He had known Redmonds was an indulgence too far, an untidy loose end that would have to be dealt with, decisively, one day. At least he had McGregor to thank for that – Redmonds' course of action and McGregor's reaction had been unexpected, but it had provided the perfect opportunity to deal with Redmonds once and for all.

And if there was one thing he could never be guilty of, it was neglecting an opportunity.

He considered. Redmonds was gone. Mark had assured him there had been no breaches or withdrawals. All that remained was to retrieve Redmonds' key and they would be secure. Again. Of course, Mark would have to be watched closely to ensure he didn't have an adverse reaction when he put Redmonds' death together with the late-night task he had been set. But that wouldn't be a problem, it was just another detail, another variable to consider.

And that, after all, was what he was paid for. To consider the details. Account for the variables. Ensure they remained invisible, discreet, restrained. Until, of course, the time for restraint was over.

9

Fettes police station sits in the north-west of the city, close to the Botanic Garden. It has the anonymous, industrial look typical of office blocks built in the 1970s, all high windows, blunt facades and flat roofs; a stark contrast to the gothic hulk of Fettes College at the end of Fettes Avenue, an exclusive private school that has produced at least one prime minister. Before Scotland's police forces had been combined, Fettes had been the headquarters for Lothian and Borders police. These days, it houses road policing, a licensing unit and lost property for the city, as well as the corporate communications unit for the East Division, which has a suite of rooms set up for press conferences and media events.

Doug sat in his car outside, trying to warm himself up as the hangover, exhaustion and shock from the previous night and morning fought a battle inside to see which would be the one to try and kill him first. He watched a slow stream of journalists drift into the building, the sight not lifting his mood. A few years ago, a news story like this would have brought reporters from every newspaper in the Central Belt scurrying to Fettes' door. These days, it was just a smattering of TV news crews, an agency reporter and snapper, and a couple of local radio stations.

"Your industry's dying," his friend Hal Damon had told him on one of his increasingly frequent visits to Edinburgh from London. "It's all bloggers and job cuts and freesheets now. But you know you can come work with me any time you want."

Hal was a PR consultant and a damn good one, but Doug always declined his half-joked job offers, saying he was a reporter and someone had to keep Hal honest. And yet, wasn't that what he was doing right now? His own personal PR job, spinning himself as the upstanding reporter and trying to keep his involvement in the Redmonds murder quiet?

He had seriously considered not coming to the press conference, avoiding the inevitable confrontation with officers who would want to talk to him for as long as possible. After all, it was only a matter of time before they checked Redmonds' phone and found the record of his late-night chat with Doug, and he couldn't afford to be slowed down by awkward questions and demands to "account for his movements the previous evening". But he didn't want to rouse Becky's suspicions any further or give her any reason to track him down, so he had decided to come along, act normally for as long as possible and see what, if anything, he could find.

Redmonds' laptop, which was now sitting in the boot of Doug's car, was an empty shell holding nothing more than a standard email account and a couple of Internet bookmarks to banking apps and soft-core porn sites. It had, ultimately, given him nothing, which was both a blessing and a curse, while the flash drive held nothing more than what Redmonds had shown him.

He closed his eyes for a moment, cheeks burning at the image that played across his mind. He was going to have to confront that, soon. But how?

He got out of the car quickly – as if he could leave the thought there and lock it in – and walked up to the station. Halfway up the path, he paused, fumbled his phone out of his pocket and sent two texts. Pocketed the phone again then headed inside.

• • •

Doug took a seat at the back of the room, behind where the TV cameras were set up, not wanting to be in the shot. On a small stage at the front of the room sat a table with three chairs, the Police Scotland logo draped over the front of the table. To the right was a small lectern, and it was this that Becky headed for when she emerged from the wings, followed by DCI Jason Burns and Bob Rankin, the Assistant Chief Constable for the East of Scotland Division. Doug watched Burns closely. He had always been a big man, projecting an air of solidity and blunt mass rather than just fat. But now he seemed smaller, harder, almost as if he had been picked up and everything non-essential squeezed from him. And his flame-red hair – that along with his explosive temper and bulldog interview style had earned him the nickname Third Degree Burns – was starting to go grey at the temples.

Doug had heard things were hard in Police Scotland, with cutbacks piling ever-increasing workloads and pressure on staff, and if Burns' appearance was the result of that, he didn't want to think about what it was doing to Susie.

"Good morning," Becky said, her voice echoing slightly thanks to the pick-up mics in front of the lectern. "As you know, officers from Police Scotland were called to an address in the Trinity area shortly before 4am today. Upon entering the premises, they discovered the body of a forty-nine-year-old male. I can now confirm that the deceased was former Lothian and Borders Police Assistant Chief Superintendent Paul William Redmonds and a murder inquiry has been launched. The family has been informed and we will be sending out a statement on their behalf after this press conference. DCI Burns, who is leading the investigation, and ACC Rankin will now take your questions."

Doug met Becky's gaze as she swept the room, looking for a reporter to go first. He lowered his head; he had questions alright, but this wasn't the place to ask them, or get the answers he needed.

He listened as the other reporters covered the ground he already had, skimming over the updated copy he had already written after speaking to Becky. He had spoken to Walter earlier and told him he would send the update as soon as the press conference was over. They wouldn't beat the live feed from the TV crews, but at least the website copy would be ahead of their rivals.

As he was reading, he got a response to one of the texts he had sent. Susie. He had asked if she was okay and whether she wanted to meet up after the presser.

I'm fine, her text read. *Usual whispers. Ignoring it. Sorry for last night. How's the PC going?*

He tapped in a brief reply, hit *Send* then typed another message: *You getting anywhere near this?* Saw the bubble that showed Susie was replying pop up almost immediately on his screen.

Not officially. But Eddie owes me a favour – I'll get him to keep me up to date.

Doug swallowed, glanced up at Becky, felt sweat prickle on his back as he typed. *Any progress? Anything to indicate motive or a suspect?* His breath quickened as he stared at the screen, willing the reply to come through. If they had checked Redmonds' phone, they'd know he had phoned him. In which case, his conversation with Susie was going to take on a whole new tone. And he was going to lie to her. He knew that now. He had to.

Finally, Susie's reply popped up on the screen. Doug stared at it, rereading it, the impossible boiled down into text shorthand.

Nothing yet. Usual checks. No late-night calls made or received, landline or mobile. Best guess is he arranged a meet and it went wrong from there. Not a random robbery – valuables still on body.

Doug tore his gaze from the phone, looked up dumbly at the stage. Burns was droning on now, asking for anyone who had seen Redmonds over the last day to come forward, reassuring the public that attacks like this were rare. Doug watched him, trying to slow his pulse, trying to make sense of what Susie had just told him.

If Redmonds hadn't called him from his own phone, then whose phone had he used? And why had he bothered to cover his tracks? To make sure there was no evidence he had ever contacted Doug? Made no sense; after all, he was rightly confident that the contents of the flash drive would be enough to keep Doug quiet. Why go to the extra trouble of concealing the fact he had contacted him?

Doug tried to put it all together in his head, but found he couldn't, the questions piling up in his mind like a slow-motion car crash. Slowly, he let the world back in, realised the press conference was winding up. He flicked to email and sent his copy to the *Tribune* newsdesk, then thumbed in a reply to Susie, asking her to meet later on, suggesting a pub just off Princes Street.

He saw Becky subtly look at him, indicating towards the door with her eyes. He nodded back his understanding and headed for the door, wishing he was heading for a pub right now.

10

He had learned the value of discipline almost thirty years ago, a little more than a mile from where he now stood. A typical student, he had been walking home after a night of thwarted pick-up lines and too many cheap shots in an overloud, overpacked nightclub. It was late June, the night mild and clear, the streets busy with other students and the advance parties of tourists who would multiply to an army in the coming weeks as the Fringe and Festival roared into life. It was a walk he had made many times before, past the old Royal Infirmary and the open swathe of playing fields behind it.

It was here that he learned his lesson.

Four kids – all poor complexions, overpriced trainers, bad shell suits and worse attitudes – emerged from the shadows that pooled in the perimeter wall of the hospital.

He smiled slightly as he remembered the leader of the group – he was about six inches taller than the rest of them, dark, glinting eyes and a cheap stud earring that glinted like a chip of copper in the soft sepia glow of the streetlights. The eldest, clearly. And not a day over sixteen.

"Gies yer fuckin' jaicket, man," he snarled, words thick with alcohol or worse. He had made his first mistake then. Rather than seizing control, definitively, he had allowed the drinks from the night to prise a dismissive laugh from him as he told the boy to "fuck off back to his mammy". He knew he shouldn't but it *was* funny, wasn't it? After all, the poor little prick had no idea of who – or what – he had just threatened.

Laughter erupted from behind the boy, his pals finding the challenge to their leader's authority and his obvious embarrassment and impotence entertaining.

"Fuckin' shut it, cunts!" the boy had shouted, head whipping back to his friends.

He should have ended it there. He was sobering up now, some dim, less evolved part of him starting to sound the alarm. But not quickly enough. Mistake two.

The boy turned back to him, eyes narrowed, mouth contorted into a sneer of hatred. "Fuckin' cheeky BASTARD!" he spat, cords starting to bulge in his too-thin neck. "I'm gonnae fuckin' kill you for that!"

The boy lunged forward, something glinting in his hand, his movements jerky and sharp with rage and the inexperience of youth.

And then he had made his third, most serious mistake. It took only a split-second, but he remembered it seemed like a lifetime. The boy coming at him. The calculations on all the ways he could stop and disarm him flitting across his mind like snapshots. The decision being made.

He got his forearm inside the boy's flailing arm, deflecting the blow and the blade with the back of his elbow. The boy staggered forward, suddenly off balance, chest exposed, and he stabbed at his throat with his fist. He felt the boy's windpipe crumple beneath his knuckles like corrugated cardboard, heard cartilage and tendon rupture with a dull, meaty popping sound.

He stepped aside and the boy staggered another half step before swaying to a halt. He fell to his knees, hands scrabbling to his throat, his friends frozen behind him. He gasped and hacked for breath, a thick, liquid gurgling sound echoing in the sudden silence. The boy opened his mouth as he clawed at his neck; blood exploding from it instead of the scream his eyes said he wanted to give. He toppled forward onto the ground and scrabbled manically around, bucking and thrashing like a fish hauled onto the deck of a ship. And in a way, that was what he was. He had been caught. Hooked. And now he was dying.

He looked from the boy to his two friends, who were caught between helping or fleeing. As he glanced around, he realised they had attracted attention. He turned and walked away quickly, not running, cursing himself for his carelessness.

In the weeks that followed, he read the papers closely, watched the TV news. The incident was reported but, amazingly, the boy had lived as his friends had dragged him to A&E. They had given the scantest description of their attacker, and it was so laughably far from the truth that he finally began to relax and not jump every time the phone rang or someone knocked at the door. When he saw the police statement that "enquiries were ongoing" and the plea for witnesses, he knew he was in the clear.

But a lack of control had left him exposed, vulnerable, on the edge of losing everything. It was a lesson he learned well, and he prided himself on applying it throughout his life.

And yet, as he put the phone down on his secretary after telling her to clear his diary for the afternoon, he felt a sudden, almost overpowering urge to let his discipline waiver, to give in to the churning rage that poisoned his thoughts and breath like acid. To lash out, upend his table, throw his coffee mug through the window, revel in the chaos and the terror and the mayhem.

But no. No. He took a deep breath, held it. Turned away from the window and eased himself into his chair and picked up his phone, rereading the message.

Redmonds' key not at his property, in car or on his person. McGregor?

He sneered, letting the phone spill from his fingers and clatter to the desk. Of course it was McGregor. Who else would it have been? The question was, how much did he know – and what to do next?

He closed his eyes, forced himself to look at the problem rationally. Consider the details and account for the variables.

Despite his assurances to the contrary, Mark had obviously not been as thorough as he had demanded: letting him find out from a third party that the key was missing. So he would talk to Mark, impress upon him his severe disappointment and make sure he knew it could never happen again. He smiled, the thought of action calming him. He tapped the keyboard in front of him, his monitor stirring to life as he did, revealing two windows on the screen: the *Capital Tribune*'s homepage and a list of stories by Doug McGregor. Glancing through them, it was clear Mr McGregor was going to have to be addressed at some point. The current situation merely moved him up the priority list. He nodded, feeling the last of the tension slip from his shoulders, the cool shroud of discipline draping itself over him again.

He picked up the phone, tapped in a quick message: *Full sweep for R. Complete inventory. No omissions.*

The situation was salvageable. Redmonds' stupidity, while dangerous, had given him the opportunity to address Mark's inefficiency, another nagging problem and the McGregor issue head on. He found himself smiling at the prospect.

11

Doug drove the five-minute trip to the Royal Botanic Garden, too exhausted from the previous night to consider making the walk. He found a space near to the main gate and headed for the café just inside, making his usual order of a large Americano for him and a large mocha – no cream – for Becky.

It had become a ritual for them not long after they had started seeing each other. After a press conference or briefing at Fettes, they would meet here and walk around the Garden, away from prying eyes. He would invariably arrive first, meeting her when she could get clear. They weren't exactly hiding their relationship, she had told him, just not advertising to the world. And by "the world" he knew she meant her bosses at Police Scotland. He smiled, imagining their response to the news that one of their senior communications officers was sleeping with the crime reporter for the city's leading newspaper. It would almost be worth going public just to see Burns' reaction.

He found a bench just past the main gate, nestled underneath a huge tree and looking out over a perfectly manicured lawn. The Garden always struck him as a calming place, an oasis of tranquillity amidst the chaos of the city. He would sometimes come here to think after visiting Fettes, to wait for the newsdesk to tell him the copy he had filed was okay or that they needed more. It was, he thought as he gulped at his coffee, better than going to the office.

As if on cue, his phone buzzed – a message from Walter that his story was running and they were looking for more, so *if you could ask your contacts really nicely, that would be appreciated.* He smiled at that. As editor, Walter had better things to do than pat his reporters on the head, but after what happened in the last year, overly sarcastic requests for follow-ups were the only way he knew how to look after him.

The return to work had been a slow process, the *Tribune's* owners handling the situation with a PR savvy that, Doug thought, would have made Hal jealous. Jonathan Greig, Walter's predecessor, had been gunned down in front of Doug; revenge for burying a story that could have helped a Gulf War veteran get a reduced sentence for an altercation gone wrong at an Edinburgh nightclub. With the help of Harvey Robertson – the father figure who had trained Doug – Greig had culled all evidence of the story from the *Tribune's* library, basically rewriting history as he saw fit. When Doug had uncovered all this and been attacked by Diane Pearson – the veteran's wife who had a child with Greig – Benedict Media, the owners of the *Tribune*, had put their righteous indignation into overdrive. They were profuse in their thanks to Doug for "uncovering this disgraceful conspiracy, which was an insult to the high standards of journalism that the *Tribune* was renowned for".

On leaving hospital, Doug was welcomed back like a conquering hero, offered private physiotherapy and whatever counselling he needed, all on the Benedict tab. He declined, not wanting to give the bastards another excuse to kick off yet another round of redundancies and cost savings to cover his medical bills. But while the Benedict concern was all gloss and PR, Walter's was real. It was, after all, his fault that Doug had been in Greig's office – the one Walter now used – when the former editor had been shot, as Doug was doing him a favour and covering the desk for him.

He closed his eyes as the memories crowded in on him. The sudden, panicked barks as the floor-to-ceiling window shattered behind Greig, the arc of blood exploding from his throat as the bullet tore at his flesh and spun him round…

Doug took a hitching breath, realised he was holding the coffee cup tight enough to burn his hand. He glared at the phone in his other hand, focused on it, forcing himself not to remember that morning, seizing the thought and using it as a shield against the memories.

The phone. According to Susie, Redmonds' call to Doug hadn't shown up on his home or mobile phone. So what did that mean? Two obvious answers: either he phoned him from somewhere else or he had another phone. Doug scrolled through his call history, found the number with the date and time stamp. Took a photo of the screen, committed the number to memory to be safe. He considered calling it for a moment, thought better of it. If it was a burner phone that Redmonds had used to make private calls, then it would ring out. If it was someone else's phone, someone who knew why Redmonds had come to him, and with what, then…

Doug's head whipped up as the realisation hit him. If it was someone else's number, then presumably they knew about the flash drive. And its contents. Would they want it back? He set his jaw, feeling the rage that had erupted onto Redmonds beginning to snarl and writhe. Fine. If there was someone else involved, and if they *did* know about the contents of the flash drive, let them come. If they wanted it back, let them try.

Doug glanced at his phone again, willing a reply to the second text he had sent at Fettes to flash up. It did just as Becky walked into the Garden and headed for him. The text was the answer he'd been hoping for and, for the first time in what felt like a very long while, Doug gave a smile that could almost pass as genuine.

12

They walked deeper into the Garden, following a tarmac path washed a dull grey by the passage of time and thousands of visitors. It was early September; the trees still lush and green, rich with the promise of life and vitality. They passed the Victorian palm house, a massive sculpture of sandstone, glass and white-washed steel that dated back to the 1840s. When they found a relatively quiet section of path Rebecca took a half step back and slipped round to Doug's right, taking his hand in hers. She didn't like holding his left anymore, not after what had happened.

He smiled, and it struck her again how tired he looked. He had always been wiry and, being tall, he always had a slight stoop, but before now it had always seemed natural on him, and there had been a strength to his grip and a warmth to his touch. Now though, his hand was all hard angles and bone, the gentle strength replaced by something more desperate, the heat from his body a more urgent, feverish thing. He moved differently as well, the quiet grace and keen gaze replaced by a choppy, disrupted stride, eyes jerking around as he tried to take everything in at once.

She took a sip of her mocha to play for time. Grimaced. Far too sweet.

"So, how you doing?" she asked, wincing internally at how contrived it sounded.

"I'm fine." His gaze skated away from hers. "Just tired. I was working late, then Susie turned up early, and I couldn't sleep after she left, thought I might as well get the jump on the story."

The sudden flare of resentful anger surprised her. She thought,

That the only reason you called me? She forced it down, nodded. Pulled them to a slow halt and tried to find his gaze with hers. "That's not what I meant, Doug, and you know it. It's me, remember? You weren't yourself on the phone this morning, and you sure as hell aren't looking any better now." She took a step towards him, placed a hand on his chest. "I'm here, okay? If your hand is giving you problems, or the nightmares are getting worse again, tell me. I want to help."

He looked at her face for a moment, the shimmering of the wind in the trees filling the silence. She watched his Adam's apple bob up and down, as though he was swallowing something rancid. He looked up, over her head, searching for an answer.

"Becky, I'm sorry," he said. "Not being much of a boyfriend, am I? I'm fine, honest. The hand…" – he raised it to chest level – "well, it's not great, but I'm fine. Promise. It's just I didn't get a lot of sleep last night, and Susie turning up threw me off balance a little."

She nodded slowly. *Threw me off balance.* It was ridiculous to be jealous of her own friend, she knew. But there it was. She had spoken to Susie about this when she and Doug had first started seeing each other; got the scoffing, incredulous assurance that there was "absolutely nothing there, never would be. I mean, *God*, Rebecca, Doug?"

But still…

She focused back on him. "So, did you get what you needed straightened out, or is there something still bothering you?"

He blinked at her, confusion and what could almost have been panic flitting across his eyes. And there it was again, that ability to throw him off his stride with one simple question.

"I, ah…" he fumbled.

"Susie," Rebecca said. "When you called me, you said something Susie told you didn't make sense. Have you sorted it out, or is there something you're still working on?"

He gulped at his coffee quickly. "Oh, that. Sorry. Yeah, it's fine. I spoke to Susie. Seems like they're in the dark on what Redmonds was doing out last night and a motive for the attack. No calls in or out, so the thinking is he met someone and they attacked him. Question is who – and why? I take it you're making the usual CCTV checks, trying to trace his movements?"

Same old Doug. When in doubt, dive right back into the story. "We're checking the CCTV cameras closest to his home from last night through until his body was discovered, yes. Problem is there aren't a lot of cameras in that part of town, and any pick-ups we get would only give an indication of where he was heading. So not too much to go on."

He nodded. "And no other possible motives at this stage?" he asked, eyes finding hers for the first time. "No money problems, old enemies recently released from prison?"

"Oh, come on, Doug," she said, surprised by her own impatience. "I'm the PR on this, not the investigating officer. They tell me what they're doing when they think I need to know it – and that's usually thirty seconds before I get a call from someone like you."

He held up his free hand in apology, gave the one holding hers a gentle squeeze. "Sorry, force of habit. Always thinking. You're right, you've already given me more than enough. I'm sorry I'm turning this into another media briefing, okay?"

"Okay," she said, her tone telling him she didn't quite believe it.

"So how about I make it up to you?" he said, his voice warming. "Dinner tonight when you get done? Who knows, I might even cook."

She gave an exaggerated sigh. "Thought you were trying to get back into my good books? I've no idea how long I'll be working, depends on what, if anything, breaks on the case. But I'll call you, okay?"

"Fine," he agreed, voice cooling again. "It's not as if I'm likely to be sleeping anyway."

They shared a brief kiss, little more than lips touching, then headed back towards the main gates. They tried for small talk and let it die out, walking in silence, dropping hands on instinct as they approached the more crowded paths. They said their good-byes at the gate and Doug ducked into his car and drove away, waving as he did.

She returned his wave, watched the car dwindle into the distance. Considered for a moment. The coldness in his voice. The way she had been able to throw him off balance. Nodded to herself as she made a decision. She dumped the too-sweet mocha into a bin then flicked through her contacts, finding the number she wanted. She dialled it and listened to it buzz in her ear as she started the walk back towards Fettes, knowing that her first call when she got there would be to Susie.

13

Mark called back less than an hour after he had conveyed his displeasure at his earlier sloppiness to him. The speed of his return call both pleased and concerned him. Obviously, he had delivered his message eloquently, spurring Mark into such quick, decisive action. But had this haste driven him to make another mistake, another omission that endangered them all? Only one way to find out.

"Mark, thank you for calling back so promptly, did you carry out the necessary checks as discussed?"

The voice at the other end of the phone was cracked glass, brittle and ready to shatter. He cursed himself quietly. He had pushed the boy too hard: now he was a sliver away from panic. And panic could be fatal.

"Ah, yes. Yes, sir. I did. I carried out a full inventory. As you've already been told, the key is not among Mr Redmonds' effects, either from his home, person or car, or been logged into police evidence anywhere so far."

He nodded to himself. He had expected that much. "Has the key been used?"

"Well, ah, yes, sir. There was one use and withdrawal at 12.37am last night. Since then, no activity."

He reached for his coffee mug. Squeezed it hard to bleach his knuckles white. "A withdrawal," he said, jaw tight. "And yet, when we spoke earlier, you told me there had been no withdrawals. How is that possible, Mark?"

A harsh, panicked gulp of air down the line. "I, ah, well, ah..."

A nervous cough. "I'm sorry, Mr James, I am. There was so much to check, in so little time, and it was only one withdrawal. I'm… I'm sorry."

"And are you absolutely certain that you've missed nothing else? No other withdrawals or activity? You understand the paramount importance of this, don't you Mark?" He let the fury bleed into his voice. Just a little. Just enough.

"Yes. Yes, sir. Yes, I do. I've checked everything. Other than the withdrawal, there has been no other unexpected activity. And Mr Redmonds' key has not been used again."

"I have your word on this?"

Mark's voice was a whisper. "Ah, yes sir. I checked thoroughly."

He forced himself to let go of the coffee cup, flexed his hand. "Good Mark, very good. Because we cannot afford any further mistakes. Further mistakes could be, well, fatal. Mark. Do you understand me?"

A murmur of agreement came down the line. He knew the boy was stifling tears on the other end of the phone. Found he didn't care.

"Very good. In that case, Mark, keep monitoring for further withdrawals or activity and let me know if anyone attempts to use Redmonds' key."

Another sniffled agreement down the line. Tears now, no doubt.

He leant forward in his chair, hunching his shoulders, his shadow engulfing the coffee cup. "And Mark? One last thing. I understand that you are being put under significant pressure, and the temptation to do something rash, or talk to someone about this situation, must be great. But I can trust you, can't I, Mark? You know that any rash action would be unhelpful for everyone involved?"

The answer came in a rush. "Yes, sir. Of course, I would never. Never…"

"Good," he said, cutting the babbling off, the discordant mewling an insult to his ears. "Keep me appraised."

"Okay," Mark said, the conviction in his voice all show. "But, sir. What about the key? If McGregor does have it…?"

"That's not your concern, Mark. I'll deal with that. You just do what we pay you for, understood?"

He got a reply and cut the line. Stared at the phone for a minute. The boy had the two most valuable traits he needed for this – skill and greed. But he also, judging from the call, lacked a backbone or the strength of character to do what needed to be done. And he had made a slip. Missed something vital. Something that he would have been in the dark about if not for the contingencies he had put in place.

He thumbed down the phone, found the number he needed. A number he had not used in a very long time. He got a reply on the third ring and dispensed with pleasantries quickly. Outlined what he needed, the message to be sent, and gave the relevant details. As he spoke, he stared at the image on his computer screen. The image he had kept there since this morning.

The byline picture of Doug McGregor.

14

Susie was in the canteen at Gayfield Police Station, one of the three CID hubs in Edinburgh along with Corstorphine and Craigmillar. The place was quietening down after the commotion of shift change, officers grabbing coffees and teas to fortify themselves for the hours ahead. For detectives, the shift started with a case briefing: the senior officer bringing the team up to date then giving out assignments. She knew the Redmonds case was being led by Burns, also knew she wasn't going to get near it after he had called her into his office earlier in the day.

"You know I can't put you on this, Susie," he had said. "Given your, ah, history with the deceased, can you imagine what the rest of the team would say, and what the press would do with it if it got out? Last thing I need is to be fielding questions from your pal McGregor about how the death of a former copper is being handled by the girl who ended his marriage."

She opened her mouth to speak, felt embarrassment and rage burn her cheeks as her chest prickled with the stress rash she always got at moments like this. "Sir, I really don't..."

Burns held up his hand, shook his head. He suddenly seemed tired, almost vulnerable, Third Degree gone, replaced by an overworked man who had a family he never saw and a job that was threatening to break him.

"Before you say it, I know, I know. It's shit. You did nothing wrong, and it's not fair that you're being sidelined from another major case because of one stupid office party fumble. But Susie, you've got to understand. After the kicking we've been taking and some of the mistakes that have been made recently, I just can't run the risk of this turning into a story that makes us look bad."

"Look bad?" she said, her voice chilled by rage. "You mean worse than leaving two people to die in a crashed car because we missed the call? Worse than officers being pinballed around the country to cover staff shortages? Worse than us spying on reporters and fellow officers? Sorry, sir, but I really don't think this is in the same league."

He shook his head again and reached for a pen on his desk, engulfing it with one massive hand. "You're right, it's not. But that's the point. There's been enough shit written about us recently, this case can't be seen to be adding to that. And, besides," – his chair creaked as he sat back – "I really don't want to give the bastards out there any more ammo to throw at you."

Susie blinked at him, stunned. Thought back to the shower, the promise she had made to herself. "Sir, I can assure you I'm more than capable of handling any puerile jibes that may be directed at me in the course of the investigation."

"I'm sure you could, Susie, I'm sure you could. But could your career? This is the type of shit that sticks, Susie. The last thing you need is to be branded as a disruptive influence, especially at the moment with staffing being the way it is. Please. Trust me. I'm keeping you off the Redmonds case for your good as well as mine."

She didn't like to admit it, but he had a point. Being seen as a problem in a tight investigating unit wouldn't do her prospects any good at all. Not that they were looking particularly bright at the moment anyway. Again, she thought of Doug. Wondered if the benefits of having him as a contact and friend outweighed the damage it seemed to be doing to her career. Burns knew of their relationship and made no effort to disguise his disgust for McGregor, and he had hinted that the big bosses were no fans of Doug's either. She wondered what would happen if they found out about him and Rebecca.

"So, if you're not putting me on the Redmonds case, can I ask what you are assigning me to?"

Burns pressed the pen against his cheek, then slid an A4 folder across the desk to her. "Theft in Leith," he said. "A high-end graphic design firm has been broken into over the last couple of weeks, had expensive equipment stolen. Probably a grab and reset job, but they've got some big-name clients, so see what you can find."

Susie felt the rage snarl behind her eyes again. This? This is what she was reduced to? Chasing up computer thefts while a major murder investigation was going on around her? And why? Because of one stupid mistake, one worthless shag.

Fucking brilliant.

She got out of the office before she said something they would both regret, something that would put the final nail into the coffin of her career. Headed for the canteen and pretended to read the file in front of her as uniforms and CID officers milled around, the crowd slowly thinning out. She spotted DC Eddie King, nodded to him as he made his way to the coffee machine. He gave her the briefest of nods back as she pointed to the tabletop. She had worked with Eddie last year on the Pearson case, found him more competent than others had given him credit for. She smiled at that: she was the last person who should be paying attention to office gossip.

After the case, she had mentioned Eddie's performance to Burns who had, in turn, told King. Since then, Eddie had been like an over-loyal puppy, always willing to help Susie out on a case or do the routine legwork that drove other detectives to distraction.

She watched Eddie go, heading for the CID suite and the briefing, sat quietly as the canteen grew still around her. When it was almost deserted she got a coffee then headed back to the table and waited. Eddie had understood. He would come and find her after the briefing, tell her what he knew.

Burns may be keeping her away from the case, and though she hated to admit it, he may even be right in doing so. But there was no way it was going to run without her.

15

The text Doug had received just before he met Rebecca was simple and direct: *Your parking space will be ready.* And, sure enough, as he drove on to Forth Street he spotted a space just outside the offices of Capital Events Management, a single bollard reserving it. Doug hopped out, lifted the bollard onto the pavement then reversed into the space, being very careful not to get near the flame-red Audi TT that was parked in front of him. It looked so new that the tyres still had the glossy garage sheen to them, and the personalised number plate told him that Janet had been splurging again.

He picked up the bollard and headed for the stone stairs that led down to the basement offices of Capital Events Management. He dropped the bollard into a stack that sat in the small, enclosed courtyard then stepped into the office.

Janet MacFarlane looked up from the desk in the main reception area, mouth splitting into a smile that spread across her face like a fracture, crumpling and scoring it with creases so deep they could have been ravines. She was a short woman, surely in her late fifties or sixties now, trying to hide the fact with skin dyed the colour of stained teak by weekly sunbed sessions, hair bleached blonde and styled to perfection and whitened teeth which were already starting to dull and take on the cold tea hue associated with chain-smoking.

"Douglas!" she said, voice as Lanarkshire as the Falls of Clyde, as she stood up from the desk and walked towards him, arms outstretched. "It's been an age, son. Where you been? And what you been doing to yersel'? Ye look way too skinny!"

She seized him in a rough, surprisingly tight hug, doughy arms wrapping around him and crushing him into her ample chest. She smelled of cigarettes and cloying perfume.

"And ye feel like a bag o' bones." She let him go, held him at arm's length, looked into his eyes. "Ye've been through the wars, son. If there's anything Rab and I can do, you just let us ken, okay?"

Doug smiled, bent down to place a kiss on her cheek. Her skin was cold and slack, caked with make-up. It reminded him of his gran. "Thanks. Janet, but I'm fine. Just a few too many late nights, is all. And you and Rab are helping me, that's why I'm here."

She held his gaze for a minute, something hard and unforgiving flitting across the motherly concern. She and her husband, Rab, had started CEM back in the 1970s, moving from the West Coast to escape the gang violence and the razor gangs. They quickly grew and, by the mid-1980s, CEM was the biggest private security operation on the East Coast, the company logo almost as much a part of doormen's uniform as the black T-shirts and unsmiling eyes.

Which was how Doug had met Rab. He'd initially approached him for comment on a story about the licensing of doormen in the city, and they had quickly formed a bond, Doug instinctively responding to Rab's natural good humour, while Janet had fallen into the role of over-protective mother hen. But Doug was under no illusions. Rab's good humour was matched by a fearsome reputation, and he was known as a man who was not afraid to resort to violence when the need arose. But Janet was the real power behind the throne. She marshalled their door staff with military precision and watched over them personally.

A few years ago, one of their doormen had been knifed while working close protection for a B-rate actor who was in town to promote a straight-to-DVD movie. The doorman, a slab of muscle who answered to the nickname Johnny 300 because of what he could lift in the gym, was stitched up and sent home to recover from the eight-inch gash that had been carved across his stomach. The rumour was that, a week after he got out of hospital, Janet paid him a home visit with three gifts: a pot of her homemade soup, an envelope stuffed with £20 and £50 notes to "tide him over until he was on his feet again", and a Jiffy bag filled with his attacker's teeth.

Doug didn't think it was just a rumour.

He nodded towards a door at the opposite side of the room. "I got a text from Rab, saying he had a little time to see me. Okay to go in?"

She released her hold on him, the gaze warming up again like a dying fire getting another gasp of air. "Aye," she said, "he's been waitin' for ye. Go on in."

Rab MacFarlane was on his feet and striding across the office as Doug stepped inside, arm outstretched. He was dressed in an impeccably tailored suit, which accentuated his wide shoulders and thin waist. His thinning, iron-grey hair was swept back from his forehead, showing off the small, silvery scar that cut through the frown lines. Doug held out his own hand and let Rab engulf it with a massive paw, suddenly glad that handshakes were right-handed.

"Doug, how you doing, son?" Rab asked. "I'm assuming Janet already said you look like shite, so we don't need to go over that again?"

Doug surprised himself with a laugh. "Yeah, Rab, we've already been over that. Thanks for seeing me at short notice."

Rab released his grip on Doug's hand and waved aside the thanks. "No bother," he said, gesturing for Doug to sit down. Rab busied himself at the drinks cabinet that sat behind the desk, producing two crystal tumblers and filling them with a generous amount of malt whisky. He never asked Doug if he wanted a drink, and Doug never refused. He had learned early on that, to Rab, drinking was as much a part of business as pen, paper and contract clauses. In this office, he was the host, you were the guest.

And the last thing Doug wanted was to be an unwelcome guest of Rab MacFarlane.

Rab handed him one of the glasses, clinked his own off it then settled into his chair. Watched as Doug took a deep drink from the glass, nodded as though confirming something to himself.

"Joking aside, son," he said after he took a sip of his own drink, "you've looked better. Something wrong?"

Doug bit back a sudden urge to laugh and the answer that played dangerously close to his lips. *Wrong? Naw, Rab, I'm great. I'm implicated in a murder, I'm going to break my friend's heart, my arm's numb and I can't get the image of a man being shot in front of me out of my head, but other than that, I'm great. You?*

Instead, he lifted his glass. "No, I'm fine Rab, thanks. Just a few too many late nights recently, too many stories to write, not enough hacks to write them. Which is why I'm here actually…"

Rab grunted a laugh. "Aye, I guessed as much. This about that ex-copper getting killed in Trinity? Not sure what help I can be though, Doug, didn't know the man, hadnae really heard of him before today."

"Actually, it's not him I'm interested in, Rab. Well, not directly anyway. It's the Falcon's Rest brothel in Morningside, and its owner."

Rab nodded. "Dessie Banks," he said slowly. "Aye, I heard Dessie wasn't too happy about that." He nodded towards Doug's glass. "You want another one?"

Doug looked at the glass, surprised to see it was almost empty. He hesitated for a moment, torn. He could feel the whisky coursing through him, wrapping itself around the pain in his hand and arm, soothing it. One more wouldn't hurt. But…

He shook his head. "Better not, Rab, I've got the car. Thanks though. Anyway, as I was saying, everyone knows about the raid on the Rest, but what's not commonly known is that Redmonds was there that night."

Rab leant back in his chair, tapping his glass gently against his lips. "So he liked to get blown by hookers, so what? What's that to do with Dessie? And what do you want from me?"

"There's a rumour," he said slowly, "that Redmonds may have been linked to Banks, and that he was at the Rest that night at the invitation of the management. If so, and Redmonds was getting worried that someone, say a certain crime reporter, was digging into the Rest and Dessie and was getting close to something, then that might be a pretty strong motive to shut him up, permanently."

Rab nodded agreement. "Aye, I see that, but what makes you think that Redmonds was getting nervous? One of your polis pals say he was getting ready to make a statement or something?"

The image from the flash drive darted across Doug's mind, searing away the pleasant whisky fog. "No, it's not that, but I know he was keen to stop me looking into him for some reason. I'm wondering if that's got anything to do with Banks, and I'm hoping –"

"That I would ask around quietly, see if there were any rumours that Banks had a former copper in his pocket?" Rab finished for him. "Christ, Doug, you never ask for the easy stuff, do you? You know Dessie's reputation, how he'd react if he knew someone was poking the hornet's nest."

"I know, Rab, and if it's too much to ask, then I'm sorry. But it's important. I need to know why Redmonds was killed. At the moment, the possibility of Banks' involvement is all I've got. I'm just asking for a few discreet questions to people who won't talk to me. Please?" He heard the pleading in his voice, hated it. He had heard it in his own father's voice too many times. The weakness, the mewling.

Rab finished his whisky. "Okay, I'll ask around for you. Quietly. But Doug, if I find anything that's going to lead to trouble for either of us, this is over, got it?"

Lead to trouble? I'm already fucking there, Doug thought. "Thanks, Rab. I appreciate it."

Rab shook his head, gave an impatient growl. "Aw no, you're

not getting off that easy. I do this for you, you're going to do something for me, okay?"

Doug fought to keep his voice even. "What's that?"

Rab sat back in his chair again, studied him closely. "Firstly, take another drink and tell me what's goin' on with you. Christ knows, you look like you need it. I'll get Chris to drive you home; he can get a taxi back. Second…" He let the sentence hang for a moment, just long enough for Doug to twist again in his seat. "Second, on the way back, you're going to get a meal. Something proper. Janet's right, you look like shite, Doug. And when she's worried, I'm worried. So you are going to get a meal and look after yourself for once and leave whatever the fuck it is that's bothering you here. Okay?"

Doug nodded his agreement. *If only it was that fucking easy*, he thought.

If only.

16

Susie got back home just after 9pm, eyes burning and body jangling with too much caffeine and too little sleep. But while her body was exhausted, her mind refused to rest. She briefly considered a trip to the gym, but compromised with following a workout DVD she had ordered from a teleshopping channel months ago and had largely ignored. She took a quick shower then flopped onto the couch, considering the takeaway menus strewn across the coffee table. Selected the menu of a nearby Indian, phoned in an order she knew she would only pick at, then went to get a bottle of white from the fridge and poured herself a healthy glass. She rolled her head back, trying to massage the tension of the day that had made a gnarled nest for itself in her neck, then leaned forward slowly, glancing across at the empty couch opposite her.

Doug's seat, she thought. Surprised, she pushed the thought away. They had worked hard to maintain their routine of takeouts and wine nights after long days, but with what had happened in the Pearson case, and Doug starting to see Rebecca, it wasn't as easy as it used to be.

Rebecca. She had called that afternoon, not long after Eddie had updated her on progress in the Redmonds case. Or rather, the lack of it. They had arranged to get out of the office, heading for a small pub on nearby Comely Bank Road. Susie arrived first and took a table overlooking the door, ordering a vodka and soda for herself and a gin and tonic for Rebecca. Normally she wouldn't drink on duty but, to hell with it, it wasn't as though Burns had given her much taxing to do – just the break-in at the graphic design company. Before leaving to meet Rebecca she'd phoned the firm, called the Docking Station, and made an appointment to meet with the owner in the morning, asked him to have a list of the equipment that had been taken ready for her. She listened to the complaints that they had already given these to the officers who had first attended the scene, uttered a reassuring "just to speed this along", through gritted teeth then hung up. Probably a fucking insurance job anyway. And a total waste of her time.

And all because she was seen as a disruptive force. She raised her glass, toasting the thought. Fuck it.

Rebecca arrived just as Susie was considering a top-up. She stepped into the pub tentatively, head moving in a slow, graceful sweep that took in the room and gave everyone just enough time to notice her perfect make-up and camera-ready hair. She was wearing a long, camel-colour jacket over the blue business suit Susie had seen on the press conference footage from earlier. What the TV cameras didn't pick up were her shoes – designer brand, worth at least four-figures. Rebecca always loved her labels.

They had met when they were both starting off in what had been the Lothian and Borders Force in Galashiels, Susie a PC and Rebecca a junior press officer. Their careers took them on different paths, until they ran into each other again years later when Rebecca had joined the new media team in Edinburgh. It was, she thought, only natural that Rebecca would meet Doug at some point, and Susie had to admit to feeling a pang of guilty pleasure at watching him squirm his way through their first meeting. But now they were dating. And Susie had found herself reassuring Rebecca on more than one occasion that she and Doug were only friends. Even, she thought, at times when it didn't seem Rebecca needed the reassurance.

Rebecca spotted her at the table, nodded her head to the bar in a *Want anything?* gesture. Susie hesitated for a beat then shook her head, watched Rebecca glide to the bar before returning with a bag of salt and vinegar.

"Sorry," she said as she sat down. "Starving all of a sudden, you know how it is. Missed lunch because of the presser follow-up."

"How did it go?" Susie asked.

"Pretty standard," Rebecca said, tearing the crisps open and offering them to Susie. "Not much more to be said at the moment. We're appealing for witnesses, investigating his last movements, picking the house apart. You heard anything else?"

Susie thought back to what Eddie had told her after the CID briefing. "Not much," she admitted. "They've not found any calls that would explain who he went to see or why, no unusual cash withdrawals. Not a robbery, so whatever caused this, it was personal." She spotted Rebecca's quizzical gaze, smiled. "And no, it wasn't me, Rebecca. Bastard was a stupid drunken mistake I made one night a long time ago, nothing more."

"You think you'll be interviewed as a possible suspect?" Rebecca asked, her tone telling Susie the question wasn't friend-to-friend but professional. Made sense. *Former fuck buddy quizzed in ex-cop slaying* was a hell of a headline.

Susie shrugged. "Doubt it. Like I said, he's ancient history. Not had any contact with him for years. If I am asked, I'll tell them that. There's nothing else to tie me to him. Besides, I'm not the interviewee you should be worried about."

Rebecca nodded, grimacing as she took a sip of her gin and tonic. "You mean his ex, Alicia Leonard? Yeah, I heard that too. Burns is handling the interview himself tomorrow, dragging poor Eddie King along as a human shield, I'm told."

"She as bad as they say?" Susie asked, staring out the window.

"I've not had any direct dealings with her," Rebecca replied. "But she sits on the Police Authority Board and I did get a pointed call from their press team, impressing on me the 'importance of discretion and sensitivity at this distressing time for Mrs Leonard.'"

Susie thought back to some of the pointed stares and whispered jibes she had been the brunt of after she had spent the night with Redmonds. *She likes attack dogs*, she thought, taking another sip of her drink.

"Anyway," Rebecca said, "Doug told me you saw him early this morning. How you doing, Suse? Bullshit aside, this can't be easy."

Susie took a deep breath, remembered Doug that morning, the way she had fallen into his arms. Felt embarrassment burn her cheeks. And the tang of something else, something deeper.

Guilt?

"I'm okay," she said softly. "Just really didn't need all this shite getting dredged up again. It's not like I've got the best career prospects as it is, but this has cost me another major investigation, which is the last thing I need."

Rebecca took another sip from her glass then laid it aside. Too early in the day. "I know," she said. "Burns told me. But, Suse, it's the best thing really. You know that. Last thing you, or he, needs is you becoming part of this story. You made a mistake, had a drunken fumble. It helps no one if that gets dragged into the headlines again, and you being part of the investigation would only increase the risk of that."

Susie grunted. Rebecca was right, she knew it deep down. Just like she knew Burns was only trying to protect her. But still…

"… getting everything sorted with Doug's help?"

Susie was startled from her thoughts, blinked at Rebecca. "Sorry, what?"

"Doug. He said there was something this morning that didn't make sense, but that you'd both managed to straighten it out. I was just wondering if it is something we should be looking at?"

Susie rubbed at the back of her neck, shaking her head slowly. "Sorry, Rebecca, not sure what you mean."

Confusion flitted across Rebecca's dark brown eyes. "He called me after you left his place this morning, wanting to go over what we knew. Something about the possible motives for Redmonds' murder."

Susie chewed her lip slowly, replayed her early-morning visit to

Doug's flat, the conversation by text before the press conference had started. Shrugged. "You sure it wasn't another ploy of his to get the drop on you and a quick quote?"

Rebecca gave a small laugh, mined the crisp bag for the last crumbs. "Hardly," she said. "He knows me better than that now. Ah well, nothing important, I'll see him later tonight, ask him then."

"You going down to Musselburgh?" Susie asked.

"Dunno yet," Rebecca replied. "Have to see how the rest of the day pans out. You want to join us for dinner if the timing works?"

Susie shook her head. "No, thanks, Rebecca. It's already been a long day. I just want to get it over with, get back and lock the world outside, okay?"

"Okay," Rebecca said, "But the offer's always there. I don't want me seeing Doug to come between you two, or us, okay?"

Susie had agreed and they parted ways soon after. And now, here she was, sitting in her flat, waiting for an Indian she didn't want, drinking a bottle of white at a rate that would put Doug to shame.

Doug. What had he meant? Something that didn't make sense? True, she hadn't been at her most incisive or articulate when she had visited him, but confusing? No. There was nothing in what she had said to Doug that didn't make sense, nothing that didn't fit. Unless she had missed something. Unless he had seen something she hadn't, was working an angle no one else had seen. Which would also explain why he was lying to Rebecca.

Wouldn't it?

Giving a frustrated sigh she reached for the phone and called Doug. Time for him to answer some questions for a change.

17

The van slid round a corner, tyres squealing as they fought for grip on the rain-slick tarmac.

"Fuck's sake, Lee, calm it!" Vic McBride snarled as he braced himself in the back of the van, struggling not to fall off the wheel arch he was perched on. This was the problem with rush jobs: you had to use the manpower that was available at the time. If he had been given time to prepare, Lee Donald would have been his last choice for a job like this, or any other for that matter. But he was keen, obedient and, vitally, had been available.

And when Mr James called with a rush job, you didn't waste time sifting CVs for the best candidates.

"Sorry, sorry, wee bit too fast there, likesay. Fuckin' Ednb'ra streets," Lee whined in the front, his fingers drumming on the wheel to some internal soundtrack only he could hear.

Vic shook his head, looked down at the ruined heap lying on the floor of the van. In the dim light he could see dark patches where blood had seeped through the old dust sheet they had wrapped him in. They glistened like oil in the gloom. There was something almost poetic about it.

The van bumped over a speed hump, the soft thrum of tarmac giving way to the hiss of gravel beneath the wheels. A couple of turns – still too fast, the speedfreak waster in the driving seat was pushing it – and they slowed to a halt, old brake pads protesting as they did.

Vic craned forward, trying to see out of the front of the van. No use, it was too dark out there, the world reduced to dull shadows. Perfect.

"We here?"

"Yeah, yeah, we're here. Want a hand wi' that?"

Vic said nothing, but hauled himself to a hunched stand in the back of the van. He leant forward and opened the panel door, sticking his head out into the cool, rain-swept night. He paused for a moment, straining to hear for any sounds of someone walking nearby, the telltale blue flash of the police. Nothing. Just the faraway moan of traffic, the occasional hoot from some pisshead on a night out.

He leaned back into the van and bent over the lump of rags at his feet, drawing his blade from his jacket. With one quick flick of the wrist he cut open the sheet – and the body beneath it – then put his foot on the lump of rags and pushed. The body rolled out of the van, flopping to the ground like a sack of rubbish, giving a dull, heavy thump. Vic nodded approval. He always loved that noise – the satisfying sound of a job well done.

"Let's get the fuck out of here," Vic said as he closed the door. "You know where our next stop is. And Lee, drive carefully, or I'll cut your fuckin' throat next."

Lee stared out into the night intently as if it held an answer. Then he drove the van away as though he was a learner setting off on his test.

Vic allowed himself a small smile as he sat back on the wheel arch. He could hardly make out the razor in his hands, but he knew it was there.

More importantly, Lee did too.

18

Doug sat in the quiet of Rebecca's flat, the smell of the bolognaise he had made earlier hanging in the air. Susie had tried to call him several times that evening, but he'd not had the courage to pick up.

After the drinks with Rab he had, on a whim, got Chris – whose expansive gut pressed against the wheel of the RX-8 even with the seat racked all the way back – to drive him to the supermarket near Becky's flat on Slateford Road. Feeling like a prisoner on day release, or a minor celebrity trying to buy himself a bit of recognition with an entourage, he had wandered the aisles under Chris's supervision, picking out the ingredients to cook for Becky. He liked cooking; found that being able to disengage his mind and merely follow the instructions in the cookbook calmed him. He didn't do it as much now, after what had happened. Holding a knife or chopping vegetables made his wounded hand hurt.

And cutting up meat brought back other, darker memories.

By the time he had finished his escorted shopping trip, Becky was on her way back. *See,* she had texted, *would have been easier if you'd just taken the key and let yourself in. Be there in 30 minutes x.*

Ah yes, the key. She had started to mention it about a month ago, telling him how it would make sense for them to have keys for each other's places. Doug knew that on one level, she was right; with the erratic shifts they both worked, it would be useful to be able to let themselves in to each other's flats after a late night. But there was something about the gesture – and the symbolism – that bothered him. He had always been a private man, used to having his own space to retreat to. The thought of sharing that, even with

Becky, made him somehow uneasy. And, he thought guiltily, he wasn't sure how Susie would take it.

Chris had carefully parked Doug's RX-8 in one of the visitor parking bays outside Becky's flat, then heaved himself out, the car rocking under his weight. He tossed the keys across the roof to Doug, gave the car a gentle pat. "Nice motor," he growled then lumbered off in search of a taxi back to Rab's office.

Doug went into the boot, prised Redmonds' laptop from its bag and crammed it into his own. Last thing he needed was Becky asking questions about it.

Nice laptop, Doug, where did you get it?

Well, ah, about that...

He was waiting when Becky pulled into the car park, engine over-revving as she took her frustration at Edinburgh's appalling traffic conditions out on her clutch, and helped him in with the shopping. He cooked, but had no real appetite. Becky ate the majority of the bolognaise while he pushed his around his plate and concentrated on finishing the wine he had bought. He saw her sideways glances every time he topped up his glass, gave a sheepish smile. She hadn't mentioned it directly, but he knew the amount he was drinking was concerning her.

They made small talk, Becky mentioning that Redmonds' ex was being interviewed tomorrow and she was worried how Burns was going to cope with it. After dinner they settled on the couch to watch a movie Doug couldn't even remember the name of, and Becky instantly fell asleep. Not surprising, Doug thought, she had had a hell of a day. And she didn't have terror and adrenalin to keep her awake like he did.

She woke up after half an hour, smiled an apology and said she was heading for bed. Doug saw his chance, offered to head off, let her get a proper sleep before another busy day tomorrow.

"Don't you dare," she said. "I saw how much of the wine you drank earlier. Besides, it'll be nice to have the company. No rush though, just come through when you're ready."

She kissed him gently then headed for bed. He waited for twenty minutes, just to make sure she wasn't going to come back into the living room, then took out the laptops and the bottle of Jameson he had also bought with Chris. He booted up his own laptop, not wanting to use Redmonds' unless absolutely necessary. He fished the flash drive out of his jeans and laid it on the table beside the computer.

Do you really want to do this, Doug? he thought.

No, he didn't. All he wanted to do was smash the fucking thing up, shatter it into a million pieces, then burn the whole poisonous lot. But he couldn't. Whatever was going on, this was a part of it. And if the bomb was going to go off, he was going to be standing right in front of it to take the brunt of the blast.

He owed her that much at least.

He poured a large measure of whisky, then jammed the flash drive into the USB port, hands starting to shake. He double-clicked on the desktop icon, whispered an apology then opened the image that the flash drive held.

Susie lay on a double bed, naked. Sweat glistened in the light of the flash, which burned like a sun in the mirror of the dressing table behind the bed. The sheet had been pulled down to just below her panty line, exposing her small, firm breasts, toned stomach and the first hint of dark pubic hair.

Doug's jaw began to ache as he clamped down hard, shame burning in his cheeks. He felt a stab of heat in his groin as he looked at the image, screwed his eyes shut then opened them again, trying to look at the image without seeing it. It had obviously been taken by Redmonds the night of the Christmas party, the time and date stamp on the bottom left of the image told him that much. He zoomed into where the flash reflected in the mirror, saw the indistinct shadow of a naked male chest. He scrolled right, keeping the zoom on and away from the main image of Susie, over the discarded glasses of champagne, caught the edge of a TV sitting on the dressing table. He scrolled further, about three quarters of the TV coming into view before it fell off the edge of the image.

He zoomed out a little, to see what was on the TV. Wasn't surprised when his mind made sense of the smears of pink he was seeing blurred in mid-frame. Porn. What else? After all, that was how he had found out about Redmonds and Susie in the first place – the porn film on the expense accounts from the night, marked as an "entertainment event".

A thought flittered across his mind, like a gentle tap on the shoulder, and then was gone. He focused back on the details of the image, but there wasn't much else. And what was he expecting anyway? Redmonds had clearly wanted to blackmail him with this, use it to make sure Doug stayed away from him. But why? Was there a connection to Dessie Banks that he didn't want revealed, or was it something else? Something to do with this image? Doug felt another pang of guilt as he took it in, but nothing. He shut the file down, then ran another check on the flash drive, making sure he hadn't missed anything.

He knew he had to tell Susie about this. The question was, how much? If he told her about the flash drive, he would have to tell her how he got it. And then she would know he was part of the case. Would she take him straight to Burns or, after seeing the picture of her, would she even care? He certainly didn't think she was going to wrap her arms around him and thank him for what he had done, but he didn't know exactly how this was going to affect her.

He thumbed in a text to Susie. *Sorry I missed your calls, busy day. Need to talk. Meet you at my place? Noon?* Hit *Send* before he could change his mind then sat staring at his laptop. Exhaustion washed over him, fuelled by the whisky, and he slumped back in the sofa. He should go to bed. Crawl in beside Becky, wrap his arm around her. But he wouldn't – couldn't – not after looking at…

Susie

…what was on the flash drive. He hauled himself forward, made sure Redmonds' laptop was hidden in his bag then pocketed the flash drive. He called up a story he was working on for the *Tribune* – a holiday feature on a trip he had taken with Becky to a spa hotel in Perthshire a few weeks ago – then topped up his whisky and leaned back into the sofa. In the morning, he would tell Becky he had fallen asleep while working. He could see her face now, the exasperated frown, the pointed glance at the bottle beside the laptop.

He raised his glass to the bottle, toasted it, took a deep drink. Might as well make the alibi convincing.

19

The body had been discovered in Leith just after 6am, a pensioner called Dennis Winslow coming across the bloodied ruin while walking his dog and sneaking his first cigarette of the day away from his wife's prying eyes. Winslow had staggered home and called it in. Susie had been on her way to Leith anyway, planning to get in a workout at the 24-hour gym in Ocean Terminal before starting her interview with the owner of the Docking Station graphic design firm. Burns had called her just before 7am. His tone told her two things: he was pissed off, mightily; and he needed her.

"You heading for Leith this morning," he snarled, no question in the statement.

"Yes, sir. Actually, I'm almost there now."

Burns grunted. "Lucky you," he said. And through the tension, Susie thought there was the faintest glimmer of relief in his voice. Automatically, she started to ask how she could help, then caught herself. Fuck him. If he was going to ask her to do something, he would have to do the running.

Finally, Burns broke the silence, the words coming out in a torrent. "Body's been found on Dock Street, at the industrial estate close to the Scottish Government building, behind Commercial Street. Know it?"

"Yes, sir," Susie replied, tone neutral, pulse starting to quicken.

"Old man almost tripped over it. Seems like whoever the poor bastard was, someone had it in for him. Officers who secured the scene report he was badly beaten, and there's evidence of knife wounds as well."

Susie blinked, tightened her grip on the steering wheel. "Hold on, sir. Two bodies found, badly beaten and with blade injuries, in two days. Isn't that...?"

"A fucking nightmare? Yes, DS Drummond, it is. Two murders in two days. Press will have a fucking field day. And I'm due to see Alicia Leonard this morning, who just happens to sit on the Police Authority Board. So yes, it is a fuck-up. And I need it handled. So you're going to handle it for me, okay?"

"Sir? You mean...?"

"Yes, Drummond. With everyone stretched to bursting point over the Redmonds case and now this, I need you to lead on this one. Reporting to me, of course. I'll send Eddie to you once we've done with Leonard, he's yours for the duration."

Susie bit back an urge to laugh, hated the gratitude that welled up in her, and the fact that it came at the price of someone's life.

"Sir, thank you. I promise I'll –"

"Save it, Drummond," Burns interrupted, his voice leaden with exhaustion. "I told you yesterday you're a good copper. I'm trusting you with this. Handle it right and it could solve a lot of your problems. But if there's any hint of a wider link to the Redmonds case, then that's it. Understood?"

"Understood," Susie said slowly. There was that fucking name again. How long was she going to have to pay for that mistake?

Burns had briefed her the best he could and she headed for Dock Street, the car bouncing softly over the cobbles. She parked up and got out, pausing for a moment to soak in the scene. The day seemed jaundiced, milky light breaking through dirty clouds and glinting off cobbles polished to mirrors by the previous night's rain. Susie stood on the pavement, just beyond the police cordon tape, looking up the street. A little further up the road, there was a pub called the Rose Leaf. She vaguely remembered being in there a few months ago with Rebecca, laughing as their cocktails were served in old china teapots.

She turned her attention to the crime scene, a uniform standing guard as SOCOs in white suits worked behind the cordon. She straightened her back. Her case. Her lead. Fuck.

She started forward and was stopped by the chirp of her phone in her pocket. Snorted a laugh when she saw the caller ID. Who else?

"Doug, what a surprise. How did I know I'd be getting an early-morning call from you today, especially after you'd snubbed all my calls yesterday?"

"Yeah, ah, sorry about that, Susie. Busy day. Did you get my text?"

She stopped for a minute. Doug sounded harried, stressed. It might just have been the usual pressure to get to a breaking story first, get it online before his rivals, but there was something more. Something so far from his normal relaxed drawl that it set an alarm ringing in her mind.

"Yeah," she said. "I did. Was going to get back to you, but Burns has put me on something else, so I may be a bit later. That okay?"

"You mean the body found in Leith? Not much for you at this stage. Late twenties, badly beaten, serious slash wound to the upper torso and face. You won't get much back until the ID is made and Williams has ruled out a link to the Redmonds murder."

Susie felt heat rise in her cheeks as anger warmed her guts. How the fuck did he know all that? If Rebecca had told him, she was breaching just about every protocol in the book. But there was no way she would be that unprofessional.

Was there?

"Well, thanks for that, Doug. You want to write my scene of crime report for me as well and we'll call it a day? And how the hell do you know Williams is going to rule out a link between this and Redmonds?"

"Trust me, Susie, there's not a link. But I really need to see you. I'm heading for the *Trib*, going to write this one up. If you want to give me a quote to run, great, if not, I'll run it straight."

Susie blinked in confusion, the words clanging around her mind like a golf ball in a copper urn. *If you want to give me a quote, great. If not, I'll run it straight.* He wasn't pushing her for a line, an angle? "Doug, what the hell's going on? If there's something that –"

"I'm fine," he snapped. "It's just important I see you. Today. My place? I'll be there from noon, just get there when you can."

She glanced up at the crime scene, the officer guarding the cordon watching her expectantly. Thought of Burns' words. *You handle this right, it could solve a lot of your problems.* "I'll be there as soon as I can," she said finally. "If I can't make it, I'll let you know, okay?"

"Okay. This is important, Susie. Please. I can't talk about it over the phone but you'll understand when I see you."

"Fine. But Doug, if there's something about all this that you're not telling me…"

"There's not, I promise. And before you think it, Becky didn't give me anything about the body found this morning. Let just say I've got some friends in Midlothian and leave it at that."

Midlothian. Of course. Bilston was in Midlothian. And Bilston just happened to be the home of Police Scotland's emergency call-handling centre. The centre had been in the headlines for all the wrong reasons recently – missed calls, IT problems, over-stressed staff. And, naturally, Doug had covered all of those stories, built up a few favours as he did.

"You'll have to introduce me to them," Susie said.

"Yeah, right," he shot back, a glimmer of the old Doug peaking out from behind the tension in his voice. "I'll see you later, Susie."

He cut the call before she could reply. She stared at the phone for a moment, mind racing with questions. What the hell was going on? What was so important that it couldn't wait? She shook her head and pocketed the phone. Pulled her warrant card from her inside suit pocket and walked for the cordon, shoulders back.

DS Susie Drummond. Professional. Controlled. Competent. Let them whisper. Let them gossip. She would show them all. She would handle it right.

20

James reviewed events as he worked his way through his morning exercise routine, the sweat hot and cleansing on his brow. As ever, Vic had proven to be a useful, if somewhat blunt, instrument. The message had been sent and, thanks to Mr McGregor and his ilk, it would only be a matter of time before Mark received it. He smiled slightly at the thought, wondered if the little shit would have the courage to make the first move or whether he would have to seek Mark out. Was surprised by the small niggle of anger he felt when he found himself hoping it would be the latter, that Mark would need further, close, attention.

As punishment, he racked another 20kg onto the bench press, strained against the weight. Felt his muscles scream as his arms shook, the acid flooding his veins, burning them, the urge to let the weight drop a growing clamour in his mind.

"Control," he gasped, holding the weight aloft for another second before lowering it. Slowly.

He thought about the text from Vic in the early hours of this morning, short and to the point: *Message delivered. Should be found soon enough. No sign of the item, must be keeping it close. Personal attention needed?* He sneered at that. No doubt Vic thought he was being clever, trying to talk in some kind of imagined tough-man code.

James moved around the weights slowly and methodically, the only sounds in the room his grunts or the squeal of trainers on the solid wood floors. Forty minutes later, he was done, and staggered towards the mats in front of a row of floor-to-ceiling mirrors that dominated the far wall of the room. He paused in front of the mirrors, chest heaving, and considered himself. Tall, lean, muscular. His hair, which was normally impeccable, was plastered to his forehead and messy where he had raked it with his hands.

He grabbed a 12kg medicine ball from the rack in the corner, tightening his grip on the slotted handles that protruded from either side. Fixed his gaze in the mirror and held the ball out at arm's length before bringing it crashing back into his gut. He grunted, the pain exploding through his mid-section. Repeated the move again and again, driving the ball home harder each time, thoughts focused on McGregor and Mark and what needed to be done, eyes locked on his own reflection.

When he saw his eyes darken, the shadows leaking from the pupils and turning everything black, he paused. Dropped the medicine ball then drove his own fists into his stomach. After the punishment he had already inflicted on his abs, it was like hitting a raw nerve, agony white-hot and all-encompassing. He held onto the pain, savoured it like a delicacy. He lifted his T-shirt, examined the scalded flesh and nodded with satisfaction. Just enough. Nothing that would bruise, but enough to remind him of what he had done here today and what needed to be done next.

He headed for the shower, ready to make himself presentable, to slip on the suit and mask that he showed to the world. But as he went through the motions, Vic's message echoed in his mind, like a tune you couldn't quite forget.

No sign of the item, must be keeping it close. Personal attention needed?

Personal attention. Yes. Perhaps that was just what he needed. To lavish a little personal attention on someone. And it would hardly be self-indulgent. And he would be doing it for a very specific purpose. For the greater good of the group and to send a message to anyone, either within the group or without, that defiance brought consequences.

He smiled at the thought as he turned the shower to cold, the sudden shift in temperature causing him to gasp. He had identified a problem and, again, turned it into an opportunity. The thought was as invigorating as the icy water that prickled his skin like needles.

21

Doug had most of the story about the body being found in Leith written up before he even set foot in the *Capital Tribune* office. He hated the building, felt his heart hammer and his blood chill every time he stepped through the front door, and wanted to minimise how long he was going to have to be there. It was, he thought, not all that different from how thousands of people felt about their places of work. But he wondered how many of those who bitched about "going into the hell hole" for another day had seen their former boss gunned down in front of them?

He sat at his desk trying to concentrate on the screen, skim reading the copy. It was exactly as he'd promised Becky: straight, factual, steering away from making any overt links between this killing and the discovery of Redmonds' body.

Becky had got the call from DCI Burns when they were in the living room, her halfway through telling him how worried she was about his drinking. Too tired and too wired from the previous day to bother, she had taken the call in front of him, Doug picking out the highlights from her end of the conversation. It hadn't taken long to agree that it was a media clusterfuck in the making – two violent murders in two days in the heart of Scotland's capital – and Doug had agreed he would cover the story as non-sensationally as he could. The fact that it helped him as much as Becky to keep some distance between the Redmonds case and this latest killing was incidental.

Honest.

Now, at his office desk, he was giving the story a final read through when his phone pinged, a text from Rebecca: *OTR: Fife's finest coming down from the Castle to personally oversee the investigations. Might be a late one. Rx*

He rocked back for a moment as he considered that. OTR – off the record. By Fife's finest Becky meant Scotland's Chief Constable, Cameron Montrose, who was based at Police Scotland HQ at the police training college at Tulliallan Castle in Fife. It was a good line for the story – *Police Chief steps in after second murder rocks City* – and he leaned forward to the keyboard before he had even thought about it. Paused, then hit *Send*. No. Becky had done enough for him. And besides, he was putting her into enough shit as it was without that.

He waited a couple of minutes to see if the newsdesk needed anything more from him then fired off a quick email to his boss, Walter, who was hovering over the backbench, watching the last pages being put together. Doug shut down his computer and headed for the door.

Ninety minutes in the office. More than enough for one day.

He took a table at a small coffee shop across the road from the *Tribune*, watching the slow passage of students and suits as they made their way to lectures at the university buildings nearby or to the Scottish Parliament at the end of the road. The SNP had its main office halfway up an alleyway across from the *Tribune*, opposite a small BBC studio, and Doug nodded greetings to those faces he recognised.

Walter joined him about twenty minutes later, lumbering across the street like a doorman on the way to break up a fight, scalp gleaming under the salt-and-pepper stubble of hair that sat on top of his massive head.

He had taken the editor's chair shortly after Greig had been murdered, and everyone at the *Tribune* agreed it was the right move. Unlike too many career cockroaches Doug had seen emerge over the last few years – rising far beyond their ability merely by virtue of the fact their schmoozing abilities meant they avoided the P45 when the latest round of redundancies and cuts came down from on high – Walter was a proper journalist. He had worked his way up from being a local reporter to the *Tribune*, then from general reporting to political editor then assistant editor. He was a hard bastard who demanded a lot from his staff, but he was fair with it, and if he thought his reporters were in the right, he would defend them all the way, which was rare in the post-Leveson world of get the apology in first for fear of the lawsuit.

All of which made Doug feel worse for lying to him, and putting him in the position he had.

"So," Walter said as he collapsed into the chair across from Doug, the table shifting slightly to accommodate his bulk, "what's happening? Nice work on the splash, though I thought you could have gone harder on the 'two in two days' line."

Doug twitched a smile. "Call it a favour that could reap benefits," he said. "If I play straight now, we'll get first dibs on anything juicy that comes up from either this or Redmonds."

Walter gave Doug an appraising look. It wasn't a comfortable experience. "That cast iron, Doug, or just pillow talk?"

Doug held up a hand. "Easy, Walter. We'll get it as soon as they can give it. Doubt anything we get will make an edition splash, but at least we can get the exclusive online before anyone else."

Walter's face contorted in disgust. He hated the drive to digital, the marketing boys' panting insistence that being first online and "generating the page views and click-throughs was the most viable and profitable business model for newspapers in the online age". *Whatever happened to producing good quality copy on the page*, he thought.

"Aye, well, let me know. I don't need to tell you this is big, Doug. Rumour has it that the Chief Constable himself is paying a visit to keep an eye on things."

Doug looked up, his surprised expression earning a smile from Walter. "Yer no' the only one with sources, son," he said softly.

Doug nodded, made himself busy draining his coffee cup.

"So," Walter said after a moment, "how's it looking, you any-where with the Redmonds case?"

Doug wished he had something left in his mug to hide behind. *Aye, boss, you could say I'm somewhere with that. Oh, and just so you know, the splash you ran yesterday was about as close to a wit-ness statement as I could get, so you might want to check with the lawyers on that one...*

"Actually," he murmured, forcing his eyes to meet Walter's, "I'm just off to see a contact about that now. Might be a line in it. I'll let you know." *Either that,* he thought, *or I'll call you to tell you I've been arrested.*

Walter nodded, leaned back from the table. "Douglas," he said slowly, "you alright, son? I know you're still finding your feet after what happened but I dunno, you seem..."

The laugh was out before Doug could stop it, too loud for the hushed murmur of the coffee shop. He glanced around, saw others looking at him with a mixture of accusation and confusion. Guessed he might have to get used to that.

"Sorry, Walter," he said. "Really. I'm fine. Thanks. Just this fuck-ing hand hurts a lot, you know? And being back at the *Trib* always stirs up some nasty memories."

"Aye," Walter said, grabbing for a sachet of sugar from the bowl on the table and running it through his huge fingers. "I can only imagine. That's why I've no' pushed about you coming back to the desk full-time. Just keep filing the stories and checking in. Far as I'm concerned, the high heidyins need never know different."

"They still keeping an eye on me?"

It was Walter's turn to laugh. "The fuck you think? You exposed a cover-up at the heart of the *Tribune*, Doug, showed that a former editor and senior reporter colluded in obscuring vital evidence in a murder trial. Course they're keeping an eye on you. You're bad news. But they're happier with you being bad news in-house than on the street."

Doug felt his checks redden. "Thanks for looking out for me, Walter. Sorry for being such a pain in the arse."

Walter crushed the sugar sachet in his hand, gave a derisive snort. "Fuck 'em," he snarled. "Pencil-pushing wankers who wouldnae know what a newspaper should be if it curled itself up and tanned them on the arse. Just bring me the stories, Doug, forget the rest."

Doug nodded. Wondered what story he would be bringing to Walter next. Would it be the one about the crime reporter arrested for withholding evidence linked to an ongoing murder inquiry in which he had a starring role? He felt the sudden, overwhelming urge just to tell Walter everything. Knew that for the cowardice it was. If he did that, there was no way Walter would let him meet Susie.

And, like it or not, that was one meeting he couldn't avoid any longer.

22

Doug was back at his flat in Musselburgh twenty minutes later, taking the fact that he found a space right outside as a good omen that things would work out better than he expected. The illusion stayed with him all the way up the stairs, only beginning to dim when he opened the door and stepped into the hallway. He paused for a moment, then shrugged, dumped his laptop bag and threw the keys into the small dish on the unit underneath the coat rack. Got to work tidying the place up before Susie arrived.

He made straight for the living room, intent on clearing away the piles of notes, books and clothes he had left there. Knew he was in deep shit when he reached across the coffee table for an abandoned glass that sat there, a bottle of Jameson standing neatly to attention next to it. The inside of the glass was wet, as though it had been recently used. But Doug hadn't been back home since yesterday morning, so the glass should have been dry and crusted, just like the one that sat next to his seat. He straightened up abruptly, adrenalin surging through him, his ears feeling like they were twitching towards the slightest foreign sound. He swiped for the whisky bottle, grabbing it by the neck, ignoring the pain in his hand.

…the pain in his hand…

He strode back through into the hallway, making for the front door. Realised now what had bothered him when he opened it. He had used his left hand instinctively, too preoccupied by the thought of what he was going to say to Susie to remember the pain it always caused him to turn the lock. But this time, it hadn't hurt. Why?

He picked up his keys, ran his thumb along the front door key. Felt something smooth and slick there. Opened the door and wiped his fingers across the face of the lock. Found the same dry smoothness, saw his fingers came away smudged a dark grey-black. Pencil lead. It was an old lock-picker's trick – blow a little powdered graphite into a lock you were about to work on and it would lubricate the tumblers, making them easier to feel and push aside. He had used it a time or two himself. It was also great for making older locks easier to turn. Just the thing for reporters with hand injuries.

He stood for a moment on the threshold of his flat, torn, the thought of just turning and bolting down the stairs a growing scream in his mind. What if someone was still in there? What if they were waiting to pounce from the shadows, grab him, demand to know where what they were looking for was?

Ah, but what were they looking for? In answer, he fumbled into his pocket with his free hand, closed his fist around the flash drive. Thought of Susie, felt the terror give way to something colder and uglier – the same desire to lash out and hurt someone that had seized him the night he attacked Redmonds.

He tightened his grip on the whisky bottle, moved back into the flat. Slowly, cautiously, senses almost supernaturally charged and alert. He crept from room to room, braced for an attack at any second, ready to lash out with the bottle and crush it into his attacker's face. Found nothing but the small, subtle signs that the place had been searched – a draped tea towel caught in a kitchen drawer that had been carelessly closed, half a muddy footprint on a letter behind the front door, piles of clutter not quite where they should be in the living room.

Whoever had been here was gone, not finding what they came for. They had done a good job, mostly, nothing disturbed at first glance, only stopping for a quick drink. He thought of his mystery visitor, standing in his flat, his home, giving the place an appraising glance, contemplatively sipping on his whisky as they did. The anger rose in him again, scalding in his gut and he stepped forward, ready to grab the glass and hurl the fucking thing at the wall.

"Doug?"

He whirled round, raising the whisky bottle above his head in a jerky, unsure spasm. Susie stood there, hands held out in front of her, skin pale, eyes huge and locked on the bottle.

"Whoa, Doug, what the fuck?" she said, taking a half-step forward as she balanced her weight and prepared for a lunging attack. "You okay there? Door was open, thought I'd come in. I shouted, didn't get a reply. Thought maybe…"

He lowered the bottle, felt the rage and adrenalin bleed out of him, eclipsed by the churning torrent of guilt, fear and shame he now felt.

"Sorry, Susie," he said, voice hoarse with tears that suddenly threatened behind his eyes, burning. "I was just looking around. Ah, looks like I've had a break-in."

Susie tensed, head jerking around as she took in the room. "What? I don't see how. Doug? What the fuck is this about? What's going on?"

He gave her a weak smile, suddenly aware of how tired he was. The bottle in his hand was cool and heavy. And inviting. He thumbed at the cap, spun it free. Dug into his pocket and pulled out the flash drive. Held it out to her with a shaking hand, found he couldn't look into her eyes.

"I'm sorry, Susie," he said, trying to crush down the tears. "I really, really am. I think this was what they were looking for. Which means we've got an even bigger problem."

"Doug, what the…?" Susie began, her voice filling with impatience, her eyes telling him she thought he was losing his mind. Maybe he was.

He nodded to the door. "Go get a couple of clean glasses from the kitchen," he said. "Trust me, we're going to need them. While you're doing that I'll get my laptop. Then you can see for yourself."

• • •

He set his laptop up on the coffee table, poured her a large Jameson, then retreated deeper into the living room, standing with his back to the bay window that looked out on to the flats opposite.

"Just open up the file that's on the flash drive. There's only one there," he said, his voice a shaking whisper. He didn't bother with a glass for himself, just swigged straight from the bottle. Felt the whisky burn down his throat, knew he deserved much worse.

Susie gave him a confused glance, then lowered her head and got to work on the laptop. He watched the light from the screen play across her face, found he couldn't bear the silence that slowly filled the room. He heard the soft double-click of the track pad, the screen turning brighter against her face. Saw the moment of incomprehension, the flinch as she made sense of what she was seeing, heard her breathing turn harsh and sharp and shallow. Saw her eyes narrow then redden, the stress rash he knew all too well surging across her chest like wildfire.

He shuffled forward on numb legs, took another greedy slug of whisky. Started to talk quickly, the words tumbling out as he sought to fill the maddening silence between them. Told her about the phone call from Redmonds, the meeting in Portobello, how he had reacted when he had shown him the image on the flash drive.

Susie rocked back in the sofa, hands scuttling up to her mouth. The tears were flowing now, glistening in the light from the laptop screen. She shook her head slowly, eyes not moving from the screen. He realised she wasn't listening to him, felt something with sharp teeth and dull, poisonous eyes roil in his chest as he wondered if she would ever listen to him again.

The shame coursed through him again, burning his cheeks. "I'm sorry, Susie," he mumbled, retreating back towards the window. "I'm so, so sorry. I just didn't know what else to do. The thought of that bastard having that… I just, I…" He trailed off, the words drying up in his throat.

Susie blinked once, closed her eyes, shook her head. He could see her chest heaving, nostrils flaring as she fought to control her breathing. The cords on her neck stood out against her pale skin, as though she was screaming. She wiped at her cheeks angrily, as though the tears offended her. Then she opened her eyes and locked onto him, the fury and, yes, hatred, in her glare forcing him to recoil.

"A day?" she whispered, her voice as cold and hard as a marble tombstone. "You had this for a *day*? You had this when I was here, in this flat, sobbing my eyes out to you? You knew about this then? And when you called me about the Redmonds case, when I, I…" – she broke eye contact with him, staring up to the ceiling as if there was an answer there – "when I texted you about the preliminary findings. You had this? You knew what had happened?"

"Yes, Susie. I'm sorry, like I said I just didn't…"

"Fuck's sake, Doug!" she roared, exploding from the couch and covering the space between them in a moment. She stood in front of him, chest heaving, eyes wide, searching his face for something he didn't understand.

And then she hit him. A fast, hard jab at his ribs, forcing the breath from his lungs in a whooping cough that doubled him over. And as his head fell, she followed up with a hammering slap across the face, the blow rattling his teeth and blurring his vision.

"A fucking day!" she shouted, her voice a thunderclap as she turned away and stalked to the other side of the room, hands clamped firmly to her sides as though she couldn't trust them. "And what did you do with it in that day, Doug? Hmm? While I was running around wondering if Redmonds' death was going to further fuck my career? Did you have a few sneaky looks? Enjoy a wee wank over it with a whisky? Not that you need a fucking excuse to have a drink these days. You fucking BASTARD!"

She rushed back across the room to him, tears flowing faster. He saw her right hand bunch into a fist as she drew it back, eyes darkening.

"And did you even fucking think about the damage you were doing to the case? For fuck's sake, Doug, this is material evidence. You beat the shit out of a man then left the scene with evidence that could be directly related to his murder! And then" – she spat a bitter laugh, rolled her head to the ceiling again as though just coming to understand the punchline to a bad joke – "you write up the story in which you're implicated and run it in the *Tribune*. So now you're fucked, I'm fucked and, yeah, Rebecca is probably fucked too. Jesus, Doug. What the *fuck* were you thinking?"

The words hit him harder than her slap, washed away the pain and the fuzziness and the buzz from the whisky. He remembered lunging at Redmonds, his savage joy at the sounds of his pain, the feel of his body bucking beneath his kicks.

He stood up straight, locked his eyes with hers. "I was thinking," he said slowly, deliberately, "that I didn't want anyone else seeing that, that..." – he gestured towards the laptop with the bottle – "... that fucking obscenity and leering over you. I wasn't thinking about me or the story or the case or even Rebecca. I was thinking about you, Susie, that's all."

She stared at him dumbly, mouth dropping open then snapping shut. He saw the tension bleed from her shoulders, her fist uncurling. She put both hands to her face and covered her eyes, and he watched as she fought back harder, deeper tears.

"Look, Susie, I..."

She stepped forward and he braced for another blow, refusing to move. Instead, for the second time in two days, she wrapped her arms around him and sobbed. He felt a rush of awkwardness, slowly, stiffly returned the hug. Muttered something meaningless about it all being okay. Glanced over her shoulder at the laptop on the coffee table. Knew what a crock of shit that really was.

23

Alicia Leonard lived in a gated development in Inveresk, a small conservation village south of Musselburgh. It was typical pic-ture-postcard East Coast Scotland, the main road through the vil-lage was bracketed on both sides by high stone walls over which privet hedges spilled and ancient trees loomed. Behind the walls, huge houses crouched in immaculate gardens.

DC Eddie King turned the pool car up a small driveway that led off the main street, opposite a couple of houses washed orange and umber, their slate-grey roofs only accentuating the splash of colour in the drabness of the day. He pulled up to the gate slowly and hit the intercom. Waited a few seconds, got a harsh, static bark, "Yes, Mr and Mrs Leonard are expecting you," before the black metal gates slid open.

From the passenger seat Burns surveyed the estate's huge build-ings crafted in granite and sandstone, their massive white-framed bay windows carefully shuttered against the outside world. He checked off the brands of cars sitting in driveways – Porsche, Audi, Land Rover, BMW. It was, he thought, a long way from the home Leonard had shared with Redmonds in Brunton when they had been married and on the force together.

When they had split, he had moved to Trinity, while she had stayed in the family home for a couple of years until meeting her current husband, Michael Leonard. According to what Burns had been able to pull together, Leonard was a big shot in investment banking, working for one of the main players who made their home on George Street in Edinburgh. It explained the house they were drawing up to now, and the six-figure car sitting in front of it. A former copper's pension wasn't that good. A fact Burns knew all too well.

King eased the Mondeo to a halt outside the house, killed the engine.

"So, boss," he said, eyes not moving from the double front door of the house, "how do you want to play this?"

Burns let the cop show cliché pass, happy that Eddie was at least using his brain and thinking seriously about the situation. That much was apparent from the suit he was wearing, which looked brand new, the high polish on his shoes, perfectly styled hair and the small nick behind his ear where he had obviously cut himself shaving that morning.

"Respectfully," Burns said as he popped his belt. "We're here as a routine part of the investigation. The fact that Mrs Leonard sits on the Police Board is of no concern to us. But, that said," – he turned his gaze to Eddie, let the weight of it settle on him and cause him to squirm a little – "Mrs Leonard has some good friends among the high heidyins. So we answer her questions, play nice and say nothing that is going to blowback on us. Okay?"

"Okay," Eddie replied, sounding a lot less convincing than he should. Poor kid would never make it as a detective if he didn't work on the poker face, Burns thought.

"Right," Burns said, "let's get it over with, then. Wouldn't do to keep Mrs Leonard waiting."

• • •

The door was answered by a tall man with dark hair and skin scrubbed tight and flawless. He was wearing jeans and a T-shirt that no doubt cost more than Burns' entire wardrobe. He smiled warmly at them, the sentiment not reaching the eyes behind his elegant rimless glasses, and offered a hand to Burns. He took it, surprised at the firmness of the man's grip.

"You must be DCI Burns," the man said, a trace of somewhere south of the border in his soft voice. "I'm Michael Leonard."

Burns nodded. "Yes, sir, good to meet you. And this" – he gestured slightly to Eddie – "is DC Eddie King. Thanks for taking the time to see us today."

Leonard released his grip on Burns, leaned past him to shake King's hand. Burns watched the young officer, saw the skin around his collar flush darker as Leonard took his hand and shook it. Burns had seen it a thousand times before – the attempt to assert early dominance with a firm handshake that left you in no doubt who the alpha male was. He'd long since given up on these pissing contests, content in the knowledge that his grip was hard enough to crush the balls of whoever he needed to when the time came.

Dispensing with the pleasantries, Leonard ushered them along a wide, tiled hallway to the living room at the back of the house. It was a massive room, a piano tucked in one corner, peppered with family photos, a huge flatscreen TV mounted on a wall above a marble fireplace. The colour scheme was light cream and tasteful greys, chosen, surely, to maximise the light from the bay window that dominated the far side of the room, the Pentland Hills visible in the distance.

Leonard gestured for them to take a seat on one of two couches that sat at right angles to a low, dark-stained wooden coffee table. "Please, gentlemen, take a seat. Alicia will be with us in a moment. As you can imagine, this has been quite a shock for her, so I'd appreciate it if we made this as brief as possible."

"Absolutely, sir," Burns agreed. "This is purely routine given Mrs Leonard's previous relationship with the deceased." He paused for half a beat, made a decision. "Speaking of whom, did you know Mr Redmonds at all?"

Leonard shook his head, glasses glinting gently. "Only from what Alicia told me," he said, his voice adopting the appropriate level of respect for the recently deceased. He would, Burns thought randomly, make a good politician. "Alicia and I only met after Paul had filed for divorce and, as you can imagine, she was in no rush to introduce us after. He was, to be blunt, somewhat selfish in his demands."

"Oh, how so?" Burns asked. Curious. The rumour he had heard was that Alicia had been planning to file for divorce *before* Redmonds' dalliance at the Christmas party had become the source of copy shop gossip and innuendo – that the relationship was effectively over before that.

Leonard shrugged, non-committal. "Oh, the usual. Property. Money. He was quite aggressive in the divorce settlement, I understand. That kind of fight leaves wounds, DCI Burns."

Burns nodded. Wondered, not for the first time, what would happen if his Carol ever decided to leave him. Not that they had much to fight over other than the kids, but still…

"Anyway," Leonard said, "where are my manners? Can I interest you gentlemen in a tea or coffee?"

"Coffee," a voice came from the entrance to the living room. "We'll have coffee please, Michael."

Leonard crossed the room to greet his wife. She was every bit as striking as Burns remembered from a brief meeting with her years ago: tall, thin, cold green eyes framed in a face that was just a little too angular to be attractive. He thought he detected a hint more grey in her hair, but other that that, the years seemed to be kind. Remarriage and money, not a bad anti-aging formula.

Leonard kissed Alicia on the cheek then headed out of the room in search of coffee. Burns and Eddie rose from the couch, took Alicia Leonard's cool hand as she offered it to both of them in turn then gestured them to return to their seats as she perched on the other couch.

"So, gentlemen," she said, just a hint of Perthshire dryness in her measured tones, "how can I help? As you know, I identified Paul and gave a statement shortly after, so I'm not sure what else I can offer."

Burns smiled, feeling as though he had been blindfolded and

sent into a minefield. With the Chief Constable set to arrive at any time, the last thing he wanted was to piss this woman off.

"We won't take long, Mrs Leonard," he said, producing his notebook, "and we appreciate your time. But, being a former officer yourself, you know there are procedures we have to follow, steps we have to take."

She nodded, eyes not leaving his. "Not part of the job I miss," she said. "So please, ask what you need to. I'm not sure what help I can be, though. As I said in my statement, I hadn't seen Paul in months before he, ah" – she cleared her throat – "died. Tell me, have you made any progress in the investigation?"

Burns felt Eddie shift slightly on the couch beside him, found it impossible not to be impressed by Alicia Leonard. She had subtly turned the conversation back on him, knowing that her position on the Police Board ensured her an answer. She must have been a hell of an interviewer when she was on the force.

"Well, we're following the standard lines of enquiry, Mrs Leonard," he said. "Processing the evidence, trying to build a picture of Mr Redmonds' life. You said you hadn't seen him in months. When was the last time you saw him?"

"At a retirement party for a former colleague – John Wallace? Perhaps you know him? I dropped in as a courtesy to John, didn't hang around when I realised Paul was there too."

Burns murmured his thanks. He knew old John, had been on the beat in Craigmillar in the late 1980s when he had been a desk sergeant there. He was a good cop, maybe a little heavy-handed at times, but he knew the job. He had been sorry he hadn't been able to make his retirement party, but he was duty CID officer that night and, unsurprisingly, no one wanted to swap the shift or cover him.

"And your husband wasn't with you that night?"

"No," Alicia replied. "Michael was in London on business. He wasn't back until…" – she paused, made a show of considering – "the following day, I think it was."

Burns scribbled a note: *Speak to John.* It was most likely point-less, he had probably been too pished to see straight, but it might be useful. And besides, he didn't have much else to go on.

"And you didn't speak to Mr Redmonds that evening? Didn't get the impression there was anything bothering him?"

"As I said," Alicia replied, a subtle shard of impatience creeping into her tone, "I dropped in to John's leaving do as a courtesy. When I saw Paul there, I paid my respects to John and left. I didn't speak to Paul. Frankly, didn't want to."

Burns nodded, made a mental note that she didn't like being pushed. Could be useful.

"Can you think of anyone who might have wanted Paul dead?" he asked. "The violence of the attack suggests a personal motive. Is there someone who would have had enough reason to kill Paul in such a violent manner?"

Alicia Leonard laughed suddenly, humourlessly, the sound of glass shattering on stone. She saw Burns' and King's reaction, held up a hand in apology.

"I'm sorry, gentlemen, I am. You obviously didn't know Paul. I can't think of many people who knew him who *didn't* want to slap him about or knock a few teeth out. You see, he had that effect. He was totally oblivious to how he affected other people, used his over-confidence in his own abilities and arrogance to ignore what he didn't want to see. Oh, don't get me wrong, he could be charming when he wanted to be, but he was, bluntly, a selfish bastard. He used people. Said what they wanted to hear to get what he wanted, didn't give a shit about the wreckage he left behind. So yes, I can imagine there's a long list of people out there who wanted to give him a good slap. But beat him like that? Kill him? No."

It tallied with what Burns had heard of the man. *An arrogant little fuck who charmed his way to where he needed to be,* was how one detective had summed up Redmonds. He found himself won-dering again what Susie had seen in the slimy little prick.

He was about to ask another question when Michael Leonard returned, laden down with a heavy silver tray, which held a cafetière, cream, sugar and an array of biscuits. He sat it down on the table, poured coffee and then distributed the cups before perching beside Alicia and wrapping a protective arm around her shoulder. She stroked his hand gently, murmured thanks.

"So gentlemen," he said, "where were we?"

Burns looked again at his notes. Wished he knew.

24

"So," Susie said, considering Doug coolly over the lip of her coffee mug, "what the fuck do we do now?"

Doug leaned back in the couch opposite her, coffee cradled to his chest. The quiet in the flat felt charged, oppressive, as if saying the wrong word or asking the wrong question would reignite the fury and pain and guilt that had raged through the place less than a hour ago. The simple answer was, he didn't know. He hadn't thought that far ahead, had only focused on telling Susie what had happened. But now, here they were, drinking the coffee she had insisted on making, discussing next steps. It was so surreal it gave him a vague case of vertigo.

"I'm not sure," he said, sitting up straighter. He spotted the bottle of whisky on the coffee table, imagined pouring a heavy jolt into his coffee.

Susie broke her gaze on him long enough to take a sip of coffee then returned it straight to him. There was anger and hurt in those red-rimmed eyes, but again Doug had the feeling she was looking for something he didn't understand. More than just an answer to her question but... what?

He shrugged, surrendering to the inevitability that she was going to wait him out until he said something. "Okay, let's look at the options. The best thing, from a procedural point of view, would be for you to caution me right now. Tell Burns what I told you, hand over the flash drive and Redmonds' laptop as evidence. I'll give a statement, and we'll see what happens. But I don't need to tell you what that means."

He watched Susie's knuckles flush white as she gripped the mug tighter. "It would mean *that*" – she nodded to the closed laptop in front of her – "becoming public knowledge. From Burns to forensics to any other fucker who fancied a sneaky look." She closed her eyes, crushed the coffee mug into her forehead. "Jesus fuck."

Doug nodded. "So that's option one out. Which leaves us with only one other option."

"Which is?" Susie asked. She already knew, but wasn't sure if she wanted Doug to articulate it. If he did, it would be real. A choice to be made. One that would change everything.

Doug leaned forward, reaching for the whisky. Saw Susie's expression harden, let his hand fall short. "The only other thing we can do is keep this to ourselves. Try to figure out whatever the fuck is going on and see if we can keep you and that picture out of it."

"But what the fuck *is* going on?"

"I don't know yet," Doug said. "But it's definitely tied to that flash drive, Redmonds' laptop, or both. If this had been just a case of Redmonds trying to get me to back off, then why would someone suddenly decide to burgle my flat?"

He gestured to the TV on the wall, the stereo on the bookshelf. "And they weren't very good burglars, were they? No, whoever broke in here knew what they were doing, and knew what they were looking for. The only new things that have been in this flat in the last month are the laptop and the flash drive. And since Redmonds used a burner to call me that night, he was obviously trying to hide something from someone. We find them, we find some answers."

"But how do we do that?" Susie asked. "You've said there's nothing else on the flash drive, or Redmonds' laptop. And since I'm not going to call this in," – she grimaced, the idea obviously repellent to her – "we can't get forensics to pick this place apart to see if there are any traces of whoever broke in. So what have we got? An empty laptop and a revenge porn pic of me. How does that help?"

Doug considered. Susie wasn't going to like this, but it wouldn't be the first bad news he'd given her today. "I said there's nothing on the flash drive or laptop that I can see, but I'm not a computer expert. We need someone who is. To have a look at them, see if I've missed anything."

Her head darted up, eyes locking with Doug's. He saw tears threaten again, held back only by the cold fury and shame in her eyes. "Doug, no, I can't, I mean, I…"

Doug reached again for the whisky. Fuck it. "It's okay," he said. "I know someone who can help, who we can trust." He gave a small smile. "And I can guarantee you he's not going to care what you look like in that picture."

He regretted what he'd said the moment he saw the agony collapse Susie's face. Put the mug down, held his hands up. "Sorry, sorry. Poor choice of words. But Colin's a good guy, Susie, we can trust him and he'll make sure this doesn't go any further."

"Colin?" Susie whispered, running the name through her head. "Colin? You mean Colin Damon, Hal's husband? How can he help with this?"

"He's a graphic designer," Doug said, "but he's also a tech geek. Spends a lot of his time building websites for clients, writing code and scripts to make things work. He's helped me on a story or two in the past, tracking down URLs for shell companies and the like. He's good, Susie. And we can trust him. And Hal."

Susie thought for a moment. Doug had been friends with Hal for a while now and he'd introduced her to Hal, his husband, Colin, and their three-year-old daughter, Jennifer. They were a sickeningly perfect family, she thought, content and happy, although just a little too eager to push Doug and Susie together.

"You sure we can trust them?" she asked.

"Absolutely. And we need answers, Susie. We're in the dark here."

"Speaking of in the dark, are you going to tell Rebecca about this?"

Doug looked away, reached for his mug again. He had expected that Becky would find out when Susie dragged him in front of Burns. But instead, here they were, effectively concocting a conspiracy to pervert the course of justice. And why? He'd said it himself. *I was only thinking of you, Susie.*

"No," he said finally. "This is between us. When we know what the hell is going on, I'll tell Becky at the same time you tell Burns. Until then…"

"What?" Susie asked, relief coursing through her as something else squeezed at her chest.

"We do what we normally do," he said. "You grab Eddie, look into the Leith body. The beating isn't connected to the shit-kicking I gave Redmonds, you know that now. So someone else did it. So you have to find them. Burns didn't want you anywhere near the Redmonds case anyway, so this will keep you off his radar and in his good books. Meanwhile, I'll look into this with Hal and Colin, and write up the Leith story as it develops."

Susie felt disbelief wash over her. The more they spoke about this, the more insane it seemed. The two of them, working together secretly under the noses of Burns and the entire senior brass of Police Scotland, hoping to find something that would save their arses. It was ridiculous, preposterous, insane.

Yeah, she thought, *as insane as some cheap fuck taking a nude pic of you when you're passed out.*

"Okay," she sighed, feeling the urge to just lunge forward and smash up the flash drive and the laptop. Knew it was futile. "But, Doug, if we're going to do this, you need to do one thing for me."

He looked at her, mug halfway to his lips, confusion etched across his face. She took him in then, the over-prominent cheeks, the dull grey skin, black rings under his eyes, hair raked up into even more expressionistic shapes than normal. Thought back to that first night in the hospital after he had been attacked by Diane Pearson, how small and fragile he had looked in the bed, his arm in a cast. He looked worse now.

"What?" he asked.

"Put the mug down, get rid of the bottle. If we're going to do this, I need you, not the booze-soaked, self-pitying twat you've become since the Pearson case."

He stared at her, jaw falling open. She saw his eyes dart between her and the bottle, colour racing into his cheeks. After a moment, he placed the mug on the coffee table, pushed it away. Bunched his left hand into a fist, wincing as he did. She saw his eyes dart around as memories scudded across his mind. She wondered what he was seeing, felt a surge of pity for him, the sudden urge to put an arm around him. After everything that had happened, nightmares were something Doug McGregor would never be short of.

"It just fucking hurts, Susie," he whispered finally, not looking at her.

She stared at him, letting the statement hang in the air. Waited for him to raise his eyes to meet hers then nodded softly.

He was right. It did fucking hurt. Both of them.

25

After finishing the interview with the Leonards, Burns told Eddie to drive them to a small hotel and gastro pub he knew that was only ten minutes away on the road to Wallyford. The hotel itself looked like a beefed-up version of the houses they had seen in the Leonards' estate, with an added tower and ivy crawling lazily up the granite walls. The restaurant was at the back, designed to blend in as well as a go-kart in a Formula One race. They got a table in the back of the restaurant, which gave them a scenic view of the kids' play area. Burns hated seeing play areas in the rain. They always depressed him.

They ordered meals, Burns noting that King's selection matched his almost exactly in price, then sat back and waited. Eddie broke the silence first.

"So, boss, what do you think?"

"I think you should stop calling me boss for a start," Burns said, not taking his eyes from the play area. There was something about it, something triggering a thought in his mind, a vague memory that dissolved like a half-remembered dream. He pushed the thought away, concentrated on his notebook on the table, pleased to see that Eddie had been as thorough with his note-taking as he had been. Maybe the kid wasn't a total loss, after all. He had kept his mouth shut and his ears open. Vital skills for a copper.

"What did you make of them?" Burns asked.

Eddie shifted in his seat, eased his tie down and his collar away from his neck, which was starting to look angry with razor burn. "Not sure, bo... sir. It's obvious they're loaded and, if what Mrs

Leonard said is true, then neither she nor her husband would have any motive or desire to see Redmonds hurt."

"But?" Burns asked, sensing there was something Eddie wasn't saying.

"Nothing really, sir," Eddie said, glancing between his notes and Burns nervously. "It's just that when you asked Mrs Leonard about the last time she'd seen Redmonds, at the party for…" – he paused, flicking through his notes – "a former officer called John Wallace, she seemed a bit hacked off when you pushed her on whether she had spoken to Redmonds that night or not. Might be nothing – after all, she sits on the Board, isn't used to having mere grunts like us asking questions – but still, seemed a little out of sorts to me."

Burns nodded approvingly. He also remembered the sharpness in Alicia Leonard's tone when he had pushed the point with her. Which led him to another thought. Something Paul Leonard had said: *He was quite aggressive in the divorce settlement, I understand. That kind of fight leaves wounds.*

It backed up what she had said about not wanting to talk to Redmonds, but it begged another question: how deep did those wounds run?

"…you want me to check up on, sir?"

"Sorry, Eddie?" Burns said, dragged back from his thoughts.

"I asked if there was something from the interview you wanted me to check up on?"

Burns shook his head, looked down at his own notes – and the scribbled instructions he had left for himself. "No, thanks, Eddie. As you said, she's got no motive for this. Why go to the bother of killing an odious ex when you're sitting pretty with a new husband, a high-profile place on the Police Board and more money than you can spend on Botox?" He saw Eddie smile at that, hoped he had the sense to keep the joke to himself. "No, we've done our duty, assured her that the investigation is ongoing and played nice so the Chief doesn't rain shit down on us from a great height when he arrives later on."

"So what can I do?" Eddie asked, trying, and failing to mask his disappointment. His earlier nerves were gone, replaced by that puppy-dog enthusiasm to get to work, help his boss.

"You," Burns said as he leant away from the table, letting the waiter place their lunches in front of them, "can write up your take on the interview and send it to me. But later. Once we're done here, you're going to find DS Drummond and help her with the body found in Leith this morning."

Pleasure and disappointment skittered across Eddie's face, the resulting expression almost comical. Burns understood. Eddie liked working with Susie, and by all accounts they had the makings of a good team. But the office gossip told him she was damaged goods, especially at the moment, which could reflect badly on him and his career prospects. Good observational skills and an awareness of office politics, Burns thought, this kid might just go places, after all.

They ate mostly in silence, exchanging the odd pleasantry, and when they finished Eddie headed for the toilets, leaving Burns to look back over his notes. When he got to the last page, he read over his reminders to himself:

Check in with John Wallace re leaving do.

Redmonds – money worries etc?

Thought for a moment. Remembered again what Paul Leonard had said about wounds. Added another item to his list: *Check divorce papers. Grounds?* Circled the note and drew an arrow from it down a couple of lines. Wrote the word *Quietly* and underlined it three times.

It was probably a waste of time, but if there was a straw to be clutched, he would take it. So Redmonds was a bastard, fine, that meant he could have invited the kicking he got. But the savagery of it bothered Burns. As he said to Alicia Leonard, it felt personal, as if Redmonds was being punished for some kind of insult or outrage. Which was why the cause of death bothered him. A single stab wound from a long, thin and incredibly sharp, bladed

114

instrument. It seemed almost cold, clinical, compared to the savagery of the beating.

He stared out at the abandoned play area, watched the swings moving gently in the wind, the rain pooling at the bottom of the dull silver slide. Felt the niggle at the back of his mind again, a picture that refused to develop.

26

The call was as unexpected as it was welcome, injecting what was proving to be a wearisome day with the almost irresistible chance to vent his frustrations. If he believed in such things, James would have almost thought it was fate smiling on him, rewarding him for his work so far.

He sat now, considering the phone he had just placed back on his desk, trying to delete his own desires out of the situation, see it for what it was. A business transaction. Another variable to be assessed and addressed.

An opportunity.

The caller had been direct to the point of brusque. "You know whae this is?"

"Why of course I do," he said, his tone neutral and measured. "And I have to say, this is an unexpected pleasure, and I'm slightly at a loss as to how you would be in possession of this number."

"Never mind that shite," the caller spat, tension thickening the coarse accent. "I've got some information you'll find useful, something your bosses will no doubt be keen to hear."

James bristled. Tightened his grip on the phone. *His bosses?*

"Yes," he said calmly. The urge to lash out crawled through him again, a bone-deep itch to explode into anger, hurl the phone against the wall, upturn his desk, smash the computer and scream his rage to the world.

Instead, he rolled his shoulders, the leather of his seat creaking softly.

"So, you fucking interestit' or no'?" the caller hissed.

"Potentially," he said slowly, relishing the caller's discomfort. He would make them suffer, show them who the real boss was here. "But first, I have two questions. What do you want in return for this information and why are you approaching me with it?"

A heavy sigh wheezed down the line, followed by a wet, eager sucking noise. A cigarette being drawn on deeply, the smoker no doubt finding relaxation and relief as ephemeral and elusive as the smoke that drifted from its glowing tip.

"Fuck's sake, I just telt ye!" the caller shouted at last. "Yer bosses will want to know about this, especially with all this shite about Paul Redmonds flying about at the moment."

James straightened in his chair, entirely focused on the phone call. "Go on," he said, not surprised that his voice was half an octave deeper and devoid of anything resembling warmth or emotion. There was danger here. And in the face of danger, he was as cold and hard as a tempered blade. It was what he had learned to do. How he had survived.

"Firstly, I want a guarantee, okay?"

"Go on," he repeated.

"Nae killin'. Ye can fuck him up a bit, nae problem. Deliver a message. But you cannae kill. If you do that, I'll shout your fucking name from the rooftops, burn the whole bastard lot of you to the ground."

"Kill who?" James asked, forcing himself not to break the phone in his grip.

"Rab MacFarlane," the caller said, voice dropping to a whisper.

"And why would I want to 'fuck up' Rab MacFarlane?" James asked. He knew the name, of course, everyone who moved in certain circles of Edinburgh society did. He wasn't adverse to a few less-than-legal sidelines, but hated drugs. And hookers. Not a natural business associate.

"Because," the caller said, as though explaining a simple problem to an uncomprehending toddler, "he's been asking about things that he shouldn't be. Things that are liable to get him into real trouble. Things your bosses wouldn't want him, or anyone, to be asking about."

"Such as?"

"Paul Redmonds. The Falcon's Rest. Dessie Banks. Want me to go on?"

James reached for a pen on his desk, held it like a knife. "And why would Mr MacFarlane be asking such questions? What's his interest?"

"He's daein' a favour for Doug McGregor. You know, the reporter."

James felt a thrill of excitement despite himself. McGregor. Again. "Oh yes, I know Mr McGregor quite well."

A pause on the line, more sucking at the cigarette. Then, a question. Urgent. Furtive. "So what are ye going to do about it?"

"Do? Now that is the question, isn't it? But you are right, this is exactly what my *associates* would want to know. So thank you."

"Fuck yer thanks," the caller snarled. "Just remember what I said. Shut him up, fuck him up, but nae killin'. You kill him, or anyone connected with him, I'll burn you. Guaranteed."

James hung up without saying anything else. Rocked back into his chair. Considered. Rab MacFarlane, an agent of Doug McGregor? It was an interesting connection – and a troublesome one. The logical thing to do would be give the task to Vic, get him to have a word with MacFarlane, persuade him to stop poking at a hornet's nest. It would be quick, final, unequivocal.

But…

Vic had already failed him. He had delivered the message as discussed, the morning papers told James that much, but he had failed to secure the missing key from McGregor. And James was too cautious to believe that such an error hadn't alerted McGregor to the fact that he was in possession of something valuable. It raised the tantalising possibility that Mr McGregor would have to be dealt with more definitively than he had first envisaged. Which was a shame. He had seen potential in the man.

So what was he to do? Send Vic to MacFarlane's door, have him deliver another message? And if he did that, could he guarantee one or both of the men would end up dead? He cared little for Vic's fate, but he knew the caller had been sincere in their threat that, should MacFarlane be killed, they would all be exposed.

He nodded to himself, satisfied, the vague glow of anticipation tickling at the base of his spine. He would send Vic after McGregor, make sure there were no mistakes this time, that the key was retrieved. And if the reporter was fatally wounded while giving up the location of the key, then so be it. He had taken his chances the moment he had stolen it.

Which would leave him free to handle the precision work. A personal conversation with Rab MacFarlane. He felt a smile play across his lips. Looked down at the pen he was still holding in his hand, remembered the last time he had used it, stabbing it deep between the knuckles of a scrappy little shite who thought no one would know he was skimming extra bonuses from expenses on a regular basis.

But he knew. James always knew.

He remembered the man's screams, the soft, liquid sucking noise as he tore the pen from between his knuckles, blood gouting from the wound in a gloriously enthusiastic arc. He remembered lunging forward, stabbing the bloody tip of the pen into the man's chest, just below the collar bone, clamping his other hand over his mouth and squeezing his jaw, the man's eyes wide and wild with pain and terror.

He wondered what it would take to elicit such a look from Rab MacFarlane. Found he was eager to discover the answer. And he would.

He always did.

27

Susie arranged to meet Eddie at a small Italian café-restaurant she knew in Leith, not far from where the body had been found on Dock Street. It would have been more natural to meet him at Gayfield police station and go over the files they had there, but the last place Susie wanted to be right now was a crowded police station. Everyone looking at her, side glances and hidden smirks. Would they know? Worse, had they seen?

She felt a cold wave of disgust pucker her skin into goose-flesh, felt the familiar prickle of her stress rash. The urge to retch churned her guts, swallowed by the acidic rage and hot skewer of violation that rose up whenever she thought of the picture Doug had shown her.

Revenge porn. She had heard of it often enough, even worked on a couple of cases. It was an all-too common phenomenon in a world that was increasingly obsessed by likes, shares, retweets and posts. Take a few intimate snaps with your lover in the height of passion, have them leaked online as a petty act of revenge when it all goes wrong. She knew there were websites dedicated to pictures of people's exes, had read the tabloid spreads where young girls described how a former partner had emailed pictures of them to his friends and hers.

Shuddered at the thought that she was one of them now. One of those who had been used, whose trust had been violated.

A victim.

The anger bloomed in her again and she turned her thoughts to why Redmonds had taken the picture. Obviously he had known she would object, so he had waited until she was passed out. Was that his plan all along? Was that why he had spoken to her at the bar? Why he plied her with champagne? To make her vulnerable, pliant? Worse, was it for his enjoyment only, or had he shared it? She shuddered at the thought. The image of that cowardly little shite wanking himself off over the picture was bad enough, but to not know if anyone else had seen it – seen *her* – was a creeping torture that was almost unbearable.

She tried to think rationally, to be the person she was trying to prove to everyone she was – competent, professional.

Except she wasn't that, was she? Thanks to what Doug had done, she was now actively involved in lying to her boss and covering up the existence of evidence that had direct bearing on an active murder investigation – and for what? To save her skin, make sure a drunken mistake she made with a fuckwit who deserved everything that came next didn't become public knowledge or titillation.

What was it Doug had said? *I was thinking of you.* Susie writhed in her seat, embarrassment flushing through her. She thought of how she had hit Doug, how he had refused to back off when she rushed at him again. Her accusation that he had kept the image for his own pleasure. Thought of him looking at her, naked, exposed, vulnerable, suddenly ashamed that she was curious at to what his reaction had been.

Against her objections, he had insisted on keeping the flash drive and Redmonds' laptop. She had argued that, as someone had already broken into his flat looking for them once, he was a target. But Doug had waved her objections aside, assuring her that he had "a safe place" in mind to store both items and that it made sense for him to keep them so he could get them to Colin more quickly.

She had agreed, grudgingly, but only after getting him to promise he wouldn't look at the image again, that only Colin would see it now. Doug had promised with his usual lopsided "trust me" grin, but she had seen the fragility behind it, and wondered what effect all this was having on him. He was already brittle from the Pearson affair. How had thinking he was a murderer affected him?

She remembered the whisky bottle on his coffee table, of his half-muttered promise to stay away from it. No grin with that, just a flat-eyed stare that scared Susie even more than the thought of the image on the flash drive.

She was seized by the sudden desire to move, to act. Grabbed her jacket and slid out of the booth, headed for the door. Barged into Eddie at the counter, just about taking him off his feet.

"Whoa," he said, arms up in a mock "I surrender" pose. "Sorry I'm late, traffic from Gayfield after I dropped the boss off was shite as usual."

Susie studied Eddie for a split-second. No half-hidden smirk, no arrogant "I've seen it" glint in his eyes. Christ, was this how she would size everyone up from now on? She waved away his apology, acted casual. "Sorry, Eddie, my fault. Wasn't watching where I was going. I was just going to walk back to the crime scene, meet you there, show you round."

Eddie glanced wistfully into the restaurant then straightened up. "No problem, boss," he said, turning and opening the door for her.

. . .

They walked along a cobbled back street to the crime scene, the sky above heavy with cloud that threatened yet more rain to come. As they walked, Eddie filled Susie in on the interview with Alicia and Michael Leonard. He seemed obsessed by their obvious wealth and the fact that Alicia Leonard "was definitely used to getting her own way" and "didn't like being questioned by anyone".

Susie thought about that. Maybe what she had heard was wrong. Maybe Alicia Leonard didn't like attack dogs, after all. Maybe *she* was the attack dog. Not surprising. Being married to

Paul Redmonds would have anyone straining at the leash.

They arrived at the industrial estate a few minutes later. The crime scene was still marked out by police cordon tape that fluttered gently in the wind. The SOCOs had long since gone, taking the body with them back to the city morgue on the Cowgate. Susie fought back a shudder. She knew she'd have to visit the place soon enough, see the body for herself, listen as Stephen Williams, the pathologist, described what had been done to the poor bastard in excruciating detail. Perfect end to a perfect day.

"So," she asked Eddie, "what have we got?"

Eddie shot her a quizzical look then smiled. Susie pushed back a smile of her own. He had bought it, thinking this was a test to see how up to speed he was. Truth was, with everything else that had happened, she hadn't had the time to look at the files.

So much for competent and professional.

"White male, late twenties," Eddie began, voice slipping into the clipped, even tone he no doubt practiced for court appearances. "Discovered by a dog walker at approximately 6am. Initial examination shows the victim had been extensively beaten, and there was a severe wound from a bladed instrument to the chest and face. Initial trawls of CCTV at the junction of Commercial Street and Ocean Drive" – Eddie pointed off to Susie's left – "show a light-coloured Transit van being driven away from the area at speed about forty minutes before the body was found."

Susie looked up, trying to keep her expression professionally bored, not show Eddie he was telling her something potentially interesting. "Any number plates?" she asked.

"Funnily enough, the van didn't have any," Eddie said, giving her a knowing look. "It was headed in the direction of Seafield though, so we've got officers looking for it."

Susie snorted. "We're looking for a Transit van in Seafield, down by the industrial estates and the MoT centres? Aye, good luck with that."

"It's something," he said softly, his tone unconvinced.

"What about the victim?" Susie asked.

"No ID yet, wallet and cash weren't found on the body."

"So we're thinking robbery gone wrong?"

Eddie chewed his lip, looked back to the cordon. "Maybe," he said at last. "But it's just…"

"Just what?" Susie asked.

"I dunno, boss, just doesn't feel right. A beating and a stabbing just for a wallet seems like overkill to me. You'd do one or the other to get what you wanted, not both. And, with the similarities to the Redmonds killing – the beating and use of a bladed instrument – you've got to consider the possibility the two are linked."

Doug's words in her mind now. *You grab Eddie, look into the Leith body. The beating isn't connected to the shit-kicking I gave Redmonds.* Jesus Christ, was she really doing this?

"…you think?" Eddie asked.

She snapped her attention back to him, cursing herself for being distracted. "Sorry, Eddie, what?"

"I asked what you thought."

"I think we should keep an open mind. Two beatings and killings in two days could be the start of a pattern, but they could just be coincidental. After all, violence and robbery do go together. We'll look into this just now. If we find something that would appear to connect this to…" – she paused, unwilling to say the bastard's name – "… Redmonds, then we'll report it to Third Degree."

Eddie murmured agreement. "So what's next?"

Susie looked down the street. "For me, a trip to see Dr Williams and the body of the deceased. For you…"

Eddie rolled his eyes. He was about to be served what his grandfather had called a shit sandwich. And he was going to have to eat it.

Susie noticed his expression, smiled. "It's not that bad," she assured him. "But this has derailed me from looking into a theft from a graphic design firm down the road, called the Docking

Station. They're on the lane opposite the Scottish Government building. Know the place?"

Eddie nodded. Victoria Quay was a massive structure, a central stone cylinder flanked by two squat wings of stone and glass.

"Well, get along there, "Susie said. "The boss is a guy called Brian Coulter. He was expecting me but I got, ah, sidetracked. Offer our apologies and get his statement about what's been taken. And a client list."

"Client list?" Eddie asked.

"Burns said they had some big-name clients. I'd like to know who. Probably means nothing, but it's worth looking at."

"You want to meet up later, compare notes?" he asked.

Susie glanced at her watch. 3.30pm. The last thing she wanted was to be feigning interest in any of this with Eddie long into the night.

"Nah," she said. "If there's something important, let me know, otherwise take an early cut, I'll see you tomorrow. 7am. Gayfield, okay?"

Eddie's smile widened. Another reason why working with Susie wasn't too bad. Not bad at all.

28

The text that accompanied the picture message was only six words long, but it spoke volumes to Mark. Shaking, on the verge of tears, feeling his bowels loosen, he now truly understood what he was involved with. And who. He had thought it easy money, all he had to do was turn a blind eye to some of the more extreme things he had seen, keep everything running smoothly and pocket the cash.

But now he knew the truth. Six words had forced his eyes open, shaken him from his oh-so convenient self-chosen ignorance, shown him the fangs and claws of the monster he was involved with and told him his life was in very real danger.

The text, blazing out from the screen of his phone, was: *I trust you received my message?*

The accompanying image was of that morning's *Capital Tribune*, the front page headline announcing, *Murder hunt as body found in Leith* above an image of a cordoned-off industrial estate that Mark knew all too well was on Dock Street.

He glanced around the flat, eyes bulging, terror clashing with adrenalin in his blood and squeezing his heart in a cold, clammy fist. He thought about ignoring the message, realised that would only make things worse, enrage Mr James further.

And that was the last thing he wanted.

With trembling fingers, he typed in a one-word reply: *Yes*. It was all he could think of to say. Watched as the message turned blue on the screen, felt a fresh wave of dread pulse through him when the bubble that showed James was typing again popped up.

The reply was business-like. Direct. To the point. The menace

Mark infused into it was all in his mind. But he knew it wasn't a delusion. *Good. Then I trust there will be no further sloppiness or mistakes on your part? You are an important part of the team, Mark. I would hate to see that change.*

Jesus. *Part of the team?*

Mark tapped in his reply, pausing to proofread it three times before hitting *Send*. A mistake at this point would be absolutely fatal.

No more mistakes. I promise.

Again, the interminable wait as the message went from delivered to read then the bubble popped up. *Good,* read the reply. *Then get to work. You know what to do. Co-ordinate with Vic. I want results.*

Mark tossed the phone aside as though it was diseased. Toppled sideways onto the couch, grabbed a cushion and screamed into it.

James had killed him. The *Tribune* story didn't name the victim, but Mark didn't need it to. He knew who the victim was as surely as he knew his own name. James had had him killed purely to send a "message" to Mark – don't fuck up again or this is what will happen to you.

He desperately wanted just to go to the police, but thoughts of some of the things he had seen, and the faces doing them, told him that wasn't an option. He'd be dead in less than a day. Running would be the same. They would find him. And he would die. Badly.

But wasn't that how this was going to end anyway? With him dead? Either at James's hand or that psychopath, Vic? And if that was true, wouldn't it be better just to do it himself? Wash down a bottle of pills with wine or vodka, open his wrists in the bath – *remember to cut up the wrist, not along,* a small, vicious voice in his mind whispered – end it on his terms? His way?

But no. That wasn't an option. Not for Mark. He had been an awkward teenager, the late onset of puberty and his total lack of physical co-ordination and desire to fight back singling him out as easy prey for the school bullies. One afternoon, after one of the bigger kids – a child mountain of testosterone, zits and bad attitude called Luke Smith – had mercilessly ripped into Mark about "his balls dropping" in front of the class after PE, he had thought about just ending it all. He had no real friends to speak of and it wasn't as if his parents would miss him. As an only child, they had made clear their disappointment in him at every turn. He was quiet when they were outgoing. Bookish when they were outdoorsy, dragging him on camping trips and to football matches and other sporting events whenever they could.

He spent weeks plotting all the ways he could do it – step out into the road, pills, knife, jump from the top of the school – but every time it came to the moment, he backed away. Despite how miserable his life was, there was some small part of him that wanted to endure, refused to quit. His parents, he thought bitterly, would be proud. The irony was he could never tell them.

He sat up, wiping the tears and snot from his face with the sleeve of his jumper, realised that he only had one option.

Get to work. You know what to do. Co-ordinate with Vic.

He stood up on numb legs and shuffled across to the computer table. Booted up and got to work. He had Doug McGregor's mobile number, access to his work and personal email and the details of all his bank accounts. He would track him. He would find him. And then he would pass that information on to Vic, who would do the rest.

No more mistakes.

29

John Wallace looked like he was treating retirement like a title bout – and winning. To Burns, he looked almost unchanged since he had last seen him more than five years ago: the thick, silver hair still sat on his head like a halo glowing in the lights of the pub, his skin remained tight across his face and around his jaw, his massive barrel torso radiated the same sense of innate strength.

The only exterior hint that the years were encroaching was in his hands. Wallace's hands had always fascinated Burns. They were huge, blunt things, the knuckles on the right gnarled and bunched – "from ma years in the police boxing team," Wallace would say with a wink as he rubbed them on cold days – and Burns had always wondered how intimidating seeing those hands would have been to anyone brought into Craigmillar Police Station. The impression they made on Burns was the same now – blunt instruments that were designed only to deliver pain – but he could see that the fingers were starting to curl and warp gently, the first flush of arthritis starting to remould them like the naked branches of a dying tree.

"So," Wallace said, leaning over the table and grabbing his pint, "Third Degree Burns. And a DCI now, no less. To what do I owe the pleasure of this visit?"

Burns smiled, let the nickname pass. He hated it, but he was damned if he was going to let John Wallace see that. The truth was he wasn't sure what he wanted. He had arranged to meet John at his home in Eskbank, a small town off the road from Edinburgh to the Borders. John had jumped at the chance, but instantly suggested a change of location. "I'll meet you at the pub. Just drive up from Dalkeith, you cannae miss it, it's on the roundabout. It'll save you the pain of Anne's home baking, and give me an excuse to get out for a bit."

They sat at a small table in a bay window, the décor screaming 'pub chain straining for olde worlde charm and authenticity' and missing by a mile. John had ordered the first round, insisted Burns had "a proper drink with an old man".

Burns reached for his "proper drink" now. A pint of 80 Shilling. He sipped, arranging the words in his mind, then put the pint back on the table and pushed it away subtly, hoping John didn't notice. Truth was, Burns wasn't much of a beer drinker, preferring a glass of red with Carol at the end of a long day.

"Well, John," he said, "you heard about Paul Redmonds?"

"Aye," Wallace said, a glint of something hungry and eager in his eyes. "Terrible business. Dinnae get me wrong, Paul was an arrogant wee shite, especially in the later years, but he didn't deserve that. You getting anywhere with it?"

Burns shook his head. He wasn't – and that was part of the reason he was here. Everything so far was a dead end. No obvious financial problems, no enemies anyone could or would identify, nothing untoward at all. And nothing, other than the Falcon's Rest raid, to link him to Dessie Banks. And there was no way that was strong enough to follow at the moment. It wasn't the message that the Chief Constable would want to hear, so Burns had made himself busy out of the office for as long as he could. Delaying the inevitable bollocking.

"Not really, and that's sort of why I'm here. We spoke to Alicia Leonard today…"

"Ah, Alicia," Wallace said, then took a gulp from his pint that made half of it disappear. "And how is the Ice Queen?"

Burns smiled, thinking back to his interview with Leonard. The cold, glinting chip of distain when he had pushed her on the last time she had seen Paul Redmonds.

"I get the impression she doesn't like being questioned, by anyone about anything," Burns admitted.

John nodded. "Aye, you've got that right. Alicia always knew exactly where she wanted to go and who she needed to know to get there. She was always convinced that she was right too. The annoying fucking thing was that she usually was. Probably explains how she got to where she is now."

Burns nodded. Made sense. All the positive discrimination and slogans about equality didn't do much against decades of ingrained sexism. It would have taken a hell of a lot of determination to claw up the ranks the way Leonard had, especially back then.

"So, John, she mentioned that she was at your leaving do a few months ago. But how did you know her, and Redmonds, anyway?"

Wallace drained his pint, started work on the Glenfiddich he had bought to keep it company. "We worked together at St Leonards," he said. "Before your time. That's where she and Paul met actually, when they were assigned to CID together. Caused a fair stooshie at the time too."

"Oh? How?" Burns reached for his pint in spite of himself.

John drained his short, nodded to the bar. Message received.

"Well, when they first met, Paul was seeing someone else. A wee PC called…" – Wallace paused, rolled his eyes to the ceiling and clicked his tongue, as though he could call the name to him – "ah! Ritchie. That was it. Jane Ritchie. Nice wee girl. Great legs, filthy sense of humour. Anyway, things were pretty serious between her and Paul, they were more or less living together at the time. But along comes Alicia, decides Paul would be better off with her, and that's that. Rumour was they were shagging on the job – not that everyone hasn't – but right under Jane's nose. And they roped in the duty sergeant – not me, the other one – to organise her shifts to keep her out of the way. Anyway, when Jane found out, she hit the roof. Made a big stink, threatened to go to the brass with it."

Burns gave a quizzical look as the barman deposited another

pint and short in front of John. He didn't present a bill and John didn't offer to pay.

"Well," he said after he had taken a sip of his fresh pint, "there was a big thing against officers having relationships back then, especially senior officers and subordinates. Didnae mean shit, of course, there were enough affairs going on to keep the plotlines of *Dynasty* going for a few years, but the brass were keen to be seen to be taking a hard line, so…"

"So they were looking to make an example of Paul and his relationship with Jane?"

"Aye, maybe," John agreed. "Didnae matter in the end, though. She transferred, Glasgow I think, with a nice wee promotion. And Paul and Alicia got married not long after. Then she went to Perth and he stayed in town."

Burns scribbled a few notes, then flicked back to his record of the interview with Alicia Leonard. "When you saw them both at your retirement do, how were they?"

John paused for a moment. "Aye, fine. From what I remember. But I was indulging in the generosity of my fellow officers at this point, Jason, so I wasnae exactly at my sharpest. But it was a nice night. We'd been for dinner, then headed for the Guildford Bar, took over a couple of tables at the back." He nodded, gaze growing wistful. "It was nice of them to make the effort to come."

"Effort?" Burns asked.

"Aye," Wallace confirmed. His pint seemed to be evaporating in the warmth of the pub. "Ack, you know what it's like. People get promoted or move patches. Like I said, Alicia went to Perth after St Leonards. I went to Craigmillar. People drift apart. I hadnae seen either of them for years by the time I retired. The odd Christmas and birthday card, aye, and Paul was always on the blower if he needed a little local knowledge, but we hadn't spent any real time together for years. But that's what you do when another copper retires, isn't it? Make the effort. I'll make the effort for you when the time comes, Jason."

Burns smiled, returned John's small toast with his glass. "Thanks, but I've got a few years in me yet," he said. "So the leaving night, best you can remember, there was nothing out of the ordinary about the two of them being together. They didn't quarrel, no awkwardness?"

John looked for the answer at the bottom of his whisky glass. Tried to get a clearer view by draining half of it. "Not that I remember," he said. "She came in first, planted a kiss on my cheek. Insisted on buying me a drink."

"And how long was she there before Paul arrived?"

Wallace's brow furrowed. "Not long," he said. "Actually, not long at all. Maybe five minutes. I remember they met at the bar."

"Really? Why?" Remembering Alicia's words now: *When I saw Paul there, I paid my respects to John and left. I didn't speak to Paul. Frankly, didn't want to.*

"The usual shite with people these days," he said. "They were both on their bloody phones, staring at the screens. Inches from each other and in totally different worlds." He shook his head. "Maybe that's why they broke up in the first place."

Burns ignored the temptation to follow that, stuck with the matter at hand. Didn't want the whisky catching up with John's memory and blurring it before he had finished with him. "And did they speak, John?"

He paused again, looked at his whisky. Raised the glass, stopped as the memory came to him. "No," he said slowly. "Not really. She came back with a couple of drinks, whisky for me, a vodka for her. Was just making the toast when Paul made an arse of himself at the bar."

Burns sat up. "How did he make himself look like an arse, John?"

Wallace's face split into a smile that showed off teeth too white and perfect to be anything other than false. "Och, the usual shite. Again, something you lot do. He was standing at the bar, Mr Super Cool in his expensive suit, when he caught my eye and gave the usual gesture." Wallace raised his hand, holding the fingers open as if he was holding an invisible pint, and tilted it to his lips. *You drinking?* the gesture said.

"Anyway, as he did, he just about took the eye oot of this wee lassie that was standing next to him. She jumped back, yelped, caused a bit of a scene. Paul sorted it out, then he looked back up at gave me that fucking stupid Yankee thumbs-up."

Burns felt something caress the back of his neck. Cold and electric. "Yankee thumbs-up? What do you mean?"

John lifted his hand again, closed it into a fist then popped up his thumb and extended his pinkie before shaking his hand from side to side.

"You know, like the Hawaiians do?" he said.

Burns nodded agreement. "And Alicia was standing beside you the entire time?" he asked, eyes not leaving Wallace's hand.

"Aye, she laughed at him, took her vodka in a shot, then left. Why?"

"Nothing," Burns said. Thinking back to his early teenager years. He knew the sign, had been introduced to it by too many episodes of *Magnum PI*. He had been obsessed by that show, by the sun and the easy lifestyle and the friendships the characters shared in Hawaii, a world away from his own grey upbringing in Broxburn. The hand sign was the shaka, a common enough greeting. But he also knew the sign was common in Scotland, and worldwide, for something else. Something that made no sense if Alicia Leonard's statement was to be believed.

Call me.

30

Doug sat at a bar in the departure lounge of Edinburgh Airport with a double whisky – which cost him almost as much as a half-bottle from the local supermarket would have – sitting untouched in front of him.

The call to Hal had been quick and fairly vague. He'd said only that he was working on a story, and needed a laptop and some files looked at pretty quickly, wondered if Colin could help? Hal had agreed on Colin's behalf, setting only two conditions: that Doug flew down to London that afternoon to see them, and that he was staying over.

"We can have dinner," Hal said. "And you can read Jennifer *The Heroic Tale of The Red Giant* at bedtime for a bloody change."

Doug smiled into the phone. *The Heroic Tale* was his one and only attempt at fiction writing, a story he had come up with for Hal and Colin's daughter when they had been driving across the Forth Road Bridge, heading for a hotel Hal was consulting with as a favour to Doug on the Isle of Skye. As they had driven, the thumps and rattles of the car over the expansion joints on the bridge had scared Jennifer, her dark eyes growing wide and wet as her porcelain-fine skin paled. Doug had seen the rising terror in her face – wondered if the poor kid had heard the stories about the bridge being shut a few months before because of welds failing. She was only three, but she was bright. Just like her dads.

So Doug had told her a story, that the thumps and bumps were only the Heroic Giant that looked after the bridge, tapping on the underside of the bridge to tell Jennifer he was there, looking after her. She had smiled, seemingly happy, then asked for Doug to tell her more.

And so *The Heroic Tale of the Red Giant* was born. Doug had written the whole thing up, surprising himself with how much he had enjoyed it, then emailed it to Hal and Colin. Colin had taken the copy and typeset it, designed a cover then bound it. It was only fifteen pages long, but it was enough for Jennifer, who insisted on it being read to her every night.

After hanging up on Hal, he had logged on and bought a ticket to London City, slapping it on his credit card and vowing to worry about it later. It hadn't taken him long to pack: a change of clothes, Redmonds' laptop and the flash drive safely in his pocket. He only felt a glimmer of guilt for lying to Susie about having a safe place for them. After all, whoever was after the flash drive and computer wasn't going to know he was heading to London. And besides, if whoever had broken into his flat was going to try again, he wanted to be the target, not Susie. He owed her that much at least.

He phoned Becky and told her where he was going, keeping the details sketchy, his earlier words to Susie rattling around his head as he spoke. *This is between us. I'll tell Becky at the same time you tell Burns.*

Driving out to the airport, he had dumped the car in the secure overnight parking, another credit card hit to worry about later, leaving his own laptop in Redmonds' bag in the boot of the car. He didn't want it falling into the hands of whoever was after him, reasoned that they would have to be pretty stupid to try to break into his car in a secure parking zone with cameras bristling from every wall.

He had made it through security without incident, his heart in his throat as he put the flash drive into the small plastic tray that rattled through the X-ray machine, then headed to the bar, buying the whisky before he had even thought about it.

He reached for the glass. Stopped. Thought of Susie. *I need you. Not the booze-soaked, self-pitying twat you've become.* Pushed the glass away. But not too far.

He decided to bring his thoughts into focus, put what he knew in order. Pulled his notepad from his bag and started filling a page with all the names and places he knew. It was an old trick, put the puzzle down on page in front of you, then reorder the pieces until they started making sense. Problem was, the more he looked at it, the less sense it made to Doug. He wrote down *Redmonds*, circled it. Then wrote *Falcon's Rest* and *Dessie Banks*, connecting the three bubbles with lines, a question mark above the line between Banks and Redmonds.

But that was the only explanation for all this, wasn't it? Redmonds had found out that Doug was poking around the brothel raid story, and his possible connection to the brothel's ultimate owner, Dessie Banks. He had used the image of Susie to try and blackmail him into killing the story, bargaining Susie's dignity against his desire to stay out of the headlines.

Drew another question mark on the page. Thought. There was that feeling that he had seen something but failed to recognise its importance, that the picture was trying to tell him something else. He closed his eyes, pushed aside the flush of shame and guilty surge of electricity through his groin as he recalled the image from the flash drive. Remembered zooming into it, the harsh shattered star of the flash Redmonds had used in the mirror, the table with the discarded bottle of champagne, the glasses, the TV showing cheap hotel porn beside it.

Porn…

Doug bit on his lip, bore down as though it would burst and the answer would bleed into his mouth. There was something…

He exhaled in frustration, glanced back towards the whisky. Tore his eyes away and looked back at his page of notes. At Redmonds' name. Drew another line, wrote *Where was he?* and circled it three times.

According to the police reports, Redmonds had been found shortly before 4am. But Doug had left him sometime after just after 2am. So where had he been? The drive back to Trinity, especially at that time of night, should have taken twenty-five minutes at most, meaning there was at least an hour and a half unaccounted for. So where had he gone? Who had he seen? And why had whoever it was killed him? What was so important about the flash drive or the laptop?

Doug snatched for his phone, hoping action would calm the raging torrent of questions in his mind. He dialled Rab MacFarlane's mobile, was rewarded with a click as he was transferred straight to voicemail. Great. More frustration.

He searched out the departures board that was hanging above the bar, saw that his flight had been given a gate and packed up. Turned and walked away, trying not to think about the abandoned whisky. Headed for the duty free shop and an overly-expensive bottle of perfume for Becky on his way to the gate.

He didn't notice the squat, wide man who watched him from the bar, light grey suit straining at his shoulders and gut. Didn't see the picture of Doug he had on his mobile, the way he glanced between it and Doug as he walked away. The man who had been dropped at the airport half an hour ago by a jumped-up little speedfreak who liked to drive too fast and thought traffic lights were advisory rather than mandatory. The man who had taken a call from Mark an hour ago, and been told all about Doug's travel plans.

The man who had delivered Mr James' message the night before.

Vic McBride.

31

The police morgue was a small, ugly knot of pebbledash and concrete that glowered over the Cowgate. With its flat roof and dull beige walls, it could almost be mistaken for a garage or a storage facility; the only signs that it was used for something else being the gratings on the windows, the security gate on the steps and the rising bollards on the drive that let vehicles in or out.

Susie sat in Dr Stephen Williams' office, which was little more than a small anteroom just off one of the main medical bays, listening to a kettle rumble to the boil. She always found it difficult to reconcile the ordered perfection of the office with the man who used it. Williams always looked like he had forgotten something important, and was on the verge of remembering it. His dark hair was beating a hasty retreat from his forehead, regrouping around his ears and sideburns in untidy wisps and swirls. He was tall to the point of gangly, a matchstick version of a man who looked like he had been flayed of any trace of muscle. He was wearing a short-sleeved shirt, untucked and rumpled, which exposed upper arms and biceps almost as flat and slender as Susie's wrists. Yet she remembered watching Williams work on more than one corpse, sinews straining as he used the rib splitters to ratchet open a chest cavity, the snapping, rending sounds echoing off the cold sterile walls of the morgue like gunshots. Work like that took strength. And resolve.

The kettle clicked off and Williams made tea, passed a cup to Susie then retreated to the chair behind his desk. He pulled a file from a small in-tray, examined it, then slid it across the otherwise naked desktop to Susie.

"Interesting one, this," he commented, the hot tea smudging the lenses of his glasses with clouds of steam.

"How so?" Susie asked, glad he had already carried out the post-mortem. After everything else that had happened, the last thing she needed was to watch that.

"Hmm?" Williams said, as if to himself. "Oh. Oh yes, sorry. The Leith body, interesting case. I mean, pretty obvious what killed him, but there's a methodology to some of the wounds that is striking."

"In what way?" Susie asked, looking at the file on the desk. She didn't want to open it, see the pictures she knew were inside, the silent screams of torn flesh and splintered bone, testament to man's talent for brutality.

"The victim…" He looked up slightly and Susie shook her head. No luck with an ID. Yet. "Well, he died from massive trauma. There's evidence on the body that he was strung up and then beaten with something like a baseball bat. Kidneys and liver were badly bruised, both lungs collapsed, internal haemorrhaging caused his chest cavity to fill with blood."

A thought of Redmonds shot across Susie's mind. *Chest cavity filled with blood.* That's what happened to him as well. She pushed the thought down, not wanting to think about…

that image. Doug seeing that image

…Redmonds at the moment. Focus, Susie. Focus.

"Sorry, I don't follow, how is that interesting? He was beaten to death. Nasty, but not something we've not seen before."

"Quite right. But there's an exactitude to the injuries this young man suffered that I've not seen before. For example," – he splayed one long thin hand out on the table in front of him – "every finger on both hands has been broken. And I don't just mean once. I mean at every knuckle. Then the wrist, the ulna, the elbow. Shoulder was then dislocated, collar bone shattered. It must have been agonising."

Susie swallowed, not tasting her tea, felt a chill that was nothing to do with the cool of the morgue. "So somebody went to work on him, broke every bone in his hands and arms? What about other injuries? The initial report said there was evidence of a bladed instrument being used on his upper body and face?"

"Ah, yes, that. Curious, actually. Seems like that was done post-mortem. Blood pooling certainly indicates that."

Susie nodded. Strange, why disfigure a body after death? If they were trying to hide the identity, there were better ways than carving the face up. "Any indication of what type of weapon was used?"

"A knife most probably," William said, his voice as flat and antiseptic as the strip lights that glowed dully from the ceiling. "Blade's probably about eight to ten inches long, serrated edge. Maybe something like you see in the windows of the hunting shops and, ah, other establishments down Leith Walk. All big blade and attitude, there to scare. Make a statement."

Susie chewed her lip. Looked at the file. There was no way she could avoid it. She flipped it open, doing her best to look casual, relaxed. "Anything else you can tell me? Any trace materials on the body that could indicate where he might have been before he was dumped?"

"Well, we've pulled the usual fibres from the body, looks like he was bundled up in something oily either before or after death. And there are abrasions on the feet consistent with him being dragged across stone or tarmac barefoot."

Susie took another gulp of tea. Forced herself to look down. "Any useable…"

Her voice died in her throat as she looked at the post-mortem pictures. The face looked like it had been split open, the wound running up from the chin and over the lips, the nose gaping open like a fillet of raw steak, glistening pink and bluish in the harsh flash-light. The eyes were, mercifully, closed, a green and purple wash of bruising glistening on the waxy skin. On the right temple, just above a cut that was gouged into the eyebrow, there was a small mole that almost looked like a question mark.

A mole Susie had seen before.

Williams was droning on, his voice fading into the background as Susie pulled out her phone. She opened up the internet app, found the page she had been looking at earlier. A hot bristle of electricity caressed the back of her neck.

She *had* seen that mole before.

She held her hand up, silencing Dr Williams. "Sorry," she said as she found Eddie's number and hit dial, "but I really need to make a call."

She waited for a moment, unable to tear her eyes from the pictures on the table as she listened to Eddie's phone ring. It seemed to take an eternity for him to answer. It took four rings.

"Boss? How was the morgue?" he asked. "Listen, I –"

"Eddie," she cut him off, "you have any luck speaking to Brian Coulter this afternoon?"

"That's what I was about to tell you," he said, unable to keep the tang of petulance from his voice. "I called to make an appointment but they said he hadn't been in the office all day. Tried his mobile, no answer. Was just about to head to his place, see if I could catch him there."

Susie swallowed down something rancid. "Do me a favour, swing past the lock-up and get me on the way, will you?"

"Aye, no problem," Eddie said. "But what's up? Thought you said –"

"I'll tell you when you get here. And make it quick, Eddie, will you?"

He grumbled a reply then clicked off. Susie flipped back to the web app on her phone, studied the page there. She had looked it up after Burns had given her the break-in case, finding the Docking Station website with no problem. She had arranged to meet the owner, Brian Coulter, and, out of curiosity, she had clicked on the *Meet our team* tab. Found his name, opened the bio. He was a small guy with a big smile and hair that had gone out of fashion in the Eighties. His face had been what Susie would have described as plain, average. Apart from one distinguishing feature.

A small mole. Just above his right eyebrow. Shaped, she thought, a little like a question mark.

32

Rebecca sat at her desk, squinting at the press release she had written to go with the call notice she had just put on the wires. She crunched down on another Rennie as a wave of indigestion clawed its way up her throat, let out a sigh that was part frustration, part anger, then clicked on the *Send* button, pinging the press release to the Chief Constable for approval.

Cameron Montrose had only taken over as Chief Constable three months ago, which made Montrose's decision to come to Edinburgh and hold a live press conference in time for the 6pm news understandable. Totally fucking stupid, but understandable. Two violent murders in two days, one of them a former senior officer with a less-than-spotless reputation. He wanted to be seen to be taking charge, leading from the front. Reassuring the public.

Rebecca had tried to talk him out of it, tried to tell him that holding a live broadcast press conference when no significant breakthroughs had been made in either case – which Montrose was tacitly acknowledging were linked by holding the press conference in the first place – was only asking for trouble.

"Nonsense, Rebecca," he had said as he picked non-existent lint from the shoulder of his impeccable uniform. "We need to be seen to be taking action here. Showing we are doing everything we can to address these heinous crimes and bring the perpetrators to justice."

Rebecca smiled at him then, taking in the glow of his ruddy cheeks from the shave he had had that morning, the perfectly coiffed and trimmed hair and the uniform that was obviously just back from the dry cleaners. She wondered how long he had been practising that line – and how grateful he was that two "heinous crimes" in two days had given him the perfect platform to introduce himself as the Chief to the public.

Now she sat at her desk, waiting for his comments on the press release, knowing that, no matter what he said, the press conference was going to be a disaster. The only small sliver of comfort was that at least Doug wasn't going to be there.

She felt a twist of guilt at that thought, but couldn't bring herself to ignore it. It was, after all, the truth. A live-broadcast press conference was bad enough, but one with Doug McGregor there, treating it like sport, cheerfully eviscerating anyone who didn't have a quick and articulate answer for him, was asking for trouble.

At least it used to be. These days, she wasn't so sure.

She sat back, toying with her phone, unlocked it and looked at the picture she had set as her home screen. She and Doug smiled out from behind a curtain of app icons; a selfie taken on a day out to St Andrews not long after they had started dating. She was leaning back onto his chest, him holding the phone out with his right hand, his injured left carefully kept out of sight. He was smiling in the picture, but looking at it now, she could see the fragility in the smile. It was the same brittle pretence that she had seen this morning, him smiling sheepishly after she woke him on the couch, the bottle of whisky sitting beside the laptop on the coffee table.

She loved him. She knew that. The quick humour, the mind that was always three steps ahead, the ability he had to know what she was thinking. He could be, by turns, charming and disarming, thoughtful and spontaneous. And she wanted him. Even though, from the start, she had felt he had seen sex as another distraction, like the whisky or the work, she couldn't help wanting him. She still did. But now, there was something else. It had been building for months – as his hand had refused to heal and the pain had ground down on him like a weight, he had seemed to withdraw from her, increasingly seeking comfort in his work or in the whisky he insisted on having at the end of every night. He began to spend less time at her place, even when she offered him a key to try and make him feel more at home, preferring instead to stay at his place and drink alone. Or with Susie.

And there was another problem. Susie. Oh yes, she and Doug had both been at pains to underline how they were just friends, that the thought of anything else was utterly revolting. Why then, did she feel herself bristle with jealousy when Susie had mentioned she had gone to Doug when she heard about Redmonds? Why did tendrils of panic reach into her chest and squeeze? She knew, on one level, it was understandable. They had worked together on two very intense cases, the violence and trauma they had seen and experienced forging a shorthand between them that seemed to exclude everyone else.

And that was the heart of it, wasn't it? Exclusion. Even when she and Doug were together, Rebecca felt alone. There were still sparks, like a dying flame getting a breath of oxygen and flaring back into brief life, but they were becoming further and further apart. She wanted to help him, needed to, but it was as if he had shut the door on what had happened to him, as if talking to her about it would make it real, force him to confront it.

And as much as she loved him, Rebecca knew she wouldn't wait at the other side of that door forever.

She blinked away the sudden tears that stung her eyes, blurring the image of the picture in front of her. She swallowed back another acidic burst of indigestion and crunched down another Rennie.

On impulse, she tapped in a text message to Doug: *Hope the flight was okay. Tell Colin and Hal I say hello. Hope you find what you need. Here when you need me. Bx*

She hit *Send*, read back the text. Waited for the small speech bubble to pop up showing that he was typing a reply.

Waited.

Waited.

33

Doug arrived at London City airport on the 16:30 flight, fighting against the tide of suits heading the other way, bound for flights home after a day of relentless capitalism in the City. Wandering through the terminal in his jeans and trainers, suit jacket over an old jumper, he half-expected to be grabbed by a security guard and huckled out of the building. "Sorry, sir, we have a dress code here. Smart suit, over-expensive watch and an expression of bored arrogance are mandatory. Sucking on marbles and speaking to everyone as though they are beneath you is voluntary, but encouraged."

He headed for the Docklands Light Railway, planning to take a train to Bank and meet Hal. He was walking past the customer service desk on the way to the platform when a thought struck him and he stopped. Turned to head for the kiosk, and almost collided with a man who was walking behind him.

"Sorry," the man grunted, accent deep Ayrshire somewhere, the vowels flattened and elongated. Something flashed in his eyes, not quite anger, and Doug stepped back a little. It wasn't that he was physically intimidating; he was small, squat, almost a foot shorter than Doug, with a gut that seemed to be trying to burst out of his trousers. But there was something about the man – a denseness, a bluntness of purpose in those eyes – that put a less evolved part of Doug, the part that still feared fire and ran through the forests, on edge.

"Nae bother," Doug said casually, eyes darting over the man's face. "My fault, shouldn't have stopped so quickly. Forgot to get my ticket."

The man nodded something and plodded away, shoulders hunched, head down. Doug watched him for a moment, then shrugged, headed for the kiosk to buy a ticket. It was understandable, he told himself. After everything that had happened – the confrontation with Redmonds, the break-in at the flat, telling Susie everything – it was only natural that he was on edge. But he was safe here, surely. The only people who knew he was in London were Hal, Colin, Susie and Becky. Whoever was looking for him, or the laptop, was back in Edinburgh. Nothing to worry about at all.

He bought his ticket and jumped on the train to Bank, joined the herd as they made their way up the stairs, emerging into a day that was starting to dim and cool. After a five-minute walk, he came to a glass-fronted skyscraper set back slightly from the road, creating a paved courtyard that had a huge stone-sculpted wing erupting from the pavement. He smiled despite himself. Hal had only said he was doing some corporate work for some City clients, mentioned nothing about them being in the beating heart of corporate London, in the wealthiest square mile in the country. He made his way inside and found a receptionist so poised and styled that she could have been ripped from a TV make-up advert. She looked up at him and gave a smile that showed off perfect teeth but no warmth, did well to keep the disdain in her eyes from contorting her features.

"Can I help you, sir?" she asked, the thick London accent shattering the illusion for Doug.

"I'm here to see Hal Damon, he's working with City Consolidated. My name's Doug McGregor."

She nodded and peered into a screen set into the lip of the reception desk, fingers gliding across a keyboard. Doug leaned on the desk, turned away to take the place in as she worked. Double-height ceilings, tasteful works of art positioned along the marble walls. Leather couches dotted the reception area, lined up against the floor-to-ceiling windows that looked out on the bustle of the street. Hal had offered him a job before, but if working in a place like this was the price to be paid, Doug didn't want it.

The receptionist cleared her throat, demanding his attention. "Here you are, sir," she said, passing him a small pass the size of a credit card. "Just swipe that at the security gate to get through. Lifts are round to your right. Mr Damon is on the 23rd floor."

Doug took the card and nodded his thanks. Adjusted the laptop bag across his shoulder and turned towards the security gate. As he swept his gaze back across the reception area, he felt a sudden jolt, as though he was being...

hunted

...watched. Stopped dead, eyes darting around, heart hammering in his chest.

Nothing there. Just the same bustle as before, the tide of City workers being washed home or to the pub. He grunted a small laugh, embarrassed at his paranoia, then headed for the security gate.

Outside, a small man in a grey suit watched him walk towards the lift. Cursed under his breath, then reached for his phone.

34

For a man who spent his life advising people on projecting the right image or delivering a line with conviction, Hal Damon didn't hide his emotions very well. As soon as Doug stepped out of the lift, shock and concern flitted across Hal's face, lips pulling tight and accentuating his already high cheekbones, eyebrows rising up his forehead, escaping from the confines of his dark-rimmed glasses.

"Douglas," he said, offering a hand, "glad you could make it."

Doug took Hal's hand, found himself pulled into a warm, strong hug. Hal was a lithe man, obviously no stranger to the inside of a gym, and Doug could feel the strength in the hug.

They broke after a moment, Hal keeping an arm on Doug's shoulder, eyes skimming across his face. "You alright, Doug?" he asked, his voice neutral, eyes conveying the concern. "Seems like you've lost weight. Again."

Doug smiled, ran a hand through his hair, embarrassed for the first time about his choice of dress. He didn't care what other people thought, but he didn't want to make Hal look bad. Especially here. "Yeah, I'm fine. Just been a rough couple of days, Hal."

Hal nodded. "Come on, they've got me set up in an office down the hall. I'll grab my stuff and we can get out of here – Colin and Jen are dying to see you."

Doug followed Hal down a long corridor to a small corner office, just enough room for a desk with a chair on either side. Hal slid in behind the desk, motioned Doug to sit down, busied himself typing on the laptop sitting in front of him.

"Just give me a minute to send a couple of emails, then we're out of here."

"No problem," Doug said, looking around the office. It was typical Hal. Clean, uncluttered, efficient. The only hint that he was working here was the picture of Colin and Jennifer on the desk beside the laptop. Doug smiled, realising he had taken that photo himself.

"So," Hal said distractedly as he poked at the keyboard. "You mentioned something about a laptop and a flash drive on the phone, but you were pretty cagey. What's up? And why was it so urgent that you had to come down here today?"

Doug's throat felt dry, everything that had happened over the last couple of days suddenly came flooding back. The pain, the terror, the look on Susie's face when he had shown her what was on the flash drive. When he had seen that image...

He shifted in his seat, coughed. Hal looked up at him, immediately concerned. His voice was soft, urgent. "Jesus, Doug, I had no idea it was this bad. Listen, whatever it is, we'll figure it out, okay? Just tell me what's going on and we'll sort it."

Doug nodded, grinding his palm into his eyes. Relief and sorrow and fear clawed at his chest, churning his insides. "Thanks," he said. "It's a hell of a story. Might even be better than the Heroic Red Giant."

Hal laughed at Doug's attempt – as usual – to deflect anything serious or heartfelt with a bad joke or a worse pun. At least that hadn't changed. "Come on," he said. "Let's get going. You can tell me about it on the way home."

Doug nodded, took a shuddering breath that somehow felt cleaner than before. "Great," he said. Then paused. "But can you do me one favour?"

"Sure. What?"

"I wondered if we could take the scenic route back." He saw the question etch itself onto Hal's face. Thought of the small, squat man he had run into at the airport, the bluntness in his eyes, the feeling of being watched when he was downstairs.

Probably nothing.

Probably.

"Let's just say the last couple of days have made me a little, ah, overcautious. And potentially allergic to men in grey suits. So let's take the long way home, okay?"

Hal shrugged, happy to pander to Doug's whim, motioned to the door.

· · ·

Vic sat watching the entrance to the building McGregor had disappeared in from a small café-bar across the street. After Mark had tracked McGregor's credit card details, call log and internet history, it had been easy enough to get another ticket for London and follow him down. He had a moment of panic when the stupid little shit walked right into him, would have grabbed his bag right there if not for the two transport cops standing nearby.

He'd watched McGregor go into the City Consolidated building, and was prepared to wait, ready to grab the little shit the moment he walked down the wrong street or into the wrong shadow. But then he had called Mr James. And the story changed. It was meant to be a routine call, an update – the uptight wanker was crawling up everyone's arse after Mark's previous mistake. Instead, it sent Vic careering off course.

"You are to stand down," he had said in that aloof tone that was like a hot needle being pushed into Vic's ear. "Under no circumstances are you to take any action against McGregor, is that clear?"

"Then what the fuck am I doing here? Fucking sightseeing?" Vic had snarled. All this way, and for what? To watch the little fucker hobnob with the great and the good while Vic froze his balls off outside? Fuck that.

"Get Mark to put you on the first flight back, get McGregor when he touches down. Clear?" James had replied, anger glinting like a blade. "It would appear that McGregor's acquaintance, Mr Damon, has some, ah, interesting connections, including in government, and you are not to do anything that would alert him or McGregor to your presence. Is that absolutely clear, Vic? Or do I have to spell this out to you in person when you get back?"

Despite himself, Vic sat up a little straighter. He had heard the stories about Mr James. About the beatings, the stabbings, the sudden disappearances. Of people being offered the impossible choice of which limb to lose first, or whether they were going to lose an eye or tongue to a skewer that glowed white hot in James' hand. And then there was what Vic had done for him the other night. He felt no pity or remorse over killing Coulter – the snivelling little shit had moaned and whined like a bitch the entire time, and finally killing him had been a relief – but Vic knew that James would do the same to him, or worse, without a moment's hesitation.

"Okay," he said finally. "But what if I get him alone? What if –"

"What if I cut your fucking ears off and stuff them down your throat?" James exploded. "Don't fuck with me on this, Vic. Leave them alone. Get home. Grab McGregor when he gets back to Edinburgh. You know his car, you know where he parked at the airport. Wait for him to get back, grab him then. Clear?"

"Clear," Vic had replied, then listened as the line went dead.

Despite himself, he briefly considered ignoring James. Taking out McGregor and his pal, dragging the laptop home along with McGregor's severed head and dropping it onto James' desk like a trophy.

But no. No. That was madness. Better to wait for the right moment to strike. Keep James happy.

After all, thanks to Mark, finding McGregor wasn't going to be a problem. Any time.

35

Burns wandered the aisles of his local supermarket, arms draped across the front of the trolley as though it was a Zimmer frame, glancing between the shopping list Carol had sent him and the shelves on either side of him. It had, over the years, become a routine for them – when leaving the office, he would call to see if there was anything she needed him to pick up on the way home. There always was. Sometimes it was a jar of coffee or a pint of milk, sometimes a full weekly shop.

He didn't mind – to him, the stop on the way home was like a first step back into family life, a buffer between the chaos and misery and pain he so often confronted during the day, and the life he had when he closed the front door. And, if he were to be honest with himself, Burns enjoyed the mundane rhythm of shopping. There was something comforting in wandering around the store, steadily ticking off the items Carol had requested, thinking of nothing more than where the next item was, or the old dodderer in front of him who was bound to stop dead in the middle of the aisle at any moment.

But tonight was different. No matter how hard he tried, his conversation with John Wallace echoed in his thoughts. He wasn't sure why. So Redmonds and Alicia Leonard didn't hate each other as much as she had made out. So what? Who speaks kindly about an ex, even a murdered one, to strangers? Especially when their new, wealthier, husband was in the room?

But there was still something about the way she had bristled when he pushed her on the last time she had seen Redmonds.

It was a routine question. And being a former officer herself, Leonard would have known that Burns would follow up with John Wallace, so why act so defensively? After all, it wasn't as if John had told him anything revelatory about Redmonds – on the contrary, he had only underlined Redmonds' credentials as a world-class arsehole who liked to shag around and didn't care about the collateral damage.

Burns chewed his lip, tipped a bag of onions into the trolley then kept walking. So, Redmonds was a bastard. Was that what this was all about? A spurned lover? Or the spouse of a lover catching up with him? It would explain the beating he took before the fatal blow, which could have been delivered in a moment of madness. But if that was the case, why had Redmonds agreed to go out and meet his attacker in the first place?

He sighed, busied himself with Carol's list as he tried to ride out the latest nicotine craving. Cursed silently as he saw he'd forgotten the ream of paper at the bottom of the list. Which was in the stationery aisle, on the other side of the store. He turned around grudgingly, annoyed to be detoured from the wine aisle and the bottle of Merlot he had promised himself for that evening. He loved Carol, supported her in her work as a primary school teacher, but he resented the fact that he was effectively bankrolling the school by buying her what she needed to do her job. He knew the ream of paper was for printing handouts for the next day's lesson, for instance. He shook his head. An education system that couldn't afford to equip its schools or staff, meanwhile a bunch of over-privileged wankers from a very shallow gene pool lived in cosseted luxury, their only qualification for the job being that they were born into the right family. Sometimes, he thought, he was investigating the wrong criminals.

He made it to the stationery aisle, grabbed a ream of A4. Paused, then added another one. She'd need it eventually, and it would save him a trip later. He continued up the aisle, his gaze falling on the brightly coloured riot of children's soft toys on the shelf opposite the stationery. He stopped, thinking, the image of the playpark from earlier in the day coming back into his mind.

What?

Playpark. Alicia Leonard. Michael Leonard.

What…?

Michael Leonard. Playpark. Alicia.

He stopped dead in the aisle. Michael Leonard worked for Paradigm Investment Solutions. One of the big players, made their home on George Street. And didn't they, a few years ago…?

Burns opened up the web app on his phone. Tapped in the company name, added another search term. Hit *Go*. Clicked through to the news hits.

Bingo. It seemed the Leonards were not being quite as straightforward about things as they could have been.

Burns headed off in the direction of the wine aisle, added an extra bottle of Rioja to the bottle of Merlot he had promised himself.

He felt he had earned it.

36

Susie collapsed on her couch, chest burning and legs pumped full of acid from the run she had just completed. After checking on Coulter's flat with Eddie and, unsurprisingly, finding it empty, she had requested a warrant to enter, and any details of his next of kin. While his parents had been contacted and were coming down from Dundee to view the body in the mortuary in the morning, she knew it was only a formality. She had known the moment she had seen the mole above his eyebrow.

The man in the morgue was Brian Coulter. There wasn't a doubt in her mind.

She had sent Eddie off to make arrangements for the warrant, made a bet with him that his parents would arrive with a spare key before the warrant did. Then she had headed home, changed and hit the streets, trying to deaden the thoughts that clamoured in her mind.

Had Colin seen the image yet? What had he found? Had Doug kept his word and not looked, or was he peering over Colin's shoulder as he worked, leering? Sitting on the couch, she shuddered, her skin prickling with a chill that had nothing to do with her cooling sweat.

She had spent her life making herself strong, independent, despising those women who played to the perceived weakness of their sex and used it to attract men who would play their knight in shining armour. She built her strength in the gym and on the streets, making sure she could handle whatever was thrown at her on her terms by taking a few martial arts classes. She had dabbled with karate and flirted with Krav Maga, attracted by its links to the Israeli military. But it was the punchbag and footwork of boxing she loved most. She stopped short of entering the ring, but hammering away at the punchbag, or building up a rhythm with the speedball, was like a meditation to Susie.

And yet, despite all her training and preparation, despite her determination to make it in a career where sexism was a way of life and misogyny was routine, despite the fact that she had never complained, never buckled, never cried "it's not fair" and given up, here she was. Another woman humiliated by a man's base desire to control and dominate. To see her not as a person but as an object there only to fulfil his sexual needs.

A victim.

She rocked forward on the couch, trapping her hands under her thighs, not trusting them to be free. She remembered hitting Doug earlier in the day, felt a pang of shame when she remembered his words. *I was only thinking of you.* She stood, made for the shower, stepped in and turned it up as high as she could bear. Let the scalding heat wash over her, blotting out thoughts of the flash drive and Redmonds and Doug.

She got out of the shower, wrapped herself in her robe and padded back through to the living room. Checked her phone, bared her teeth at the screen that showed her Doug hadn't called. She hesitated for a moment, considered calling him, demanding an update.

But no. He had promised he would call her as soon as he had any news. She just hoped it was the news she wanted.

The thought had come to her earlier. While one picture was bad enough, the inescapable thought was that there was more than one image. And if so, where were the others? Who had seen them? Was there, even now, some sweaty little shit beating one out to an image of her lying naked on that bed, exposed, quite literally, for the world to see through the power of the Internet?

She shuddered again. She wouldn't, couldn't think like that

until Doug told her what was going on. If it was that bad, she would deal with it then. Until that time, and until Burns found out what she was doing with Doug and what they were hiding, she would do her job.

But she was damned if she was going to do it sober.

She made for the kitchen, came back with a bottle of white and a glass. Opened up her laptop and called up the files on Brian Coulter. Somewhere in here there was an answer, or at least a clue, to why he had died. Something to make sense of everything that had happened, something to help her start to impose some form of order on the chaos that was threatening to engulf her. It was here. And she was going to find it.

She let out a small cry when the phone chattered across the table in front of her fifteen minutes later. She reached for it, hand shaking. But the message wasn't from Doug. It was Rebecca: *Long day. Just done. Could do with a drink after the clusterfuck caused by the CC. Fancy it?*

Susie put the phone aside. Rebecca. There was another problem. Not only were she and Doug lying to Burns, they were lying to Rebecca as well. And, ultimately, it was her who was going to have to go in front of the TV cameras and the news reporters to explain all this.

And what would she say when she did? "My boyfriend perverted the course of justice and committed an act of grievous bodily harm so severe that it could be classed as attempted murder to save the blushes of our mutual friend, who was daft enough to shag a complete fuckwit that took candid nude shots of her for the family album"?

No. Maybe not. She typed in a reply, excusing herself with a headache. Took a moment to ponder why she didn't feel as guilty lying to Rebecca as she thought she should have, then turned back to the files.

The answer was there. And she would find it.

37

Doug crept out of Jennifer's room, *The Heroic Tale of The Red Giant* tucked under his arm. They had got back to Hal and Colin's place just after 8pm – delayed only by a short stop in a local pub. They kept the conversation light, Doug avoiding Hal's attempts to get an explanation of what the hell was going on. It could wait until they got back to his place and Colin. It wasn't a story he wanted to repeat. After finishing their drinks – a pint helping Doug relax almost as much as getting a seat watching the pub door and satisfying himself that no one wearing a grey suit was following them – they made their way home.

Colin and Hal lived in a three-bed, split-level garden flat in Kensington, which probably cost as much as a mansion in a few acres of grounds would in Scotland. They had bought it when they were young and carefree, before Jennifer came along and tore through their carefully ordered existence in a blur of nappies, sleepless nights, adjusted career goals and baby-related expenses. Stepping into the flat, Doug could see what Hal meant. The tasteful design was there: the muted colours, the artful print on the walls, the state-of-the-art TV. But instead of being the focus of the flat, they were now the afterthought, drowned out by the clutter of toys, colouring books and family pictures that seemed to encroach on every inch of free space.

Colin greeted Hal with a kiss, then turned his attention to Doug, engulfing him in a bear hug. Again, it struck Doug how different Hal and Colin were. While Hal always gave the impression he had just walked out of a tailor's shop, Colin was short, barrel-chested and always looked a little dishevelled. The first time he had met Colin, Doug couldn't see how he and Hal worked as a couple. The thought was quickly dispelled after watching them in each other's company. Yes, they bickered, argued, disagreed – especially over how they were spoiling Jennifer rotten – but they just worked together. And, despite himself, Doug never failed to feel a faint pang of jealousy at that.

"Right," Colin said. "Get your jacket off, and get up the stairs. Jennifer's waiting for Uncle Doug to read to her."

After the story, dinner was waiting downstairs. They caught up as they ate, the conversation dwindling away along with the food, finally petering out as Hal took Doug's plate and started clearing the table.

"So, Doug," he said. "It's great to have you here, but isn't it about time you told us what's going on? You said you needed Colin's help with a laptop?"

Doug nodded, stood up, took the laptop from the sofa where he'd left it and placed it on the table between them. "Before we get to that, there are a few things I need to tell you first," he said, his voice calm. It took him a moment to realise he was slipping into interview mode, hiding his fear behind his training. Slowly he laid the whole story out for them: Redmonds, the image of Susie, the fact he had effectively stolen the laptop from a crime scene and exposed the *Tribune* to legal action for the splash he had written. He didn't tell them he had kept all this from Rebecca. There was time for that later.

Colin and Hal listened quietly, eyes growing wide as he spoke. When he had finished, he paused, studied the stem of his wine glass. Thin and fragile. He knew the feeling.

"So that's it," he said softly. "That's the story. I understand I'm asking you to get into some murky shit, and I'm sorry for that. If you don't want to get involved, no problem, but I just… just didn't know who else to ask."

Colin and Hal exchanged a brief glance, an entire conversation seeming to occur in the silence. Then Colin nodded slightly, leaned forward and eased the laptop bag forward.

"Right," he said. "Let's see what we've got. You got that flash drive there, Doug?"

Doug fished it out of the pocket of his jeans, and Colin reached over the table for it, eyes holding Doug's. "Well, I'll say this, Doug, knowing you is never dull. Don't know how much help I can be, but let's see. I'm going to take this to my study, that okay with you?"

Doug nodded. "No problem."

"Good," Colin said. He turned to Hal. "You two have a drink and a chat, I'll have a look at all this, see what I can find out, okay?"

Hal nodded, squeezed Colin's leg. "Thanks," he said.

"Oh, don't thank me," Colin said, eyes dancing with mischief. "Thank Wordsworth over there. After all, he's going to owe us another bedtime story for Jennifer after this."

. . .

"So Doug," Hal said softly, sipping on his whisky, "just what the hell is going on with you and Susie?"

Doug coughed, his own whisky scalding the back of his throat. "Wha…?" he gasped, blinking away the tears. "Whadya mean?"

Hal cocked his head to the side, giving Doug a "you-know-better-than-that" look. "Seriously, Doug? I have to lay it out for you? So much for the trained investigative journalist, the keen reader of people."

"Hal, honestly, I don't know what you mean," Doug said. But he did. Hal and Colin seemed set on their view that Doug and Susie shared an unspoken attraction, that they deserved to be together. They never showed it when they had met Becky on their last trip to Edinburgh, but Doug could tell it was another silent conversation they had between glances.

She doesn't fit, those shared looks said. *She doesn't belong.*

Hal got up, paced across the room to the mantelpiece. Picked up a picture of the four of them – Doug, Hal, Colin and Jennifer – that they had taken on Skye. He studied it for a moment, as if he was looking for how to say what he wanted to in it, then put it down and turned to Doug. He looked like he should have been in a whisky advert.

"Doug, can I be blunt with you?"

"Course," Doug said, a vague snarl of unease penetrating the whisky fug.

"We're worried about you, Doug. You've lost weight, and the way you're grimacing every time you use that hand tells me it's not getting much better. And yet…"

Doug shifted in his seat. "And yet what?"

"And yet, as fucked up as you are, you beat a man half to death when he showed you a picture that would compromise Susie. You get her to lie to the police, you withhold evidence, put the *Trib* into so much shit that they're going to think they're in a manure factory… and for what? To protect a friend?"

Doug heard Redmonds' voice in his ear. Mewling, pleading. *Stop, please, I was wrong, I know I was wrong. Just stop.* Remembered the rage at that moment, the way it coursed through him like molten steel, cauterising, galvanising, washing away every other thought and feeling but one.

Revenge.

"Look, Hal, if this is another one of your misguided attempts to get me and Susie together…"

Hal waved the notion away. "No, it's not, Doug. Really, it isn't. But you're in some serious shit here, and the only way you're going to get through it is to be honest with yourself. Why are you doing this? To protect a friend? Or was there something about that picture in particular that bothered you?"

"So what are you saying?" Doug asked, looking up at Hal. "That I was, what? Jealous or something?"

Hal shrugged. "That's for you to decide. I'm just saying it's not you, Doug. You're not a violent guy. You're not the type to hit first and ask questions later. I know that. So I'm asking what drove this." He paused for a beat. "Say it had been Rebecca instead of Susie, would you have reacted the same way?"

Doug opened his mouth. *Of course I would,* he was going to say. *What, you think I wouldn't fly off the handle if that scumbag had shown me a naked picture of Becky instead of Susie?*

Instead, he closed his mouth. He didn't know what to say. Stared up at Hal, the question hanging between them.

What *would* he have done?

They were still sitting in the silence when Colin poked his head around the door, an uncertain look on his pale face.

"Find something?" Hal asked, taking a half step towards him.

"Not sure," he said, walking to the dining room table and laying the laptop and flash drive down. "Come here, I'll show you what I mean."

Doug got up, his legs numb pillars of concrete, and shuffled across to Colin, suddenly not sure if he wanted to know what he had found.

38

James stepped out into the night quietly, glanced around. He was at the bottom of an old stone stairway, the lips of the steps rounded and smoothed off by years of use. They were, he thought with a smile, a real trip hazard. Someone could take a nasty tumble down those stairs, cracking their head open with a deep, ripe crunch as they landed at the bottom in a crumpled, broken heap.

Now wouldn't that be a shame?

He made sure the door was closed securely then ran his gaze down his front. No blood, no telltale rips or tears, no outward signs of anything untoward. Perfect. Flicking up the collar of his jacket, he took the stairs two at a time, then emerged onto the street. No one was around. At this time of night, the offices were closed and the street was little more than a thoroughfare.

Perfect again.

Tucking his hands into his pockets, he started walking, deciding to savour the night. It was cold and clear, the moon a shard of bone that glowed in the dark sky.

He should, he thought, be angry with himself. This had been foolish, irresponsible. What if he had been recognised? He was under no illusions that he was some kind of celebrity, but he was self-aware enough to recognise that he did have a public profile of sorts, especially now. And if he had been seen...

No. There was no point in torturing himself with possibilities. What was done was done and he had emerged unscathed, his anonymity intact. It was everything he had hoped it would be, and more. The perfect counterpoint to a day that was replete with frustrations and setbacks. A day that, briefly, made him question whether he was losing his touch.

Mark had done well in tracking McGregor so quickly, proof if it was needed that the message he had Vic deliver had served its purpose. But then Vic had failed to act before McGregor had made it to London, and his rendezvous with Hal Damon.

James rolled the name around in his mind. Damon's involvement in this, however tangential, was a problem, but he couldn't see how he fit into the picture. Unless, of course, McGregor had decided to pack it all in and flee to the City, taking a job with his friend in PR.

If only it was that simple.

Damon was connected to the wrong people. Any action against him would bring undue attention from some of his clients. He had, according to what James had been able to dig up, done good work in the past for the Scottish Tories on a delicate story, earning the respect of just the type of people James wanted to keep in the dark. So it was a problem, but a manageable one. As long as Vic didn't make it worse.

He thought again of his earlier call with Vic. The insolent tone, the defiance, and he felt his irritation stretch its wings, fan the embers of rage that he had so recently and pleasurably quelled.

He sighed, picking up his pace. This was the problem with indulging himself: he developed a taste for it all too quickly. Like a drinker who says he'll "only have the one" and then finishes half the bottle before he's aware of it, James was acutely aware that he had an addiction. But he also knew how to control it, channel it.

Most of the time.

He thought back to his last meeting. The look of shock and confusion when he had pounced; the sweet symphony of bones grinding together under his blows; the smell of blood and adrenalin a bittersweet thrill in his nostrils; the hot, fevered feel of flesh beneath his fingers as he gouged and pulled and tore. It was a pity he had to use the latex gloves, but caution was always preferable.

And besides, he thought, remembering the broken, blood-soaked mess he had left behind him, the results had been most satisfactory.

He closed his hand around the blade in his pocket, remembered how it had caught the light, the blade seeming to glow as he swung it. The pulsing arc of blood it had unleashed, the grunt of pain and shock, the spatter as it hit the wall. He smiled, tightening his grip on the handle as he decided on a destination and picked his way through the cattle that shared the pavement with him.

The night was young. He had released his tensions and frustrations in the only way he knew. There were other problems that demanded his attention – Damon, Vic, McGregor – and he would solve them.

Every single one.

39

"So," Colin said, absently running his finger over the trackpad of the laptop, "I had a look at this thing, like you said. And..." – he laid the flash drive in the small gutter between the keyboard and the screen – "this."

Doug swallowed, heard his throat click. It was as if the flash drive had a magnetic pull, dragging his eyes to it, forcing him to see it, remember... He coughed, blinked. Hal shot him a look and Doug shook his head. *I'm fine*, the gesture said. He wished he meant it. "Well," he said, voice little more than a whisper, "what did you find?"

"Nothing at first," Colin said, picking up the flash drive and plugging it in. "Firstly, this is nothing more than it appears to be. A basic flash drive with just one file on it. Doug, do you mind if I...?"

Doug remembered his promise to Susie, not to look at the image again. He paused. Remembered his conversation with Hal only moments ago.

"Is it important?" he asked, his voice flat.

Something like sympathy flitted across Colin's face. "Yeah, I think it might be. It'll only be a minute, Doug, I promise. But I think you need to understand this."

It felt to Doug as if spiders were crawling around his stomach, caressing his guts with slender, skittering legs. He jerked his head in a nod, barely felt Hal's arm slide round his shoulders and squeeze. Colin nodded and double-clicked on the icon, the image jumping to life on the screen. Doug heard Hal take a breath then coughed.

"Oh, Susie. Jesus," he whispered.

Colin quickly zoomed into the image, scrolling away from anything that would embarrass Susie. "Okay," he said, the stress in his voice twisting his attempt at relaxed informality into something that made Doug grind his teeth. "So what we've got here is a jpeg. Pretty standard, not very high res, obviously taken by an amateur." He scrolled around the image, past the TV where the porn played, zooming in further to the flash bouncing off the mirror.

Colin pointed at the screen. "See this? That's the camera that took the picture." He traced a small rectangle around a section of the screen. "And I mean camera, not smartphone. By the looks of it, that's a small digital camera – you know, the flat ones with the retractable lenses."

"Okay," Doug said, eyes glued to the screen, unable to really follow what Colin was saying, or make connections himself.

"So," Colin said slowly, shooting a concerned glance at Hal, "that's the start of the bad news."

Doug felt as though he had been slapped. Bad news? What? "Bad news?"

"Well, yeah," Colin said. "Those cameras don't use flash drives like this, they use SD memory cards – you know, the things that look a little like a bank card? Wider. Flatter. Which means –"

"Which means," Doug said, finally seeing what Colin was getting at with horrific clarity, "that this isn't the original jpeg. That Redmonds copied this file onto the flash drive from another device. Meaning there's another copy of this out there somewhere. Along with fuck knows what else." He took a breath. Glanced down at his glass. Empty. "Fuck," he said.

Colin nodded. "Sorry, Doug," was all he said, hating how inadequate it sounded.

"And there's nothing else on the laptop, nothing linked to this? I couldn't find anything more than a couple of spreadsheets and a Word file with an abortion of a memoir on it. You find anything at all?"

Colin shut the image down and Doug stared at the screen a moment longer, feeling as if he was still missing something. Something in plain sight, something his stupid booze-soaked brain wasn't able to connect with another fact stored away deep in his brain…

"See, that's where none of this makes sense," Colin said. "This Mac is top of the range, only came out six months ago. And there's nothing on it, so you would think it's fairly new, right?"

"Right," Doug said absently, his mind still gnawing on the memory of the image. *Something…*

"That's what I thought," Colin said, fingers pecking away at keys and bringing up another menu. "But then I looked at this." He gestured to the display on the screen, a small icon showing a battery with two coloured bars sitting beside it. "This is the battery life indicator for the computer. It shows the battery has been heavily used, which indicates that the computer has been fairly consistently powered up with a lot of active programs for long periods since it was bought. For only six months old, tops, there's a lot of degradation to the battery condition, more than I would expect for a laptop of this age. And yet, for all that –"

"There's nothing on the laptop," Doug said, feeling something in the back of his head spark to life. "So what the hell has he been using it for?"

"Ah," Colin said, a small, proud smile lighting up his face, "that's where it gets really interesting. I dug down a little further, and found the IP log files. It shows that this laptop has been connecting to the Internet fairly regularly. What it doesn't show is where it's being connected to. And when you go into the web browser history, there's just the usual stuff, a handful of everyday websites."

"But what does it all mean?" Hal asked. "A seriously used laptop that's empty. A naked picture taken on a digital camera and copied to a flash drive. Records of serious Internet use but hardly any indication of what for in the browser history? What…?"

Colin shrugged, looked to Doug. "Doug, you said that this is all there was, just the laptop and the flash drive. Anything else? Another hard disk maybe, another flash drive?"

Doug thought back to Redmonds' laptop bag, which was now sitting in the boot of his car at Edinburgh Airport. He had searched it the first night, after Susie left. Found nothing but a bunch of business cards. Nothing else.

He looked at the glass in his hand, felt a stab of shame. Hal's words: *The only way you're going to get through this is to be honest with yourself.* How sober had he been when he searched the bag? How drunk? Could he have missed something? He mashed his fingers into his eyes, pushing hard enough to send bright spots of light exploding across his field of vision. Nothing. A wasted trip. A waste of time he didn't have, a …

Wait a minute.

Time.

He snapped his eyes open, glared at the screen. "Open up the image again, will you?"

Colin looked at him, shared another glance with Hal. "You sure you want to?"

"Yes!" Doug snapped. Held up a hand. "Sorry, Colin. Yes. Please. It's important."

Colin turned to the laptop and brought the image back up. Doug hauled his eyes away from Susie, forced himself to instead concentrate on the bottom right-hand corner of the image. The corner where a time stamp glowed on the screen in neon red.

02.37am.

He closed his eyes, willing his mind into action. Looking back in his thoughts. Time. That time. Something about it that he…

"Fuck," he said after a moment, realisation shuddering through him. How could he have been so fucking blind? So stupid? It was, after all, how he had found out about Susie and Redmonds in the first place. Going through the hotel records from the night of the party, he had seen that a bottle of champagne and an "entertainment event", which was hotel code for a porn film, had been charged to Susie's room at 11.24pm. So unless it was *Horny Olympians Go For The All-Night Fuckathon Record* they had been watching, the film couldn't have still been playing more than two hours later.

Which meant the porn on the TV screen was something else. But what?

He gestured to the screen in the corner, not looking at the main image. "Can you enhance that?" he said.

Colin squinted at the screen. Grunted. "Maybe, though it could take a while," he said, more to himself than Doug or Hal. "But why? Is it important what fuckfest he was watching?"

"Could be," Doug said, feeling the first shards of sobriety peek through the fog in his mind for the first time in entirely too long. "And can you have another look at the laptop, see if you can find anything else?"

"I can," Colin said, "but I'm not sure there's much more to find. It's like I said, Doug, it's as if there's something missing. You find that, maybe I can do something more."

Doug nodded, eyes locked on the keyboard and not the screen. Something missing? Yes. But if that was the case, why did he feel as if he had just found something vital?

40

The cream walls seemed to glow in the gloom, a solitary lamp throwing a small pool of light that sketched objects out in a relief of silhouettes and shadows. Alicia Leonard sat on the sofa, a glass of wine forgotten on the coffee table in front of her. She turned her attention back to the iPad on her lap, rereading the same paragraph of a Police Board paper for what felt like the hundredth time. With a sigh of frustration, she tossed the iPad aside, looked across to the sofa where the two policemen had sat earlier today.

She felt a hard, impotent anger as she thought of the senior officer. What was his name? Bryan? No, Burns. Jason Burns. How dare the pompous little prick question her about the last time she had seen Paul? And how stupid had she been to rise to it? It was only for a second, but the irritation that seeped into her voice reverberated in her ears even as she said the words. And she had seen it in his eyes, of course, that look she had seen too many times before from men who thought they had got the measure of her or slipped her up. *Gotcha, bitch.*

If only they knew.

She sighed in frustration. Grabbed the wine glass and padded through to the kitchen, passing the door to Michael's office as she did. He was out, again, either working or indulging his other passions. She was observant enough to know about the other women, but at least he did her the courtesy of not lying about it. Instead, the topic was studiously ignored by both of them as they lived the lie of a happily married couple. It was no great effort for Alicia. After all, Paul had given her the chance to practise for the role.

She thought of him then, lying naked and pale on a cold steel table at the mortuary when she had gone to formally identify him. She had only seen his shoulders and face, but it was clear Paul had been given a hell of a beating. His skin, bleached grey by the draining of his blood and the inevitable onset of decay, was a patchwork of lurid greens, purples and dusky reds, almost as though he had been attacked by a murderous tattooist. His nose, which she vaguely remembered one of her friends referring to as a "perfect Roman nose – sexy", was now a crooked mess, split open at the nostrils and bent towards his left cheek. And she could see the telltale swelling just below his ears which told her that his jaw had been broken. Looking down on him, on the man she had shared so much with, she felt a brief pang of sorrow. Crushed it down with the memory of all the pain she had caused him.

She had received a call from the Chief Constable when she was driving back home, been assured that Police Scotland was "doing all it could to bring the culprit to justice". The arrival of Burns and his minion was, she supposed, another attempt to show that the force was throwing everything it had at the case. It didn't comfort her.

She thought of calling John Wallace, using Paul's death as a pretence, then thought better of it. He knew nothing of what really happened that night beyond what he saw at the bar. Calling him would only stir his suspicions and, worse, his memory. No, better to let it lie.

She poured her wine down the sink, considered having a vodka while she waited for Michael to return. Instead, she headed for the gym in the basement – the gym Michael had insisted on installing with his last bonus – to lose herself in exercise.

After all, she was a member of the Police Board, the woman whose ex had become front-page news due to the manner of his death. She was also the wife of a successful and well-respected figure in the finance sector who had a knack of snagging column inches in the business pages of papers. All that added up to publicity. Exposure. Opportunity. And with that in mind, it would be stupid not to keep in shape, make sure she was looking her best.

Just in case the cameras came calling.

41

Doug lay in the spare room of Hal and Colin's flat, staring at the ceiling in the dark and flexing his left hand slowly. The comforting silence was doing nothing to ease the pain in his arm or his mind. So Redmonds had put on another porn film while taking pics of Susie, so what? Fucking prick was obviously only interested in his own pleasure, probably put it on to jack off to as he took those pictures. But the time difference meant it wasn't the "entertainment event" provided by the hotel. So whatever Redmonds had put on, he had taken with him to the hotel that night.

Doug shuddered slightly, an unpleasant thought coming to him. Had Redmonds been that predatory, his plan all along being to pick someone up then watch whatever it was he had with him as he took pictures of them? If so, why?

He gasped softly as he turned his hand the wrong way, needles of pain rippling up from his ring finger to his wrist. Thought again of the first blow he had landed on Redmonds, the pain a joyous wildfire. Knowing what he did now, Doug wished he had hit the bastard harder. Killed him himself.

He stopped, Hal's warning in his mind again. *The only way you're going to get through this is by being honest.*

If he was being honest, he didn't want Redmonds dead. Not really. Yes, he wanted him to suffer for what he had done to Susie, but dead? No. He thought back to the shock and terror that had screamed through his mind when Susie had told him Redmonds was dead. The revulsion at the thought he was responsible, the weight of another man's life weighing down on him, crushing, suffocating…

No. Doug knew he was no killer. But someone was. The question was who? And why?

He swung his legs off the bed, sat up and clicked on the light. Dug around in his bag for his notebook and opened it to the page of notes he had scribbled down at the airport, going over what he knew.

Redmonds. Falcon's Rest. Dessie Banks.

Doug made a mental note to chase Rab for anything he had found as soon as he got home. He grabbed a pen, flicked to a new page of his notebook. Tried to lay the whole picture out in his mind again. Asked himself what he knew. And what he didn't. Started writing.

Redmonds was scared by something I was doing. Scared enough to try to blackmail me. Where did he go after I – he paused for a moment – *beat the shit out of him?*

Why did someone kill him? Because he confronted me? Because he told them he showed me the picture of Susie?

Doug looked at the page. Was that it? Was that why he had died? But then why would someone kill him over a nude pic of a cop? The only person with motive was Susie herself, and Doug knew she wasn't the killer.

So who was?

He massaged his forehead, as though trying to coax his brain into gear. There was something missing, something that he was almost seeing, something that connected all this, made the picture make sense….

He was startled from his thoughts by the chirp of his mobile on the bedside table. He picked it up and peered at the screen, cursing when he saw Susie's name on the display. He had promised to call her with an update after Colin had looked at the laptop, and forgotten. His thumb hesitated over the *Answer* key. What could he tell her? *Sorry, nothing new to report, every chance he had more dirty pics of you and we can't tell if he uploaded any of them to the Internet. On the bright side, you do have amazing breasts.*

He shook his head, embarrassed by the thought. Hit the screen.

"Susie? What's up? Look, sorry I haven't called, we were –"

Susie cut him off. "Doug. Forget about that now. What time are you flying back tomorrow?"

"Early," he said, an alarm starting to ring in the back of his mind, unease making his breath short. "9am flight. Why?"

"We just got a call. Seems like a man has been found severely beaten and stabbed in the New Town. Late fifties."

"And?" Doug coaxed, not sure he wanted to hear what was coming next.

"Doug," – and something in Susie's businesslike tone softened – "the call came from Forth Street. The victim was taken to the ERI, he's in surgery now. Outlook is 50-50 at this stage."

"Forth Street," Doug said, his tongue clicking as he forced the words out. "You mean…?"

"Yes, Doug. The victim has been identified as Rab MacFarlane. Janet's been informed and is being taken to the hospital. But you better get back here as soon as you can. I'm not sure how long he's going to last."

42

Doug staggered out of the arrivals gate at Edinburgh the next morning, addled by too much coffee and too little sleep. After the call from Susie, his first move had been to phone Janet, see what she could tell him.

"It's nae looking good, son," she'd said, voice hard and brittle. "Someone got him at the office when he was on his own. Bastard kicked the shite out of him then stabbed him as well. Doctors say he's got one collapsed lung, internal bleeding. They're working on him now."

Doug made some supportive comments, mind racing and eyes glued to his notepad, fixed on the other name written there and circled. *Dessie Banks*. Was that who was behind this? Had Rab asked a question he shouldn't, and paid the price for it? If so, then this was on Doug's shoulders.

Fuck.

"Look, Janet, I'm in London. I'm on an early flight back up tomorrow morning, I'll come straight to the hospital when I get in."

"Bloody right you will!" Janet said, her voice jagged with something different now. Something dangerous. "He was poking around on your behalf so I think it's well past time we had a wee word, don't you?"

He had agreed and hung up, spent the rest of a sleepless night turning everything over in his mind, hitting dead end after dead end. The only thing that seemed to connect everything was Dessie Banks. But why would Banks kill Redmonds over a dirty picture or an empty laptop? And what was he so desperate to cover up that he had Rab almost killed to keep his nose out of it?

At Edinburgh Airport next morning he was so preoccupied with thoughts of getting to his car and rechecking Redmonds' laptop bag that he almost didn't see the man mountain looming up in front of him. The doughy colossus who had driven him back to Becky's flat the other day, steering wheel digging into his gut.

Chris.

Doug stopped just before he walked into him, pulling up short at the last moment. He blinked in confusion. Chris saw the look and smiled. Doug swore he could hear children start to cry in the distance.

"Mr McGregor," Chris said in his slow, deliberate voice as he offered Doug his hand. It was like watching a digger swinging its shovel arm into position. "Mrs MacFarlane told me to come and see you, drive you to the hospital."

Doug took Chris's hand. The shake was surprisingly gentle, the bones only bruised, not broken. "Ah, sorry, Chris, wasted trip for you. I've got my car here."

Chris widened his smile, exposing slabs of dirty, yellow-white concrete roughly hewn into the shape of teeth. The children's screams gave way to sobs and groans. "Naw, Mr McGregor," he said, voice growing lyrical with humour, "we know that. I'm here to drive you. Not to worry though, I've already had a shot of your RX-8. Got a feel for her now. I'll be gentle. Promise."

The drive was mostly uneventful, the only moment of excitement when Chris gave the car too much gas at the roundabout leading from the airport to the bypass and the back end kicked out.

"Rear-wheel drives," he said happily, "fucking love them."

When they got to the Edinburgh Royal Infirmary, Chris pulled up to the main entrance, stuck the RX-8 in neutral and kept the engine running. "You go on in," he said, "I'll stay with the car. Mrs MacFarlane says she'll call me when you're done and I'll get you here."

Doug was about to protest, the thought of Chris just driving off in his car not sitting comfortably with him, especially with

Redmonds' bag in the boot, but then he looked at the stranglehold Chris had on the steering wheel and changed his mind. The bag would be safe with Chris looking after the car.

He got out and headed for the high-dependency unit. Just outside it were three of Rab's men sitting in the cheap, orange plastic waiting-room seats he knew all too well from his childhood. Which was apt, as the three made them look like toy furniture.

"Mr McGregor," the man sitting in the middle growled. Doug thought he recognised him, was sure Rab had introduced him once. Eric, Eddie...

"Ernie," Doug said as the man stood up. "Good to see you. Wish it wasn't like this. How's he doing?"

Ernie's brow furrowed, the creases becoming dark crevices running across his head. "Boss is a stubborn bastard," he said, the pride obvious in his voice. "He made it through the night. Doctors seem to think he's got a good chance."

Doug nodded. "Good, that's good. Can I see him?"

Ernie held up a hand. "Stay here a minute," he said. "Mrs MacFarlane said I was to tell her the moment you arrived. She's with the boss now."

Doug murmured agreement and Ernie lumbered off into the ward. From the plastic seats, his two colleagues stared up at Doug impassively. Maybe, he thought, they were marvelling at this strange sub-species of human that was under twenty-five-stone and had clear definition between the end of the shoulders and start of the neck. Or maybe they were just jealous that he had two eyebrows to their one.

The minutes crawled past, the sounds of the hospital filling the silence: gentle coughs and splutters, the squeak of rubber soles on the floor, the plaintive beep of a monitor. And then there was a new sound, the staccato of heels on the floor, marching towards him.

Janet.

He turned and there she was. Her hair was still immaculate, held in place by enough spray to punch a hole in the ozone layer, but the deep mahogany stain of her false tan exposed and accentuated every wrinkle and crease on her face. She looked pinched, reduced somehow.

Doug stepped forward, took her in a hug. She didn't move, her body a flick-knife encased in dough. Then, after a moment, he felt her soften, and her hand go around his back.

"Douglas," she whispered, "thank you for coming."

He thought of Chris. Wondered how much of a choice he had. Let it go. "No problem," he said. "How's Rab doing?"

She pushed him away then, glanced at the two thugs sitting outside the ward. Doug could see tears glisten in the corners of her eyes. "Not here," she said. "Let's take a walk. Rab's sleeping. And if I don't get a fag soon, someone is going to end up in the bed beside him."

"So," he said, once they were outside. "What happened, Janet? Who would do that to Rab?"

She lit the cigarette she had fumbled from her bag then stopped and turned to him. Eyed him coolly as she took a deep drag, the tip of the cigarette glowing hot and angry as she did. She spat the words out with the smoke from the cigarette, both issuing from her mouth like poison. "I don't know, Doug," she said. "Why don't you tell me?"

Doug cocked his head to the side. "Sorry, Janet, I don't know what –"

"Dinnae give me that shite, son," she snarled, stabbing the cigarette at him like it was a weapon. "You asked Rab to look into Dessie Banks, and then this happens. What the fuck do you think happened? You're the investigative reporter, why don't you put the clues together for me?"

Doug stared at her, knowing she was right. "Look, Janet, I'm sorry, I had no idea that, this…" – he raised his hands impotently – "that Rab…"

She held up a hand, eyes fixed on his. "Look, son. You know Rab thinks the sun shines out of your arse. He would do anything for you. I would too. But whoever did this to him, they were sending a message. So now I'm sending one. Whatever it is you're looking into, whatever it is you think you've got, walk the fuck away. Otherwise it'll be you in there next time, not Rab."

Doug was lost for words. He had heard about this side of Janet, but never seen it. He knew protective mother hen, the loyal wife, the shrewd operator. But he had never seen… this before.

"It's not as easy as that," he said at last. "I'm sorry, Janet, but it's complicated. I'm not sure I can leave this alone."

She took another draw on her cigarette, shook her head. Something Doug couldn't read twisted across her face, like an undercurrent rippling across the surface of still water, then it passed. She tossed the cigarette away, didn't bother to stub it out with her toe.

"Then I'm sorry, Doug," she said. "Just be careful, okay? Rab would be broken-hearted if anything happened to you. And…" – she paused, considering – "so would I."

"Thanks, Janet," he said with a lot more warmth than he felt.

"No bother son. I've got to get back. I'll tell Chris to meet you at the main entrance."

He watched her walk off then, a small woman stooped over by the weight of the world. What was that? A warning? A threat? A plea? Just what the hell was going on? And what had Rab found out?

Doug started walking back towards the front door of the hospital. He didn't notice the car parked outside the Casualty unit, its window cracked open, a squat man in a light grey suit jacket watching him closely.

43

Burns sat in his office, print-outs, folders and old newspapers fighting for every available inch of space on his desk. A coffee cup sat forgotten on top of one pile that was taller than the others, like a flag planted by a mountaineer.

The morning conference had gone as well, and as briefly, as he had hoped. Officers reported that the sifting of CCTV – to try and trace Redmonds' movements on the night of his murder – should be completed by the end of the day. They'd picked him up heading along the coast towards East Lothian, so were now checking the cameras in Portobello and Musselburgh. The final forensic report was also back, confirming what Dr Williams had sketched out in his preliminary findings: death was caused by a slim, incredibly sharp blade puncturing the chest cavity and rupturing the inferior vena cava, which then caused internal bleeding and, ultimately, Redmonds' heart to stop.

Ironic, Burns thought, that a heartless bastard like that would be killed by a broken heart.

He divided up duties for the day, made sure everyone was co-ordinating through him. He nodded his approval at an update from Drummond, telling him that she and Eddie had a strong lead on the identity of the body from Leith: Brian Coulter, who ran the graphic design company that had been burgled. It was an interesting link, and Burns made sure Eddie and Susie would follow it up. If there was something there, they would find it. They had the makings of a good team.

The only piece of new business was the attack on Rab MacFarlane. Officers who attended the scene at Forth Street had described it as being like "something out of a horror film", blood pooled on the floors and spattered up the walls, MacFarlane lying draped over his desk, mangled like a discarded chew toy. Burns had seen the SOCO pictures from the scene – from the damage to the room, the owner of the chew toy must have been somewhere between Cujo and the Hound of the Baskervilles. Glass glittered on the floor in the glare from the flash, legs and supports from pulverised pieces of furniture littered the ground like pieces of flotsam left on the beach by a retreating tide. And the blood. Jesus, the blood. But the picture Burns kept returning to was the last one – a smeared, bloody handprint trailing down a cream wall, no doubt where MacFarlane had propped himself up before staggering to his desk and collapsing.

Burns wondered briefly who would do that to MacFarlane, and why. Pushed the thought aside, resigned himself to the knowledge that the Major Investigations Unit would be looking into it. A team had been investigating MacFarlane for years, trying to get a handle on his more illicit practices and his role in punishment beatings of low-level drug dealers across Edinburgh. It wasn't out of any concern for the scum he was targeting, but there was a feeling that the fragile peace between Dessie Banks and MacFarlane might be about to crack. And a gang war on the streets of Edinburgh was something no one wanted to see.

Satisfied that the bases were covered, Burns dismissed the meeting and retreated to his office, the print-outs he had made the previous evening when he got home from the shop waiting for him.

He settled into his chair, gave the door another quick glance. The lock may have been broken, but he had folded up a few old cigarette packets and wedged them in door. If the chief came knocking, Burns wanted a few moments to get what he was working on out of sight. It may be something, it may be nothing. Either way, the powers that be weren't going to be pleased with his line of inquiry.

It had been back in 2008, the length of time just long enough to blur the memory in Burns' mind and make it a persistent nag rather than an instant recognition. He hadn't worked on the case, but he remembered it – everyone in the force at the time did. It was one of the few occasions when there had been an almost tacit approval for what had happened, and a certain reluctance to find whoever was responsible.

His name was Greg Davidson, a former teacher in Newcastle who had been imprisoned for luring a fifteen-year-old pupil into his home and then his bed. The story had come to light when she had fallen pregnant and his response had been, "Get rid of it." In that moment, his victim saw Davidson for what he was: not the sophisticated older man who had seen beyond her youth to the woman she really was, but a craven little shit who was after only one thing and not interested in the repercussions.

Maybe that was why she had lunged at him with a pair of sewing scissors.

The judge had, stupidly, taken the attack into account and given Davidson a reduced sentence. Some of the tabloids followed the story for a while, Gemma's brave decision to have the baby, Davidson's cushy life in prison, his new identity on release, before the story petered out and they moved onto the next scandal.

That was until Davidson turned up in the village of Glenview, wrapped in the swings of a playpark. He had been badly beaten, a small placard hanging from his neck with the word *Paedo* scrawled across it in Davidson's own blood, a crumpled-up piece of paper stuffed into his mouth as a gag.

It didn't take local police long to fill in the blanks, the local community eager to decry the "filthy wee bastard". Davidson had been drawn to the area by the promise of work, project managing a new housing and leisure development that was being built on the outskirts of the village. As his previous life in Newcastle prevented him from working as a teacher or with children, it made sense to Burns. New start. New life.

Problem was, the old urges remained.

The rumours soon began about the well-dressed guy who would always just happen to be checking the site's perimeter – with a camera – when the schoolkids from the local high school were filing past at the end of the day. Officers who searched his home found the camera, along with a neat bundle of print-outs that had been cropped to focus in on the girls. They also found evidence that he was using chat rooms to contact a range of kids in the area, posing as a gangling, smiling teenager called Matthew. The profile image he used was ripped straight from Google Images.

Though no one in the village would say what happened, it was pretty clear that Davidson had pushed it too far, and a relative of one of the girls confronted him. Given that the piece of paper stuffed into his mouth was a newspaper spread on his Newcastle conviction, it was clear that the locals had recognised him and decided to dish out some punitive action.

Enquiries were made, and while the police investigation stumbled to a halt, the press, sensing a moral outrage story that had a way to run, went looking for other targets, in this case, the owner of the home and leisure development.

Paradigm Investment Solutions.

Burns flicked to a newspaper article from the time. The company faced some fairly sharp questioning about its employment and vetting practices, while local MSPs eager to jump on the bandwagon called for greater regulation and scrutiny of those working near schools. It was a potentially damaging story for Paradigm, and they fell back on the tried and tested PR formula often employed by big firms: throw money at the problem.

The company sent a senior director to Glenview, armed with a fat cheque that was to be split between Glenview High School and Kidsnet, a charity set up to curb online grooming and abuse of children. The picture accompanying the story featured the local MSP, sporting an epic combover, and the director from Paradigm. The director who lived in a gated estate in Inveresk and served them coffee yesterday.

Michael Leonard.

Burns studied the picture for a moment longer, then put it aside, picking up the investigation reports and interview transcripts from the Davidson beating. All present and correct, properly filed and signed by the investigating officer.

DI Alicia Redmonds.

So did Leonard and Alicia cross paths at the time? Burns remembered Michael Leonard's words just yesterday: *Alicia and I only met after Paul had filed for divorce.* There was the problem, wasn't it? The newspaper article was dated August 2008, but Redmonds hadn't filed for divorce until 2009. Maybe an innocent mistake. Or maybe the truth: perhaps he and Alicia hadn't met in Glenview. But it was a hell of a coincidence, and Burns had a copper's natural disdain for coincidence.

And then there was Alicia Leonard's reaction to him pushing her on the last time she had seen Redmonds alive. That hard, bright anger snarling beneath her veneer of sophisticated control.

The image of John Wallace reared up in Burns' mind: his massive hand held up in a fist, thumb and pinkie jabbing out.

Call me.

Burns reached into his desk drawer and grabbed a handful of tobacco from the small tin he kept there and started chewing slowly. The bitterness helped him think, and it was easier than trying to hang out of the window for a puff.

There was something here that didn't add up. He had been lied to or misled, both about when Michael met Alicia, and about what happened the last time Alicia saw Redmonds alive. There was no escaping it, no avoiding it. No matter how thin the ice he was on, no matter how pissed off the top brass would be, he would have to speak to Alicia Leonard again.

He just hoped the ice didn't crack under him when he did.

44

Chris was waiting at the front door of the hospital as agreed. He was leaning against Doug's car, massive arms crossed on the roof. Doug was sure he could see the metal bow a little.

"Here she is, Mr McGregor," he said slowly, hefting his massive bulk off the car, one hand trailing gently over the roof as he did, as though reluctant to break the connection. "Keys are in the ignition. Oh, and I ran the engine up, so she'll have spun, nae risk o' the rotary flooding."

Doug nodded as he took a step closer, Chris slowly stepping back and opening the driver's door for him, the world's most grotesque parking assistant. "Cheers, Chris," he said as he slid into the seat. Chris slammed the driver's door shut, the car juddering sideways with the force. Then he leant down, massive face taking up the entire driver's side window, which he'd left open. In the distance, Doug heard the kids starting to scream again.

"Drive safe, Mr McGregor," he said, his breath rich and sour with something Doug didn't want to think about. "She's a real beauty. If you ever want shot of her, let me know, I'll give you a fair price."

Doug ran his hand over the steering wheel. It was still warm from Chris's touch. "Thanks, but I think I'll hold onto her for a while," he said. "Kind of attached to her."

Chris nodded as though this made perfect sense, but there was a childish disappointment in his gaze. And something darker too. Something that told Doug this wasn't a man used to hearing the word no. A man who was only on his best behaviour at the behest of his boss. But who, Doug thought suddenly, was that? Rab? Or Janet?

He started the engine, gave Chris a wave and drove away slowly, easing in behind a double-decker that was queuing at the traffic lights at the exit of the hospital. He jacked his seat in, glanced up and started to adjust the rear-view mirror back to a useful position after Chris had used it.

Froze when he saw the silver Ford behind him, the man in the light grey suit sitting in the driver's seat.

He tried to ignore the sour thrill of adrenalin telling him to floor the accelerator. Looked again. It was the same man who he had bumped into at London City Airport, he was sure. Same wide shoulders, close-cropped grey hair. That same purpose in his eyes, which were nothing more than dark, empty pools fixed on him. And now he was here, following him again. Why? The answer was obvious: the laptop and the flash drive, both of which were safely with Colin and Hal in London. But what was this guy's plan? Tail Doug then grab him, or engineer an accident on the road? What should Doug do?

He shifted his gaze forward, locked them on the brake lights of the double-decker as he gently hit the central locking control on the door panel. Watched the traffic lights turn from red to amber then green, the bus pulling away in a rising diesel growl.

Doug eased the handbrake off. Waited. Heard the impatient blare of a horn from a few cars back, glanced in the mirror. Saw nothing but the same dull glare back at him, two hands strangling the steering wheel. Looked back at the lights. Waited. Licked his lips.

Show time.

The RX-8's engine gave its high-pitched whine, the rotary engine spinning into life as the car shot forward, back end wiggling with the sudden acceleration. The engine warning started to blare and he shifted into second as the Mazda hit 60mph, pulling out and shooting past the bus as it laboured its way up a steep hill. He overtook another two cars, then jerked back into the left again and hammered on the brakes, ignoring the flashing and gesticulating from the driver behind him. Flicked his gaze to the rearview, waiting for the Ford to appear. But he couldn't pass the bus now because of the oncoming traffic. Trapped. Perfect.

Doug thought fast. Where to go? If this was the same guy who had broken into his flat, then he would know where he lived. But if that was the case, why follow him here? Why not just wait for him at the flat, get him there? He couldn't go to the *Tribune* – there was nowhere to park and with Redmonds' bag in the boot he didn't want to be exposed. So where could he go? Where could he…?

He was snapped out of his thoughts by the sudden blare of horns behind him, the silver nose of the Ford pushing out from behind the bus.

Shit.

Doug glanced up, gauging the road in front of him. Not ideal, but traffic was light, and he was in his car.

Fuck it.

He downshifted back into second and hammered the accelerator, the Mazda surging forward. He swung out, dodging the central reservation bollard by inches and powered up the hill, not sure if the sudden appearance of blue lights in front or behind him would be the worst or best news of the day.

He got to the next junction and saw traffic snarled up on the main road ahead. Doug hauled the wheel right and feathered the accelerator, drifting the car around the junction and narrowly missing a Fiesta that was about to merge into the road from the opposite lane. He flew along a smaller road, driving deeper into the thicket of red-brick maisonettes and former council houses that stood like sentries on either side of the street. He glanced in his mirror, saw no sign of the Ford. Made a quick left into a cul-de-sac and doubled back, pulling in behind a small Asda van and poking the nose out just enough so he could see the road he had just pulled off.

The wait was almost as excruciating as the pain in his arm, seconds dragging past as he felt sweat cool on his back. After a minute, the Ford gunned its way past, the driver leaning forward in his seat, grimly intent on the road in front of him.

Doug couldn't help but smile. He waited for a few more seconds, wanting to make sure Mr Grey Suit wasn't going to double-back, then inched the car back out to the junction. He paused for a moment, seriously considering turning the game around and following whoever it was that was after him. Then he remembered Redmonds' bag, and Colin's insistence that he must have missed something.

No. He had to look at the bag. And losing Mr Grey Suit had bought him time. He would head to the flat, lock the door, see what he could find. Call Susie for back-up.

• • •

Doug headed back the way he had come then out on to the bypass that led to East Lothian, red-lining through the gears, revelling in the simple joy of driving too fast. At this speed, he could forget the pain, the shame, the mistakes he had made. At this speed, all he had to focus on was the road in front of him and the next second.

Pity it couldn't last.

He made it back to Musselburgh without incident, amazed to find a space outside the flat. He revved the engine then killed the ignition, listening to the rotary system whine to a halt. He might have to make a quick exit, and the last thing he wanted was to come down to a flooded engine. He moved quickly, jumping out of the car and retrieving Redmonds' bag, then bounding up the stairs to his front door.

He got his key in the lock, swung the door open and stepped inside. He was just turning to slide the locks back into place when a warm slab of muscle slid around his neck and jerked him violently backwards and off his feet. Doug's hand scrabbled for the arm holding him, the laptop bag dropped and forgotten as his lungs screamed for air.

"Fuckin' quit it, ya wee shite," a voice hissed in his ear, the blackness pulsing through his head as the pressure was increased on his neck. He was birled round and marched toward the living room, then dumped roughly at his assailant's feet. Doug collapsed forward, hands clawing at his throat as he took in gasping gulps of air. It felt as if his throat was on fire, and it sounded as if someone was beating an anvil in his ears.

Fuck! All for nothing. Fuckers knew you would come here and now they're going to get whatever's in the bag and have a nice long chat with you…

Conscious thought gave way to a flickering slideshow of memories. Diane Pearson, giggling and cackling as she danced around him, kicking and clawing and biting. The whimpering of Paul Redmonds as Doug had kicked him again and again and again. And now it was going to happen to him, and there was nothing he could do and nothing he could…

"Mr McGregor?"

The voice was low and soft, but commanded the attention of the room. It was one of those voices that carried an innate authority with it. A voice you knew to listen to. A voice you knew not to fuck with.

Doug forced his head up. It felt at though it weighed a tonne. He blinked away the tears in his eyes, focused on the figure standing in the bay window that looked back down onto the street. Felt his bladder spasm as recognition hit him like a hammer. A small, cadaverous-looking man – waxy, jaundiced skin pulled tight over high cheekbones and a skeleton that seemed too angular to be contained – stood before him. He was wearing a black suit, the narrow shoulders flecked with ash from the cigarette that now hung in the air, halfway up to his thin, bloodless lips.

Dessie Banks.

Banks shook his head slowly, eyes not leaving Doug. "Phillip, you seem to have been a little too rough with Mr McGregor. Get him a drink, will you?"

Doug sensed a massive presence behind him lumber off, heard the soft rasp of glass on the coffee table as his whisky bottle was picked up. A huge hand thrust a brimming glass over his shoulder. He wasn't going to argue. He took the glass. Drank. Blinked back the fire in his guts. It was nothing compared to what Dessie was going to do to him.

"Better?" Banks asked, thin lips pulling into a contorted leer that was as close to friendly as he got. "Good. Please. Take a seat, Mr McGregor. We need to chat."

Before Doug could move, he was grabbed by the shoulders and roughly dumped into his sofa by Phillip, who then retreated to the door to stand guard.

Banks stared at Doug for a moment, letting the silence draw out. Then he nodded, as if confirming something to himself. "So, Mr McGregor. I understand you've just been at the hospital visiting Rab MacFarlane?"

Doug nodded like a naughty child. Oh Christ, it was Banks who had hit Rab. And now he was finishing the job.

"Good," Banks said slowly. "It's important to pay our respects in difficult times, isn't it?"

Another dumb nod from Doug as he fought back the urge to down the rest of his whisky in a gulp. After all, might be the last drink he would ever get. But then Banks spoke. And Doug felt the world tilt and then fall away from under him.

"I know your work, Mr McGregor, and I know you've been asking questions about the Falcon's Rest and my possible involvement with Paul Redmonds."

Doug felt numb. "Yes. But, Mr Banks, I…"

Banks raised one skeletal hand, the cuff of his shirt dangling loosely from the branch-thin wrist. "And am I to believe you also asked Rab to look into this on your behalf?"

Doug felt the terror claw its way up his throat again, threatening to throttle him. His gaze darted around the room as his grip tightened on the whisky glass. He could throw it at Banks, make a break for it. Couldn't he?

Instead, he just gave a slow nod. "Yes, but I…"

Banks shook his head again. "Enough, Douglas," he said. "You really don't need to talk at the moment, but you really, really need to fucking listen. Do we understand each other?"

Doug blinked. When he spoke, his voice was a dull, listless whisper. "Yes, we understand each other."

"Good," Banks said. "Then understand this. I knew Rab was asking around for you, and when I heard about Rab I knew you would jump to the conclusion that it was me who had him hospitalised. I know the two of you are, ah, associates. But I'm here to tell you, Douglas, on my word, it wasn't me. If I ever decide to call on Rab MacFarlane, it won't be as messy. Or incomplete."

Doug shook his head, confusion punching through the numb terror that was rolling across his mind like a low morning haar. He spoke before he thought, Banks' warning forgotten. "Hold on, you're saying that you didn't…"

Anger sparked in Banks' small, dead eyes, and Doug sensed Phillip take a half-step into the room. He ignored it. "But if you didn't have Rab attacked, then who did? And why?"

Banks glared at him then stepped forward, his movements remarkably fluid and lithe for a man who looked like an animated corpse. He folded himself into the seat opposite Doug, rested sharp elbows on bony knees and leaned forward. Doug had to force himself not to flinch back.

"That I do not know, Douglas," he said. "But this is bad business. With Rab out of the picture, those Clarkson fuckers from the West are already looking to step into the void. And the last thing I need is a war on two fronts under the glare of the media spotlight you and your nasty little colleagues will bring. So here's what I'm going to do. I'm going to tell you what I told Rab. About the Rest, about Redmonds. And then you are going to find the fucker who did this. And when you do, you are going to tell me who it is. Are we clear?"

Doug couldn't tear his eyes from Banks'. Was this a lie? A trap? If Banks really hadn't taken out Rab, then who had? And why?

And then Banks started talking, his voice a parchment dry hiss in the silence of Doug's living room. And as he spoke, Doug began to see a picture. A picture he didn't want to see but knew he had to.

A picture that threatened to tear down the world around him, Becky and Susie, one brick at a time.

45

Lauren Carmichael had the kind of bored, disconnected beauty Eddie King had become all-too familiar with during his student days in St Andrews; women who had been handed the world on a silver platter, thanks to family wealth or connections, and who always assumed the world would work the same way – in their favour. He wondered, as he always did when he encountered such a woman, what it would take to shatter that glacial facade, knew he wasn't the type of man who would or could do it.

They were sitting in a small office in the Docking Station in Leith, Eddie watching as Lauren picked through the company's records for what they were looking for. The office was almost as stylish as she was, the table and chairs a mix of glass and stainless steel that sparkled in the strategically positioned spotlights above. A couple of abstract prints hung from the cool blue walls, along with a smattering of design awards that meant nothing to Eddie.

He sensed Susie shift in the chair beside him again, risked sneaking a glance. She was worrying at her phone again, refreshing the email app then, best he could tell, flicking back into the text messages. Eddie hadn't seen her like this before, and he didn't like it. She was normally so cool, focused, even when half the cops in the station – him, he hated to admit, included – were having a joke about her shagging that stupid little prick Redmonds. It was, he supposed, understandable that she would be on edge – Redmonds being murdered had reignited all the old gossip, but he got the feeling it was something more than that, something deeper.

He shrugged internally and turned back to watch Lauren work. The one thing he had learned about Susie Drummond was that she would tell him what she wanted to, when she wanted to.

"Ah, yes, here it is," Lauren said, her accent warm with west central Scotland and upper middle class. Eddie dimly wondered if she was going riding with Daddy dearest and Farquhar at the weekend.

"You've found Mr Coulter's employee file?" Eddie asked.

Lauren looked up, the glow from the iMac's monitor playing across her perfect cheekbones as her face contorted into a smile so condescending it had to be practised. "I have Mr Coulter's records, yes," she said. "But he was hardly an employee, he built this place from the ground up. It was him who got the funding for the start-up, won the first big clients."

Eddie nodded. This much he already knew from digging around the company's website and the brief conversation he had had with Coulter's parents. Nice people, he thought, normal, and having the normal reaction to the sudden death of their child: incomprehension.

Coulter had started the Docking Station back in 2002 out of university, taking on freelance gigs at first, cashing in on the emerging boom as companies finally twigged that their online presence needed to be more than a website with a logo and some contact details. He specialised in making websites and online content interactive and user-friendly, and the Docking Station grew from a small start-up to the largest independent graphic design and web content provider in Scotland, its only real rivals being in London. From all accounts, Coulter was successful and respected by his peers.

So why then, was he dead, less than twenty-four hours after the theft of computer equipment from his company?

"Can you give us a print-out and email the files to this address?" Susie asked, pocketing her phone and sliding a business card over the desk towards Lauren, who regarded it coolly.

"Well, I suppose I…"

"If you're worried about commercial confidentiality, then don't be," Susie said. "We're not interested in who your clients are, or how much you're charging them. But we are interested in why Brian was killed, and the answer might be in here. We can get a court order and go the long way round, or you can help us out. Your choice." Susie stared across the table at Lauren, her gaze unflinching. The ice maiden didn't take long to buckle. She clicked the mouse and a small printer behind her started to whirr gently to life.

"So this will give us his client list and his diary for the last week?" Eddie asked.

Lauren shot him a look. "As you requested," she replied as she handed over the sheaf of paper.

Eddie gave her a smile then took the sheets, started shuffling through them absently, finally coming to the week Coulter had died. It didn't look much different from the other entries he had seen, a series of coloured boxes flagging up the different meetings, each box marked with initials.

Eddie spotted something marked for yesterday and paused. Looked over to Susie.

"Did you make an appointment to see Coulter about the break-in?" he asked.

"Yeah, 9.30am, why?"

Eddie ran his finger across the page to an entry marked, *SD – Pol Scot*. Coulter had blocked out half an hour for the meeting. Generous. Eddie turned back to the print-outs and read out another as he looked up at Lauren. "MH, SG cont. ATD," he said. "This was marked out for 6pm to 8pm the night before Mr Coulter's body was found. Any idea what this could be?"

Lauren looked at him for a moment, as though he was a species she had never seen before. "I thought you wanted the client list to cross-check this yourself," she said, before tapping away at the computer. "Ah, of course," she said after a moment, more to herself than Eddie or Susie.

"Well?" Susie asked, an edge of impatience in her voice. Eddie saw that her phone was in her hand again.

"It's a Scottish Government contract we're advising on, a website built for new services they're launching next year. Brian was heavily involved in that one, government work is always a big deal."

Susie nodded. Made sense. "And MH? Who's that? And what's ATD, the name of the project?"

"MH is Mark Hayes," Lauren said. "Used to work here a few years ago, got headhunted by the government in the run-up to the Games. But" – her brow furrowed – "the project is called Online Access Accounts, giving people all their information in one place. OAA. So I'm not sure what ATD means. At the Dock? They might have been planning on meeting here, although Mark just works across the road."

"By across the road you mean Victoria Quay?" Eddie asked, conjuring up the image of the massive Scottish Government building in his mind.

"Yes, quite," Lauren said, the boredom creeping back into her tone. "I suppose you could just nip across and ask Mark. After all," she gave the sheaf of papers Eddie was holding a pointed glance, "you've got his contact details sitting in your lap."

46

Doug watched Dessie and his men file out of the tenement from his living room window, Banks dwarfed by Phillip in front of him and another goon he hadn't seen in the flat behind him. Christ, had he been in here as well? Or, worse, had he been in the stairwell the entire time, watching, and Doug had failed to spot him?

Banks got into a sleek Jaguar and then they were gone. Doug looked at the empty street for a moment, then turned back to the room. He had work to do. And, if he was right, not a lot of time to do it.

He walked through to the kitchen, grabbing a small stool that acted as a mini stepladder for the top cupboards, then headed for the front door. He locked and bolted it, propping the stool up at an angle. It was the world's crappiest barricade, but it would hopefully slow down anyone who was determined enough to come through the door.

And someone *was* definitely coming through the door. After what he had been told, Doug was convinced of that.

He grabbed Redmonds' laptop bag from where he had dropped it, dug out the cricket bat he kept under the bed, and sat down on the living room sofa, laying the laptop bag down in front of him.

The whisky bottle seemed to push its way into his line of sight, distracting him from the bag. He considered it for a moment, rubbing his hand across his throat where Phillip had grabbed him. One was okay, wasn't it? After all, it wouldn't be the first of the day, and he needed something to calm his nerves, help him think straight.

He glanced across to the other sofa, where Susie had sat only a couple of days ago. Remembered her words: *I need you, not the booze-soaked, self-pitying twat you've become.*

He looked back at the laptop bag. Remembered the shame he had felt in London. He had already searched the bag, but how sober had he been when he had done it? What could he have missed? And just now, the thug he hadn't seen in the flat or in the hallway. Christ, if he was missing things like that, what else was he missing? And for what? Because he was being a typical taciturn Scotsman, turning his problems inward, letting them fester and grow into self-loathing as he tried to drown them with booze?

He weighed the bottle in his hand, decided. Placed it on the floor and slid it under the coffee table.

Time to get to work.

He went through the exterior pockets of the bag first, finding nothing but a charger cable and adaptor and a user manual that had obviously never been opened. Then he unzipped the main compartment. It was as he remembered, a couple of sheets of paper in the bottom where the laptop would sit, the pouches in the other half of the bag empty apart from a stack of business cards he had absently flicked through while they were still in the pocket.

Cursing his earlier sloppiness, he reached for them, eased them out of the pocket. They were cheap cards – probably bought from one of those Internet companies that offer to print a million for a fiver – bearing Redmonds' name, his number and the title *Security Consultant* on them. Doug shook his head contemptuously, fanned the cards out and inspected them. All the same, nothing illuminating. Another dead end.

He turned his attention back to the bag, saw nothing out of the ordinary. Colin must have been wrong, there was nothing. If there was another flash drive or hard disk, it wasn't here. But if it did actually exist, where the fuck was it?

Doug picked up the small stack of business cards, tapping them on the table as he thought, a Morse code of his impatience. What the hell was he going to do next? He sighed, reached forward to stuff the cards back in their pocket. They slid in, or at least the front half did. He felt the back of the stack hit something, splitting the deck and stopping him from pushing them into the pocket fully. Doug felt the hairs rise on the back of his neck. He put the cards aside, fished into the small pocket with his finger, fumbled around, felt something small and cool and hard at the bottom, wedged half in the pocket and half in the lining of the bag. He managed to get it between his thumb and forefinger and tease it out.

It was a memory card. Not like the flash drive with the image of Susie on it, but a flat, credit card-shaped device that Doug had seen photographers at the *Tribune* use in their digital cameras. What was it Colin had said? The camera that took the picture of Susie would have used a memory card like this, not a flash drive? Shit, was this it? Was this the master file, the card that Redmonds had first used?

Doug grabbed for his own laptop, booting it up, bouncing on the couch as he waited the eternity it took for the system to spring into life. Too long. He stood up, striding through to his bedroom, grabbing the digital camera he kept on his chest of drawers. He had bought it a few years ago to use on stories: quickly found that, as a photographer, he made a great reporter.

He ejected the memory card that was in it and slotted in the one he had just found. Switched the camera on and flicked it to *Review*, excitement and something he couldn't quite place making his breath sharp and shallow and raw. But nothing came up, the display on the back of the camera merely reading, *Card not recognised.*

Doug frowned, felt the weight of disappointment and frustration bear down on him. What the hell was going on? Why had Redmonds hidden a faulty memory card in the lining of his laptop bag? And what now?

Doug heard his phone chirp in the living room and he made his way through. Saw the caller and smiled. Good news. Finally.

"Hal," he said. "How's it going?"

"Fine. Doug, listen, Colin managed to do something with the background on the, ah, picture, you showed us. He managed to get some faces, didn't take me long to recognise them."

Doug felt a small pang of guilt for what he was about to do. He could hear the excitement in Hal's voice, the thrill of the chase, and here he was about to beat him to the punchline. He thought back to what Banks had told him then gave Hal two names. A guess. But a good one.

"Yeah, that's right," Hal said. "But how the hell did you...?"

"Contacts, Hal, contacts," Doug said. "Listen, can you tell Colin that I found another memory card in Redmonds' bag, but it's useless. Tried it in my camera and it's corrupted or something."

"Hold on," Hal said, "you can tell him yourself." There was a hiss of static as the phone was passed from Hal to Colin, the dull sound of discussion as Hal filled Colin in on what Doug had just told him.

"Doug?" Colin asked, "you moonlighting as a psychic now, or do you like me wasting my time?"

Doug laughed. "Yeah, sorry about that. I was just telling Hal that I've found another memory card, but it's knackered."

"How do you mean, knackered?" Colin asked, his voice all business now.

"Well, I tried it in my camera, it's saying 'card not recognised'. Must be corrupted somehow. I'll try it in my laptop in a minute, see if there's anything I can do with it."

"No," Colin said urgently. "No, don't do that. Is it a standard SD card? Shaped like a small credit card?"

"Yeah, that's it. But what?"

"Yeah, yeah, that makes sense," Colin said, more to himself than Doug. "Don't use it in your laptop, Doug, might cause problems. Listen, we're on our way anyway, Hal wanted to give you the flash drive back in person and check on Susie. And my mum had been nagging us for some granny time with Jen anyway. We're at City now, will be with you by 3pm. Just keep that card safe until we get there."

"Why?" Doug asked. "What's so important about a knackered memory card?"

Colin couldn't keep the smile out of his voice. "Come on, Doug, I thought you were psychic. Don't you know?"

Doug swore into the phone, arranged for them to text him when they arrived so he could go and collect them, then wished them a good flight and hung up. Hal and Colin, once again going out of their way to be there for him, help him. They deserved a better friend than he was, an over-demanding journalist who once wrote a nice story for their daughter.

He didn't know what he could do about that to redress the balance. But for now, he had other friends who needed him. Least he could do was be there for them. He glanced towards the front door, then dialled Susie's number.

The clock was ticking. Time to fill her in.

47

Mr James placed the phone on his desk gently, deliberately, focusing on his breathing. He tried not to think of the crunching sound it would make if he threw it at the pine floor or the toughened safety glass that looked out onto a dull grey sky. Instead, he paused and considered his options.

The call from Vic had been brief, littered with expletives and vows to ensure Doug McGregor would become intimately acquainted with the feeling of holding his internal organs in his own hands. He had, apparently, been scooped up at the airport by MacFarlane's men then driven to the hospital. It was irritating but unsurprising to learn that he had spotted Vic when he left the hospital and given him the slip – Vic was nothing if not dependable in his stupidity and inability to stay out of sight.

And now, just to top everything off, Vic had arrived in time to see Dessie Banks himself leaving McGregor's flat. So he had called to give an update and ask what to do next. Which, amongst the growing fuck-up this was becoming, offered a ray of light for Mr James. At least Vic was following orders. The situation had changed and he had checked in before taking action. Hopeful.

James stepped to the window and looked out. That McGregor had been taken to see MacFarlane was predictable, but the addition of Banks was a problem. He had acted against MacFarlane to stop him poking around Banks and Redmonds, and yet now Banks was visiting McGregor.

What had they discussed? Had Banks attacked him? Was McGregor now lying in his flat, lifeless? It was a pleasant thought, but James was forced to rule it out. If Banks wanted McGregor dealt with, he would have sent one or two of his men to deal with him, not visited the little shit personally. So he had gone there with something else in mind.

What?

The only possible conclusion, he was forced to admit, was that Banks had gone to McGregor because of what happened to MacFarlane. And he had either told him what Redmonds was doing at the Rest, or warned him to back the fuck off. And while Mr James hoped for one, he knew to prepare for the other.

He forced himself to see it as just another problem, ignoring the growing itch of frustration, that maddening, bone-deep ache that nothing would reach or soothe. If Banks had told McGregor about Redmonds, even if it was only a piece of it, then the missing key was the least of his problems. The risk of exposure was too great, not just for him, but for all those involved.

A small bell went off, a reminder to James and his colleagues that they were needed elsewhere. From the corridor outside he heard the clatter of feet on wooden floors, the squeal of doors opening, the low chatter that always came from a group of people moving together in one direction.

Cattle. All of them.

He sat at his desk, tuning out the noise, thinking. Considering the variables, the possibilities, the solutions. He saw it all as a chessboard, the pieces his to move and control. McGregor. Banks. MacFarlane. Vic. Mark...

Mark.

He stopped. Considered. Took the idea and looked at it from all angles, testing it for flaws. Felt himself smile as he found none.

Yes, Mark. Mark was the key to this. Now that he had received his message and understood the consequences of failure, he would do what James asked. Quickly. Efficiently. The only loose end remaining would be McGregor. He sighed, imagining the sharp snap of the reporter's fingers as he broke them one at a time, the meaty resistance of his eyeballs as he pushed his thumbs deep into the eye sockets, gouging, rupturing, the ruined eyes eventually running down his cheeks like raw egg yolks as he screamed in blind agony. The thought gave him a thrill of pleasure, tinged with the disappointment of knowing that the circumstances wouldn't afford him the opportunity to make it a reality.

He pushed the thought aside, focused on the task in hand. First, he would send a message to the group, advising them to stay away for the moment. Then he would call Mark and outline what he needed him to do. Finally, he would let Vic loose on Doug McGregor.

And perhaps, just perhaps, he would ask for a souvenir. Nothing flashy or ostentatious. Nothing that would attract attention, something that could be easily hidden. An ear, perhaps. Or a finger.

Or, even better, he thought, he would ask Vic to bring him the annoying little cunt's tongue.

48

Mark paced around the flat, panic squeezing his chest like a band of steel, making it hard to breathe, hard to think, hard to act. He walked through to his office, stared at the computer, swore, then rushed back through to the living room, felt his eyes bulge as he tried to see everything at once, adrenalin amplifying the scene, making edges sharper, shadows deeper, colours gaudy and overbright.

"Fuck, fuck, fuck, fuck," he whispered, his voice a tremor on the verge of tears.

The call had come five minutes ago. At first he thought it was Mr James calling back with a reminder for him, some detail he had failed to emphasise, but the reality was worse. Much worse. The caller was a police officer named DC Eddie King who "wanted to talk to him about his work with Brian Coulter at the Docking Station."

When he heard the words, Mark had had to dig his fingernails into his palm to stay calm.

"I tried to call you at your office," King had continued, his voice a study of apologetic civility, "but they told me you were working from home today and gave me your number. Would it be possible for me to nip round and have a chat?"

"Why yes, of course," Mark said, his voice sounding alien to his ears, as though he was listening to a playback of the conversation rather than participating in it. "But can you give me an hour or so first? I am actually *working* from home, rather than flopped in front of the TV, and I've got a project I've really got to finish up. Would that be okay?"

King laughed down the phone, the sound like grinding glass to Mark's jumbled, frantic thoughts. "No problem at all," he said. "Would half three work for you?"

"Ideal," Mark said, his lips numb. He gave King his address then hung up, dropping the phone as if it was burning hot.

Fuck, fuck, fuck.

He moved back through to the office/bedroom, looked at the computer set-up in front of him. It seemed to glare back at him like an accusation.

It had been such a simple plan at the time. One of the server blades had developed a fault, and it was quicker and easier to change the whole thing rather than try to identify the problem and fix it. But it was 11pm at night and besides, the local PC World was hardly likely to have what he needed: a top-end replacement with a five-figure price tag. Luckily enough, he knew a man who did.

Mark knew Brian from his days at the Docking Station, the pair quickly bonding over their love of online gaming, IT and design. Over time, they had found they shared other passions as well. Passions that, ultimately, got Brian killed and left Mark in the shit that he was in now.

Brian took one of the servers from the Docking Station and brought it round to the flat. They had it installed in less than an hour, Brian doing a quick check that everything was running as it should before declaring all was well.

And it would have been, Mark realised, if they'd left it there. But somewhere in the night, fuelled perhaps by too much Jack Daniels and too many episodes of *Breaking Bad*, they had decided they would be clever. They would go back to the Docking Station, mess the place up a little, make it look like the server was stolen, along with a couple of older laptops and some other crap that Brian had been meaning to upgrade anyway. That way, he could claim the insurance, replace everything and get paid twice – once from Mark's clients and once from his insurer.

Everybody wins, right?

Mark glared at the server as it hummed away in the corner of the room. Would King want to look around the place? Could he? Was he just here to talk to Mark about his work with Brian, or did he know more?

Mark froze, a sudden realisation making sweat spring out on his skin. Was this a coincidence? From what James had said, Brian had been killed as a message, a warning to ensure Mark made no further mistakes. But was it more than that? Was he now cleaning house, making sure every possible link back to him and the other clients was being closed off? Was Brian killed as part of that agenda? Was that why he had called, with very specific instructions, just before the police? Was that why the police were coming? Was he setting Mark up?

Mark shook his head. No. That didn't make sense. If James was setting him up, the last thing he would want was police involvement. No, he would deal with him personally. Finally.

Just like Brian had been dealt with.

Mark was vaguely aware of the tears beginning to streak his cheeks. His breath was becoming more shallow and frantic, and he recognised the warning signs of an impending panic attack. He closed his eyes, concentrated on his breathing. In, out. In, out. In, out.

Calmness crept through him slowly, cooling, comforting. He opened his eyes and looked again at the computer. Thought back to the episode of *Game of Thrones* he had been watching when James had called three nights ago and started this nightmare. The character impaled on a sword, mouth frozen on the screen in a scream of agony.

Mark wasn't impaled yet. And while he didn't have a sword, he did have a blade. And with it, he could perhaps find a way out of this. He glanced at the clock, realised he had just over forty minutes until King arrived. Time enough to put Mr James' plan in action. And time enough to act on one of his own.

Mark sat at the computer and began working, relief flooding through him as, once again, the world drained away, replaced by the single point of focus that the monitor provided. His typing, at first tentative, became faster, more fluid as he lost himself in the work. He had time. He would do as Mr James asked. And prepare a small surprise for him too.

After all, Brian hadn't been the only one who knew a thing or two about insurance.

49

After getting the call from Doug, Susie had sent Eddie to chase up the lead with Mark Hayes then headed for Musselburgh. She pulled into a space up the road from Doug's flat, not wanting to waste time searching for a non-existent space any closer.

She killed the engine and sat thinking in the car. He hadn't said anything on the phone, and her mind was churning almost as badly as her stomach. What had he found? Were there other pictures of her? Had Doug kept his promise and not looked at the image again, or had he leered at it with Colin and Hal? Christ, what had they thought when they saw the image? She felt the heat rise in her cheeks again, the hot itch of her stress rash as it flushed across her chest and crawled up her neck.

She slammed the palm of her hand onto the steering wheel, seizing the sudden anger and holding onto it. Redmonds. The fucking bastard. He had used her in every way, made her a pariah and, worse, a victim. He got what he wanted: a feeble orgasm and a picture to remember her by. What did she get? Shame, regret and the worst shag of her life. She felt cold revulsion as she remembered kissing him, his touch as he grabbed impatiently for her breasts, tried to choke her with his tongue.

Bastard. Fucking bastard. Whoever had killed him, they hadn't done it slowly enough.

Susie got out of the car, seized by the impulse to move. She wasn't sure she wanted to see Doug again, but it was better than sitting there and remembering. She hurried along the pavement, her attention focused on the tenement door as she fought to compose herself, determined not to show him how rattled she was. She didn't notice the man walking towards her until it was almost too late – he took a step to the side and mumbled an apology as she marched up the road.

After Doug buzzed her in, she took the steps up to his flat two at a time, and was surprised the door wasn't sitting open as usual for her. She heard Doug moving behind the door, something being dragged, then the thunk and jingle of the door being unlocked and the chain being pulled back. Whatever was going on, he wasn't taking any chances.

He swung the door open, appearing behind it. His face was just twitching into the start of a nervous, welcoming smile, and then it dissolved into a look of utter horror. She started forward, the question already forming on her lips.

And then, suddenly, she was flying. Propelled forward with brutal force as someone shoved her from the side and towards the door. Pain exploded in her shoulder as she crashed into the door and collapsed in a heap in Doug's hallway. She tried to get up, was stopped by a sudden kick in her side that sent dark stars of agony flashing across her field of vision. She screwed her eyes shut, tried to focus past the pain.

Get up, her mind screamed. *Get the fuck up!*

"Stay the fuck down, ya wee bitch," a vaguely familiar voice growled. "Ah swear I'll fuckin gut ye after ah finish with this wee cunt…"

She rolled onto her back, heard Doug grunt and cry out as he tackled her attacker and was thrown off. She felt the shudder as he banged off the hallway wall, yelping in pain. Was aware of their attacker's breathing, harsh and ragged, like a winded bull looking for one last victim before it met the matador's sword.

Victim, she thought, just another victim. Be easy to lie and take it, wouldn't it? Just lie for a minute, roll over. Let them win. At least the pain would stop.

Susie scrabbled for the thought, grabbed it. Victim. She had been made a victim. By Redmonds and his perverted desires. She had rolled over for him, and look where it got her. She was fucked if she would be made a victim again.

She forced her eyes open, pushed past the agony that pulsed in her side. Saw a short, stocky man hunched over Doug, slamming his head back into the hallway wall.

"Where is it, ya wee fuck?" he snarled. "Gimmie it and I'll no' fuck you up too badly."

Doug's head lolled on his neck, drooping down to his shoulder. Blood oozed from his nose. The bastard who had him was so focused on getting what he wanted that he didn't realise he'd knocked Doug stupid by slamming him into the wall.

Which gave Susie a chance. Just one. She pushed herself back, getting more distance between her and their attacker, then staggered to her feet. "Get…" She gasped, the words unwilling to come out as her lungs still tried to fill themselves. "Get off him. Now."

The stocky man whirled round, as though he had forgotten Susie was there. "I told you to stay down, ya fuckin hoor," he said, twisting his hands tighter into Doug's shirt. "Now dae as yer fucking telt, or ah swear I'll…"

Susie surged forward, delivering a quick, savage jab to his jaw. The snap of his teeth clattering together was satisfyingly loud and he staggered back, releasing his grip on Doug, who slid down the wall.

"You fucking bitch!" he barked, hand wiping at the blood that was flowing from his bottom lip. "I'm gonna fucking kill you for that."

"Aye, Vic," Susie said, only recognising him when she spoke his name. "Let's see if you are."

He bellowed and charged forward, grasping wildly for her. Susie darted to the side, dodging him. She glanced around, noticed her bag on the floor. If she could get to that, she could get her CS spray, empty the can into the fucker's eyes. She looked away from the bag and back to Vic. Realised she didn't have time – and that somewhere deep down, some feral, hate-fuelled part of her didn't want to.

He lunged for her again, hands splayed as he scrabbled for a grip on her. Susie sidestepped, pulling her fists into the defensive position she had practised so often in the gym.

Vic's face contorted into a smile, uneven teeth framed by the blood from his lip. "Aye, very fucking funny, Rocky," he hissed.

The knife appeared like a conjurer's trick, winking and glittering, and Susie backed off before McBride sprang again. Susie turned to the side, grabbing for his forearm and trying to break his grip on the knife. No use, it was like grabbing a knot of steel cable. She shifted her weight, trying to use Vic's momentum against him, get him off balance. She felt his breath, hot and sour, on her cheek as she twisted him around her hip, trying to get him into a fall. He staggered, grunted, but was too heavy for her to pivot him. He flailed out with his free hand, grabbed her hair. She screamed as he tightened his grip, pain flaring in her scalp as he pulled her back into him. She focused on her grip on his forearm, digging her fingers in as hard as she could. He yanked her head back, hard, her eyes dragged to the ceiling even as she felt him trying to raise the arm holding the knife.

"I'm gonna fucking gut you," he hissed, the arm rising.

Frantic, Susie let her knees buckle. The pain in her scalp was excruciating, but she felt Vic stagger and lose his balance. She drove her head back as hard as she could, hearing a wet crunch as she forced his own hand into his face.

She felt the grip on the knife ease and punched his wrist as hard as she could. Vic yelped and the knife clattered to the floor, skittering away across the polished wood.

He let go of her, taking a faltering step back. His hands were clamped to his face, blood oozing between the fingers, eyes glittering malevolently like twin pits of hate.

"Fugging cunt!" he spat. He took a half-step forward then stopped, eyes darting about. Susie saw the calculation in his eyes and he stepped back into the stairwell and bolted down the stairs. She also started down the stairs then froze, remembering Doug. She heard the tenement door banging open as she retreated back into the flat.

Doug was sliding himself up the wall, face pale and eyes huge. He was cradling his left arm against his chest, dabbing at his nose with his right.

"You alright?" she asked, as she helped him to his feet.

He smiled weakly. "Yeah, fine. I love having house guests. You okay?"

She nodded then reached into her pocket for her phone.

"Who you calling?" Doug asked.

"Control," Susie said as she hit *Speed Dial*. "I'll get patrols to pick up that shite McBride then get SOCOs here."

Doug held up his right hand. It was smeared with blood. "Wait a minute," he said. "You sure you want to do that?"

"Why the hell wouldn't I?" she asked, incredulous.

Doug shook his head, kept his eyes on hers. "Think about it, Susie. You call in the cavalry, they're going to want to know why this guy McBride was here and what he wanted. And once the questions start, they'll just keep coming. Meaning there's a good chance that they're going to find out what Redmonds did. And I don't want that."

She glanced at the phone, then back at Doug. "Fuck," she spat. "But I can't just let him –"

"And you won't," Doug interrupted. "But for now, let it go. First, let me tell you what I've found. I think there might be a way out of this, but I'm not sure you're going to like it."

Susie felt something leaden drop in her stomach. "How do you mean?" she asked, her voice heavy.

Doug shook his head. "Later. First, let me tell you what I've found. It'll kill the time until Colin and Hal get here."

50

She should have seen it sooner. Would have, Rebecca told herself, if it wasn't for aftermath of the Chief's shambolic live press conference the night before, the constant calls for comment and updates and the acid indigestion that felt like it was a scalding tide splashing up her throat with every breath. And then there was the package that sat waiting patiently in her bottom desk drawer, ready to answer a question she didn't want to ask. So yes, she had been busy. Distracted, even. So not seeing it sooner was understandable. Maybe even forgivable.

Maybe. But she also knew that was, ultimately, an excuse. She hadn't seen it until now because, bluntly, she hadn't wanted to. But now, sitting in her office, the cuts from last night's press conference and this morning's headlines about *Lack of progress in City murder probes* and *Fresh questions for police after attempted murder bid in New Town* strewn on her desk, it was right in front of her. Or, more accurately, it *wasn't* there, all the more conspicuous by its absence.

One name. A name that should have been splashed all over the coverage of the last few days.

Doug McGregor.

His byline was nowhere to be seen. Not on the follow-ups to the Redmonds murder or the Leith body find or the Chief's car-crash TV appearance. True, he had written the initial splash on the Redmonds murder, along with the first follow-up, and he had filed copy on the discovery of Brian Coulter's body in Leith. But what leapt out at her now was the complete lack of his byline in connection with the Chief's STV disaster or the attack on Rab MacFarlane.

And that made no sense whatsoever.

She had initially though that perhaps he hadn't heard, that he was so wrapped up with whatever he was doing in London that the news hadn't filtered down to him. But she had quickly chided herself for the stupidity of the thought. She knew he and Rab were close, knew MacFarlane's wife – what was her name, Jane, Janet? – would call him and let him know. Either her, or one of his other…

Susie

…contacts.

So he knew. He must do. And yet, despite that, he hadn't been in touch. No call, no text. Not even an acknowledgement of her message wishing him a good trip.

So just what the hell was he up to?

When he told her he was going to London to see Colin and Hal, Rebecca had been too relieved to push too hard on why he was going. Something was bothering him, that much was clear, and if she couldn't help, then perhaps Colin and Hal could. She knew they had grown close, Hal looking out for Doug like an over-protective elder brother, and she had liked both him and Colin when they met. But why was he going to London now? Two murders in Edinburgh in two days, a new Chief Constable floundering on TV and now an attempted murder on a close friend and contact – and the *Capital Tribune*'s crime reporter decides to take a working trip to London?

No. There was something else. Had to be.

She wanted to call him, make sure he was okay, ask what was going on. Knew she wouldn't. She had never been *that* woman; the girlfriend who felt the need to fill the silence and uncertainty with forced contact and contrived conversation. If he needed to get in touch with her, he would. And yet, the thought of the last message she had sent him burned worse that the acid in her throat. *Hope you find what you need. Here when you need me. Bx*

Was it so much to ask for a response?

He was scheduled to fly back this morning, but she had heard nothing from him, despite checking her phone and email every chance she could in between the incessant media calls and demands for reassurance from a clearly rattled Chief. With the attack on Rab, Doug surely must have headed home. Had he been to the hospital to see him already? Maybe, but there was nothing in the last edition of the *Tribune* or on the website to indicate he had been. And if he wasn't working the story, what was he doing? A thought rose up, shameful and petty, and Rebecca swallowed it down with another Rennie.

Susie. He had said he was following something up for Susie. Had he come back and gone straight to her? Were they working together now, the two of them talking in that shorthand they had, the outside world excluded?

She thought back to last night. At Susie rejecting her offer of a drink after a hard day, saying she had a headache. Innocent enough. And plausible. But was that all it was? Or was she working on something with Doug? Something they didn't want her knowing about.

And, if so, what?

Rebecca sighed. Another question she wasn't sure she wanted to know the answer to. Her eyes drifted to the bottom drawer of her desk, an image of the small package sitting inside drifting across her mind.

Unanswered questions. When, she thought, would she have the courage to face them?

51

Eddie King's first thought when Mark Hayes opened the door was simple and unequivocal: *high*.

He was a tall man, about two inches taller than Eddie who, at 6ft 2ins, wasn't used to looking up to people. Sweat glistened on his brow below a mop of thick, dark hair that was trying to be fashionably unkempt and missing the fashion part of the description. His eyes were a disconcertingly pale blue trapped behind a set of rimless glasses, darting all over Eddie's face as he sized him up in the doorway. Eddie gave him what he hoped was a reassuring smile and stuck his hand out. Hayes returned the gesture, a thin, bony arm with skin the colour of old bread reaching out to his. His grip was cold and anaemic.

"Mr Hayes?" Eddie said, keeping his eyes on Mark's. "I'm DC Eddie King. We spoke earlier on the phone. Thanks for taking the time to see me, can I come in?"

Behind the glasses, the blue eyes squinted for a moment, as though Eddie had gripped too hard when they shook hands. Then he seemed to remember where he was, and his face reorganised itself into something approaching a smile.

"Oh, of course, of course," Hayes said as he swung the door open, the movement as erratic and halting as his speech pattern. "Sorry. Not thinking. Head full of work. Please. Come in."

With a nod of thanks Eddie stepped into flat, waited for Hayes to shut the door and lead him into the living room he could see at the end of the hallway. He noticed a toilet to his left and a kitchen on his right. Just before they hit the living room, there was another door. It was the only one pulled shut.

The living room itself was large and surprisingly bright, with high ceilings and a huge window. Eddie took the room in with a quick sweep of his gaze: top-notch TV, stereo system with stack speakers, DVD player, Apple TV, games console. The typical lair of a well-paid IT geek.

Hayes stood in the centre of the room, gesturing to one of two couches that formed an L-shape around the wall-mounted TV. "Please," he said, "take a seat. Can I get you anything? A drink, perhaps? As you can probably tell, I'm no stranger to coffee."

Eddie smiled at the joke. Could it be that simple? Just another desk jockey hopped up on coffee? After all, he had been working at home, on what he described as an important project. And if it was for the Scottish Government, then they were hardly likely to be forgiving with the deadlines. It made sense – and explained his appearance. Too much caffeine, not enough sleep, a punishing deadline and a surprise visit from the coppers to round the day off. No wonder the kid looked tweaked. He was running on nerves.

But still, there was something about him. Something that put Eddie on edge.

"No, no, I'm fine, Mr Hayes. Thanks, though. I just need to ask you a few questions about Brian Coulter. You know he was found murdered in Leith yesterday?"

Mark sat down on the couch across from Eddie. He leaned forward, thin arms crossed over his chest, as though trying to hug himself. "Yes," he said as he stared at the coffee table, "I saw the news on the *Tribune*'s website just before you arrived." He shook his head. "Poor Brian," he said. "Makes you wonder how anyone could do something like that, doesn't it?"

"Yes," Eddie said, reaching for his notepad. "Yes, it does. That's why I'm hoping you'll be able to help me."

Hayes jerked his head up, eyes returning to their almost-frantic search pattern sweep across his face. "Help you?" he stuttered.

"How can I…?"

"You knew Brian," Eddie said as soothingly as he could. "I wondered if you could tell me about him. Your work together. Anything that might explain what happened."

Hayes twitched a smile of understanding at Eddie. It wasn't a pleasant sight. "Okay," he said as he glanced towards the door of the living room. "I'll try."

● ● ●

Hal and Colin texted from the airport and, once they heard about Doug and Susie's house guest, it was agreed that they would get a taxi straight to Musselburgh.

"No point in making yourself a moving target," Hal had said in the call he made two seconds after he got the message, "and if he knows Susie is police it's unlikely this guy's going to try your place again any time soon."

Doug wasn't sure he agreed with Hal's logic. But he was too tired and sore to argue, so he just murmured agreement and said he'd see them when they arrived.

It took about forty minutes, more than long enough for him to fill Susie in on what he had found, and the first rough outlines of his plan. They sat opposite each other as they had so many times before, but the woman sitting across from Doug now was as good as a stranger. At first he thought it was her anger at him – for grabbing the laptop from Redmonds, for dragging her into the confrontation with McBride and everything that was about to follow. It was only when the entry phone buzzer echoed through the flat, causing them both to jump, that Doug understood. It was just an instant, but it was enough – uncertainty and fear flitting across her gaze, the knot of muscle in her jaw pulsing once as she bore down on her emotions. He realised she had been preparing herself to face Colin and Hal – another two people who had seen what Redmonds had done to her, seen her vulnerable and used and exposed.

Unable to think of anything to say, he smiled and made for the door, using the spyhole to check it was Colin and Hal before he slid the deadbolt clear. After brief greetings, Doug began bustling them through into the living room. "Susie's waiting," he said, sharing a glance with both of them, hoping they understood.

They did. Hal strode into the room, dropping his bags and covering the space between him and Susie before she had a chance to properly get to her feet. He had his arms around her before she could protest, burying his head into her auburn hair. Doug couldn't hear what he said, but watched as Susie tensed then relaxed, her weight falling forward into Hal's embrace. He couldn't be sure, but looking at the way she was breathing, he thought she might be crying.

Colin squeezed Doug's arm briefly then stepped past him, joining Susie and Hal. He said nothing, just put one hand on Hal's back and one on Susie's head. He leaned in, kissed her on the head then backed off, leaving her and Hal.

After a moment, she pulled herself from Hal's embrace, wiping tears from her eyes as she smiled uncertainly at him and nodded her head slightly. Doug wished he knew what Hal had said. He shook his head. Colin and Hal. Again, being better friends than he could ever hope to be. And they had made it look so easy.

Which begged the question, why was he finding it so hard to be what Susie needed in all of this?

And why did he want to be that so badly?

"So," Colin said, "we going to stand around here all day or do we want to get to work? Though I'm not sure what more we've got to add, after you stole our punchline, Doug."

Doug looked at Susie, pushed down the glow of embarrassment he felt as he explained about the porn playing in the background of the picture Redmonds had taken.

"You see," he said, "the times didn't match. Your records showed that the film you and Redmonds ordered was earlier in the evening, so whatever was on the TV had to be something else.

So I asked Colin to see if he could clean the picture up. And he did…"

Colin unzipped his own laptop bag and produced a brown A3-sized envelope. He handed it to Susie without a word, watched as she opened it. She slid out the image, a blow-up of what had been on the screen, any trace of her carefully cropped out, just as Doug had requested. From where he was standing, Doug couldn't see the image that was draining the colour from Susie's face, but he didn't need to. He knew who was in it. Had known since the visit from Dessie Banks.

Susie looked up, eyes darting between him, Hal and Colin. Despite everything, Doug had to suppress the urge to smile. He had missed this. Being one step ahead. Knowing what was going on.

Well, some of it.

"But that means that…?" Susie said, her voice little more than a whisper as she put the pieces together in her mind.

Doug nodded. "Probably," he said, agreeing with her. "And your first job after we're done here is going to be to call Burns. But there's more to it, isn't there, Colin?" He reached for his camera and popped out the memory card. "But I don't see what use this could be? Unless it was holding a copy of the same image and others like it and Redmonds tried to destroy it? Is that why it's corrupt?"

"Maybe," Colin said, taking the SD card from Doug and inspecting it. "But I don't think so." He sat on the couch, taking Redmonds' laptop from his bag and booting it up. "See, I couldn't make sense of this. Why would a new laptop have such a knackered battery and show extensive use, yet be essentially a blank slate? Why didn't it even have a password lock on it?"

"Nothing to hide on it?" Doug suggested.

"Possibly," Colin said. "But remember what we found in the log files – that this was launching a web browser but not registering log files?"

"Yeah," Doug said slowly. "But what does that…"

Colin held up a hand. "Remember the games consoles you played as a kid?" he asked. "You know, the ones that you loaded the cartridges into?"

"Yeah, what about them?" Doug asked, vague memories of PlayStations and Mega Drives flitting across his mind.

"Well, what if it's like that?" Colin said. "What if this" – he held up the SD card – "isn't a memory card, but something else?"

"Like what?" Doug asked. "A cartridge? Or a boot disk?"

"It's not unheard of," Colin said. "Programme a memory card to act like a boot disk for a specific computer and get it to run a program on the system. The two fit together like a lock and a key. Bit like this…"

He slotted the SD card into the side of Redmonds' laptop. At first, nothing happened, the screen showing its standard landscape screensaver. Then, after a moment, there was the gentle whirr of the hard drive, and then, slowly, the mountains dissolved, replaced by a plain black screen with a hand clutching what looked like a trident etched in red. The screen seemed to dim, then, slowly, a single line of white text crawled across it from left to right.

Hell is empty, it read.

Doug blinked at the screen, looked around the room. Saw Hal, Colin and Susie were as lost as he was.

"What the…?" Hal muttered, looking to Colin.

Colin shrugged. "Could be a password challenge," he said. "Looks like it's trying to log on to something, the SD card acting as the boot disk and the browser. But what the answer could be, fuck knows."

Susie stood up, paced to the window, arms folded across her chest, one hand massaging the rapidly reddening patch of skin just below her neck. Doug knew the signs well enough.

"Susie?" he said slowly.

She shook her head, stared harder out of the window. "Hell, hell, hell," she chanted softly. She whirled back, eyes widening. "Something about…" Then she stopped, looked at the laptop as though seeing it for the first time.

"Try 'Tempest,'" she said.

Colin looked at her blankly, then shrugged and started typing. Hit *Return*. Nothing. "Susie, you on to something?"

She nodded, eyes not leaving the laptop, as if scared it was about to leap from the table and attack her. "I think it's a quote from Shakespeare," she said. "*The Tempest*. 'Hell is empty. And all the Devils are here.' But if it's not…"

"All the Devils," Doug said. "Colin, try that."

Colin turned back to the laptop, keyed it in. For a moment, nothing happened, and then the screen dissolved again, replaced by what looked like a list of numbers and file names.

"What the fuck is this?" Hal whispered.

"Files," Colin said. "Look at this: .rar, .jpeg, .mov. They're files." He moved the trackpad to one subdirectory, marked *Dom*, then double-clicked, opening the folder. He scrolled to a random file and double-clicked. An image sprung onto the screen: a man strapped to a bed, naked but for a mask that did nothing to hide the agony as the woman straddling him poured wax from a lit candle onto his exposed genitals.

Colin closed the image. Doug stood for a moment, not breathing, eyes locked on the screen. Files. Screens and screens of them. Movies and images and audio files. All carefully catalogued, the folder names making Doug's skin crawl.

Dom. Anal. Snuff. Kids. Four legs good.

And down in the left-hand corner, tucked away from the somehow banal horror of the descriptions Doug had read, a window that made his blood run cold. One line of text that made everything fall into place at once.

31 guests. 7 online. All the Devils are here. Welcome back, Paul.

"Copy it," Doug said suddenly, lunging forward and placing a hand on Colin's shoulder. "Copy as much as you can, as quickly as you can."

Colin nodded, understanding. Fingers blurring across the keyboard. "On it," he said.

Susie blinked at Doug. "Doug, what is all this? And what –"

"It's a file-sharing site," Doug said. "Porn, from the mundane to the extreme. Looks like a darkweb site, you know, one of those hidden sites where like-minded weirdos can get together and enjoy their perversions."

He nodded to the guest counter at the bottom of the screen. "I'm sorry, Susie, but Redmonds almost certainly put the pic of you on here…" His voice trailed off and he glanced at the files in front of him.

Files.

"Hal, open up the flash drive, get me the filename of the pic Susie was in, will you?" He felt her gaze on him, hard and unflinching. Ignored it. Didn't have time. "Colin, can you search for that filename, and anything associated?"

"I can try," Colin said, the warning in his voice all too clear. Doug understood. He could find the files, but this was only a directory, not the home location. He couldn't delete them. Not from here.

Doug nodded. "Get as much as you can as quick as you can," he said.

"Why the rush?" Susie asked, sounding dazed. "If we've got access, can't we take our time, go through whatever this is methodically, try to figure out what the fuck is going on?"

Doug felt as though the ground beneath his feet had been electrified. He could feel the seconds ticking away as they spoke. He shook his head. "Time's one thing we don't have," he said, gesturing back to the screen and reading out the message. "'All the Devils are here. Welcome back, Paul.'"

He searched her eyes, saw understanding bleed into them slowly. "That's right. We just logged into a closed porn-sharing site with at least thirty-one members, according to that. And we used a dead man's ID. Sooner or later someone's going to get interested in that. They killed Redmonds and sent Vic McBride to stop us getting this far. Who or what do you think they'll send next?"

52

To Eddie, the sound from the other room was like the electronic cheep from an alarm clock: strident, insistent, annoying. But from the way Mark Hayes reacted when it started, it could have been the two-minute warning klaxon for the nuclear apocalypse. He stopped talking, halfway through a rant about "data packaging and multi-phase encryption", which sounded to Eddie like English that had been dumped into a blender. Hayes' mouth hung open in a slack-jawed gape of surprise, blue eyes growing wide and terrified behind his glasses as he stared past Eddie towards the living room door.

Eddie glanced over his shoulder, towards the source of the alarm, half-expecting to see the Grim Reaper standing in the doorway. Nothing. He looked back at Mark.

"Everything alright, Mr Hayes?" he asked, trying to keep his voice casual. The last thing this guy needed was more stress.

"Fine, fine," Hayes said, head darting to face Eddie then back to the door in a jerky, halting spasm. He twitched his face into that awful not-smile of his again, teeth glistening with spittle. "Sorry," he said, trying and failing to force nonchalance into his voice. "It's work. Alarm tells me when a program is running. Would you excuse me for a moment?"

"No problem," Eddie said, glancing down at his notes. Things were close to wrapping up anyway.

Hayes nodded and bustled out of the living room. Eddie heard another door being opened then pushed shut – the closed door he had seen adjacent to the living room. Must be a home office.

He looked back down at his notes, disappointed. There was nothing here beyond basic background: they'd worked together on various things, most recently on a government project. Yes, they were friends, socialising outside of work. No, Hayes couldn't think of any reason why someone would want Brian dead. A case of mistaken identity? A robbery gone wrong?

Eddie sighed. Nothing useful. And he wasn't looking forward to telling Susie that. But what had he expected, really? For Mark to open the door, bloodied knife in one hand, signed confession in the other? *Dream on, Eddie*, he thought to himself. No, this was going to take time. Patience. Real police w…

"Ah, SHIT!" the cry echoed through the flat, only slightly muffled by the closed door and the wall between the spare room and the living room. Eddie suppressed a small smile and stood up, taking a step into the hall.

"Mr Hayes?" he called to the closed door. "Mark? Everything okay in there?"

Mark's voice was a wavering screech, tears and hysteria fighting for supremacy. "Yeah, yeah, fine," he called back. "Just a small work problem, nothing I can't… Oh, mother-*fucker*!"

There was a moment's silence, then the sudden, brittle sound of plastic snapping. The shock of something bouncing off the wall reverberated around the flat. Eddie took a step forward, hammered the door with the flat of his hand then grabbed the door handle. "Mark? Mark? What's going on? If you don't answer me now, I'll –"

"Fucking bastard!" Mark shouted, the hysteria poking through his voice like coastal rocks at low tide. There was another crash, the almost musical sound of something shattering.

Right. Enough.

Eddie turned the door handle and barged into the room. Mark whirled away from the desk on the opposite wall, hands clamped to his head, eyes glittering and rimmed with tears. A laptop sat at his feet, broken like a child's discarded toy. In the corner, a tower that looked like an oversized hard disk gave an asthmatic grunt, as though struggling to breathe past the boot-sized dent that had been put in its high-gloss casing.

"You want to tell me what's going on here, Mark?" Eddie asked, eyes strobing across the room, taking it all in. He saw the shards of plastic from the ruined laptop. They looked sharp. And lethal. The last thing he wanted was Mark getting his hands on one of them and some sudden ideas.

Mark looked at him, uncomprehending, eyes searching Eddie's face for an answer he knew he wouldn't find. He shook his head, small hands bunching in his hair, pulling clumps of it painfully taut. The thin tendons in his arms bulged and flexed with the effort.

"He warned me," he said, shaking his head faster and faster.

"Who warned you, Mark?" Eddie asked. "About what? Tell me what the problem is and maybe –"

"I did what he asked," Mark said suddenly, looking down at the ruined laptop. "Took all the precautions, put the safeties in place. But I didn't expect, didn't know he'd know how to use the key, let alone access the site. How could I? How *could* I?"

Eddie felt his head spin. What the fuck was going on?

"Mark, look, I –"

"And now he's going to be so angry. So, so angry." Tears were streaming down Mark's face now, his face draining of colour, leaving nothing but slack, doughy flesh. "He told me what would happen if I made any more mistakes. Used Brian. Made sure I got the message. But now. Now…" His voice trailed off as he focused on a horror only he could see.

Eddie felt as though he had just been slapped. Wait. What?

"Mark, what did you just say? Brian? What's Brian got to do with this? Did he give you a message? Something to do with your work?" He nodded towards the ruined laptop.

Mark laughed, a high, wavering yelp, the sound of an adult laughing at an uncomprehending child. "No, no, no," he said.

"Don't you see? Brian was the message. For me. To show me what would happen if I did anything wrong. And I did. Fuck, I did..."

Eddie took another tentative step forward. He had to calm this guy down, get him to tell him what he knew.

"Look, Mark, I'm here to help, okay? I don't know what's going on, but whoever is angry with you, they're not going to hurt you when I'm here, okay? So just take it one step at a time, start from the beginning, and tell me. You mentioned Brian. What does he have to do with all this? Is it connected to his death? Is there something you're not telling me?"

Mark smiled again, the closest to genuine Eddie had seen. It made his skin crawl. "You don't understand, do you?" he said. "He doesn't care about you, you're nothing to him. You think you can protect me, keep me safe? What, the same way Brian was? Or that wanker Redmonds? No one is safe from him, no one."

Eddie's mind was a pile-up of thoughts and ideas. Jesus Christ. Redmonds. Brian. What the fuck did this guy know, and who was he so scared of? What the fuck had he stumbled on to here?

"Mark, please. Take a breath. I want to help. And I promise I'll protect you. But first, you have to tell me what's going on. What has all this got to do with Brian and Paul Redmonds? And who are you afraid is going to hurt you?"

Mark seemed to consider him for a moment then looked down at the laptop. Eddie braced himself to lunge, convinced Mark was about to try for one of the shards of plastic and use it. On whom, he wasn't sure. But then he seemed to sag and he staggered back, resting his butt awkwardly on the edge of the desk. He pushed his glasses up his face, took a hitching breath and rubbed at his eyes. Then in a dull, dead tone, he started talking.

And as he did, two thoughts occurred to Eddie at once. The first was that he needed to call Susie as soon as he could.

The second was that Burns had been right all along.

53

The tobacco was bitter and cloying in his mouth, the effort of chewing doing nothing to ease the pulsing headache that throbbed like a discordant soundtrack to his thoughts. After reviewing what he had found on the Leonards and deciding he had no option but to interview them again, Burns' day had quickly descended into what an old boss of his would have termed a "total fucking fuckado".

Before he had managed to make it out of the office, Rebecca had called asking – no, actually, almost pleading – for any update on the Redmonds and Coulter murders. He couldn't blame her, after the car-crash that the Chief's TV presser had been the night before, he understood all too well the need for Police Scotland to be seen as on the front foot and driving the investigations forward. Problem was, there wasn't much more to be done. The CCTV review was ongoing, Drummond and King were following up leads on Coulter, including who he was working with at the time he died. Standard police work. Routine, methodical. Unsexy.

And exactly what the press didn't need to hear.

Eventually they had worked out a line that could be given to the press that didn't overegg the investigations but gave the impression of steady progress being made. After promising Rebecca he would update her with anything he heard from either team, Burns set about trying to arrange a second interview with Alicia Leonard about the night she saw Redmonds at John Wallace's leaving do. However, getting hold of Alicia Leonard had proved almost impossible. Her phone was diverting straight to voicemail, and a quick call to the Police Board secretariat showed she was in meetings with the Chief for most of the day.

Perfect.

Giving up on Alicia, Burns focused on Michael Leonard. He wasn't sure what, if anything, he could glean from asking him about the 2008 paedophile case in Glenview – and if he had met Alicia then, despite saying he only met her later – but it seemed worth pursuing.

He called the contact number on the card Leonard had given him, got put through to his secretary at Paradigm Investment Solutions. She explained in a breathless, West Coast lilt that "Mr Leonard was in a series of meetings with clients for most of the morning and afternoon", leaving Burns in no doubt that she had much better things to do with her day than spend time talking to the police.

Burns had clamped down on his mouthful of tobacco, his thoughts as bitter as the taste flooding his mouth. "It is," he hissed, "somewhat important. And related to an ongoing murder investigation. Perhaps you could see if you could find some time in his diary this afternoon. Either at his offices or here at the station, I really don't mind."

He left the threat hanging on the line, heard a sigh he knew was accompanied by a pout and then the not-so-gentle clatter of a keyboard.

"I can give you a slot at 4.30pm here on George Street," she said eventually, sounding as if she was doing Burns the world's greatest favour.

He bit back the urge just to tell her to forget it – that he would send a patrol car for Mr Leonard and have him driven to the station – and instead thanked her for her time. He spent an hour going through paperwork then headed out, wanting to be away from the station and possible calls from Rebecca. He needed time to think.

He walked up from Gayfield into town, cutting through the back of St James Centre and then through Multrees Walk, past all the designer shops and boutiques that Carol secretly loved. He stopped outside the Mulberry store, thinking, as he always did, that he should just go in, put a bag on his credit card and make Carol's day.

It wasn't as if she didn't deserved it, putting up with him all these years.

He was just trying to figure out which bag he should buy when his mobile chirped in his pocket. He fumbled it out of his pocket as one of the shop assistants watched him a little too closely through the window.

"Drummond," he said as he hit *Answer*, "what's up?"

"Sir, ah, there's been some developments in the Coulter case." She quickly filled him in on Eddie's encounter with Mark Hayes, the destroyed computer and the story he had told him.

"Tell me King has him at Gayfield," Burns said.

"Yes, sir, he has. Eddie's getting a formal statement from Hayes now. Though I'm not sure how much he'll repeat on the record, Eddie said he was absolutely terrified in the flat."

"Fuck him," Burns growled. "He should have thought about that before he got into this." He glanced at his watch, made a quick calculation. "I can be back at Gayfield in fifteen minutes, I assume I can meet you and King there?"

Susie took a breath on the line. "Actually, no, sir. I was hoping we could meet up first. I've got something else as well, something that may be connected to this. And the Redmonds case."

Burns blinked for a moment, trying to take in what Drummond had just told him. "What?" he whispered. He was suddenly very aware that he was standing on a busy shopping street. "Redmonds? What the fuck has any of this, or you, got to do with the Redmonds case? I thought I told you to stay away from that, Drummond. What part of that didn't you get?"

"Sir, please," she said, her voice hardening, "I didn't go looking for this, but it… well, it dropped in my lap. And I think it's connected to Redmonds' murder, and what happened to Brian Coulter."

Burns turned what Drummond had told him over in his mind, trying to see it as one picture. It was no good, he couldn't get the pieces of the puzzle to slot together. He turned back and started walking up the street, taking a right into an alley. He didn't want to talk about this in the open. "Go on then," he said, "enthrall me, Drummond. What have you got?"

"Not on the phone," she said, defiance in her voice. "Sir, I'm really sorry, but you've got to trust me on this. I think I can connect the Coulter murder to Redmonds' death, and even what happened to Rab MacFarlane. But I can't tell you over the phone, or at Gayfield, could you meet me?"

Burns felt the anger roil in him. Enough of this shit. She had called him out of the blue, telling him she was up to her ears in an investigation that he had explicitly warned her away from. And now she was playing a game of cat and mouse with him? Forget the fact that she was contravening a whole manual's worth of regulations, he was through with her fucking him around.

But then again… If there was something that linked all this together, wasn't it worth giving her a little latitude? He cursed under his breath. Why the fuck did Susie Drummond have to be such an intuitive copper? If she was shit at her job he could find a reason to get rid of her. Yet here she was, again, offering him a lead on two major cases. A lead that, as usual, would probably get messy for them all.

"Okay," he said, looking up at the grey, mesh-covered front of an old 1970s office block that was being demolished, "tell me where you are. But I swear, Drummond, if this is a waste of time, you'll be directing traffic by the end of the day."

Susie paused. He heard a click on the line as she swallowed, took a steadying breath. Then she told him where they should meet. And as she did, Burns was suddenly seized by the urge to wade into the building site and tear the office block in front of him down with his bare hands, one brick at a time.

• • •

The buzzer to Doug's flat sounded twenty-five minutes later. Susie exchanged a brief glance with Doug, who was sitting on the sofa in front of Redmonds' laptop. He gave her a brief nod and, again, the magnitude of what she was about to do hit her. It was like a crushing weight bearing down on her, crippling, buckling. But what choice did she have? Both she and Doug knew it was the only way to keep both of them in the clear, Colin and Hal already being sent off to enjoy a daughter-free stay in Edinburgh with promises that they would be kept out of it.

It was the only way. And it was, broadly, the truth. With a few omissions.

When Burns appeared at the door, his face was set in dark rage.

"Sir, thank you for coming, I…"

He glared at her as though she was speaking a language he didn't understand, jaw working furiously. "Where is he?" he hissed.

Susie led him into the living room, Doug rising from the couch as they entered. He offered his hand to Burns. "DCI Burns," he said. "Thanks for coming, I can appreciate this is a little out of the ordinary."

"Skip it, McGregor. I see that, once again, you've managed to drag Drummond into the shit with you. But she says you've got something that might link two murder investigations. So why don't you tell me what the fuck is going on and then I'll decide if I'm going to charge you with anything?"

Doug let his hand drop slowly and lowered himself back onto the couch. Susie saw something dark flash across his own face, said a silent prayer that whatever smart-ass comment he had just thought up would die on his lips. Amazingly, it did.

"It's about this," he said, gesturing to the laptop and the brown envelope beside it.

"And what, exactly, is that?" Burns asked.

Doug let the obvious answer slide. No point in antagonising

Burns any further. They were going to need him on this. "This laptop came into my possession a couple of days ago, along with a memory stick and an SD card," Doug said slowly, keeping his eyes locked on Burns. "I believe they belonged to Paul Redmonds."

Burns' jaw pulsed. "Why would you think that?" he asked. "And how did you come by these items?"

"They were sent to me," Doug said, keeping his voice level. "And as to why I think they belong to Redmonds... well, either they're his, or there's another Paul Redmonds out there who used to work for Lothian and Borders who wants to write the world's worst autobiography. Also, this was on the flash drive." He handed the envelope to Burns.

Burns took it, slid out the picture Colin had produced for Doug. A simple blow-up of what was on the screen behind Redmonds and Susie. That original full image had, of course, now been deleted from the flash drive, and they had found no record of it or any other associated images on the Devils website. *The camera never lies*, Doug thought, feeling the sudden scampering of hysterical laughter in his chest, *but I do.*

He watched as comprehension dawned on Burns' face, his jaw slackening as his eyes went wide. "The date stamp... 2008," he said after a moment. "Is it accurate?"

"No reason to believe it isn't, sir," Susie said. "But that's not the reason I wanted to see you here."

Burns tore his gaze from the picture. "Then what the fuck is?" he said, the anger reasserting itself in his eyes as he spoke.

"This," Doug said, tapping the laptop. As I said, I had a look at it, and then I inserted this SD card. And look what happened when I did."

He slid the card home, watched as the boot sequence ran and the landing page for the website appeared. He waited for the prompt, typed, *All the Devils*, then swivelled the laptop round on the table towards Burns.

"We think this is what caused Mark Hayes' outburst, sir." Susie said, moving closer. "As you can see, it's a personal log-in under Redmonds' name. It must have triggered the alarm DC King spoke about hearing at Hayes' flat when we logged into the site."

"But what is it?" Burns asked, squinting down at the laptop.

"It's a porn-sharing site," Doug said as he started to call up images and files, his fingers feeling cold and alien as typed, disgust rising in the back of his throat. "Best we can tell, the users are taking pictures or filming stuff, then uploading it here so they can enjoy it with their 'friends.'" He spat the last word as though it was an obscenity. He gestured at the small message at the bottom of the screen: *31 guests. 1 online. All the Devils are here. Welcome back, Paul.* "It looks like Redmonds was a member, probably with the people in that picture you've got there."

Burns blinked, trying to take in what he was being told. "So you're telling me this is what Redmonds was killed for? This image and his access to a porn site? Why?"

"See for yourself," Doug said, gesturing to the images he had called up. He saw Burns flinch away when he looked at the screen, felt a sudden irrational hope. So he was human, after all. "It's pretty nasty stuff. Most of it illegal. Kids, bestiality, date rape." He fought the urge to look up at Susie. "I've not had time to go through all of it, but some of the files seem to have identifiable faces in them. If you were involved in this type of shit, wouldn't you kill to keep it quiet?"

Burns shook his head, trying to get to grips with it all. He pushed down his fury that McGregor was involved in this. That could wait. Right now, he needed answers.

"So you're saying that Mark Hayes looked after this site, and panicked when you accessed it?"

"It fits with what Eddie told us," Susie said, nodding. "He said his employer was angry at him for a previous mistake he made, that he thinks Coulter was killed purely as a warning to him not to fuck up again. If his boss finds out that we've accessed this site, can you image how angry he'll be then? I would say Hayes probably had good reason to panic."

Burns took a moment to calm his raging thoughts. Then a memory hit him. "Hold on, you said this was also connected to what happened to Rab MacFarlane. How?"

"That's my fault," Doug said, his voice flat and cold. "I asked Rab to ask around about Redmonds' possible links to Dessie Banks after the raid on the Falcon's Rest."

"And?" Burns said, unable to keep the sharp glint of excitement out of his voice.

"And he found a link, alright," Doug said, looking past the screen to something only he could see. It all made sense now. Almost. "But not the one any of us was expecting. Seems Redmonds was using the Falcon's Rest as a venue to indulge his amateur filming enthusiasms. And someone didn't want us knowing that. Someone who has a vested interest in keeping all this quiet."

Burns glanced back at the printed out photograph Doug had handed him, then to the screen. He was starting to see it now. It made sense. Jesus. It was obvious, really. He suddenly saw John Wallace in his mind again, making the *Call me* sign.

Doug shut the laptop, pushed it to Burns. "So, what do we do next?" he asked.

Burns felt the anger flare in him again as he looked down at the reporter.

"'We' are going to do nothing," Burns said, straightening up and glaring at Susie. "You're not going to write up one word of this – clear, McGregor? If you do, I'll have you done for perverting the course of justice and tampering with police evidence before you can squeal NUJ. Fuck knows you've caused enough problems by handling material evidence as it is, but if I find out that you're sniffing around this…" He jutted his jaw to the laptop.

Doug held up his hands. "Look, I get it," he said. "You don't like me. But credit me with some fucking common sense, will you? There's kiddie porn and fuck knows what else on that site. Getting to who is responsible for that is a little more important to me than a fucking byline. I'll write what I want to write when I think it's time to write it. In the meantime…" He heard his voice rise in anger, saw Susie give him a warning glance. Didn't care. "In the meantime, DCI Burns, I've laid enough of the pieces out for you here, how about you go and do your fucking job? Inveresk is just up the road. Pretty sure even you could find it from here."

Burns took a step forward and Doug shot up from the couch. He bunched his fists, embracing the pain in his hand and arm. He'd attacked a man, been throttled by a gangster, followed, chased. If this cunt Burns wanted to have a go after all he'd done to try and help him, so be it. Fuck it.

"Sir, Doug," Susie said. "This isn't getting us anywhere. Boss, Doug has already agreed to keep this quiet for the moment; I say we believe him. We can take the laptop and drives into evidence now, then set up the interviews we need to."

Burns stared at Doug for another moment, his eyes dancing from the little shit's jaw to temple to throat. All the places he wanted to hit.

"Fine. Get all this logged. We'll get a formal statement from you" – he pointed a blunt finger at Doug – "later."

Doug nodded then Burns turned away, already fiddling with his mobile. Behind him, Doug and Susie shared a glance. So far, so good.

Doug just hoped Susie didn't see in his eyes what he was planning next.

54

Susie followed Burns on the short drive to Inveresk, mind racing as she drove. She had been so intent on what she and Doug were going to tell Burns – about making sure he believed their version of events – that she hadn't thought about what the next step would be. She should have seen it, though; interviewing the Leonards was the obvious move. She just wished it wasn't in front of Burns. She understood the context of the picture Colin had managed to salvage now, but how could she confront the Leonards, especially Alicia, with that whilst Burns was in the room?

Alicia Leonard. For years, Susie had been known as the woman who ended her marriage. The stupid slut who tempted a senior officer and left Alicia to pay the price. She knew differently now, but the knowledge didn't make the prospect of meeting the woman any easier.

They walked up to the front door, Burns' anger evident in his determined march and the hunch of his shoulders. He was pissed off, and Susie had no doubt there would be hell to pay later on. She just hoped what happened next would lessen the impact of it a little.

Alicia Leonard appeared at the door before the echo of the bell had faded. Her skin was tight and flushed, patches of hectic colour glowing behind her make-up. Her hair was pulled back in a severe bun, and her green eyes flashed as she took in Burns and then Susie.

"I don't know who you think you are, DCI Burns," she said, "demanding that I cut short a meeting with the Chief Constable and the Board to meet you here. But I'm sure you're about to give me a very, very good explanation."

Burns' face twitched in a tight smile as Susie saw his grip tighten on the brown envelope he held. "Mrs Leonard, I'm sorry for the inconvenience, but this is urgent. And relates directly to the death of your ex-husband. I apologise for disrupting your schedule, but I think you'll understand why this couldn't wait."

Leonard stared at him for a moment, then turned and headed into the house, beckoning them to follow. They headed for the living room at the back of the house, the same room Burns had been in with Eddie only a few days before. Leonard took up a place in front of the massive fireplace, as though she was posing for a picture. She didn't ask them to sit.

"So, what's all this about?" she asked.

"Is your husband joining us?" Burns asked, making a show of looking around the room.

"No, Michael has meetings in town, but then, as I know you already had an appointment to meet him at his office, I'm sure you're already aware of that. I saw no point in disrupting both of our days with this nonsense."

Burns nodded in agreement. Made sense. And it kept him out of the way while they were discussing delicate matters. Nice move. Appear to be the considerate wife and keep the husband in the dark at the same time.

On the drive up here, Burns had gone over dozens of ways to handle this in his head. She was, after all, a member of the Board. On first names with the Chief Constable. She was also a massive pain in the arse and, as Burns now knew, a liar.

Fuck it.

"Mrs Leonard, when I was here previously, you said that the last time you saw Mr Redmonds was at John Wallace's leaving party. Is that correct?"

He saw something in her chin tighten. "Yes. As I told you at the time: when I realised he was there, I left quickly. We didn't really speak."

Burns nodded. "I suppose you didn't need to speak much there," he said, more to himself than Leonard. "After all, you would have had plenty of time to chat and do whatever else it was you were doing with him when you met him later that night at the Falcon's Rest in Morningside, isn't that right?"

Leonard blinked as though she had been slapped, eyes darting between Burns and Susie as the colour drained from her face. "Wh… what?" she whispered. "What exactly do you mean by…?"

Burns waved his hand, time to push it a little. And hope what that little shit McGregor had told him was true. "You know exactly what I mean, Mrs Leonard. We have information that Mr Redmonds was given exclusive use of a suite at the Falcon's Rest by the owner of the establishment. And the owner, being a cautious sort, gave us a description of a woman Redmonds would frequently visit with. Tall, blonde with hints of grey, striking green eyes. Sound familiar, Mrs Leonard? Not that we really needed the description, the CCTV we've been provided has some good shots of you."

"How dare you," Leonard whispered. "This is preposterous. Leave. Now. And you can rest assured, DCI Burns, I will be raising your scandalous accusations and slurs with the Chief Constable immediately."

Burns shrugged, fought back the sudden urge to smile. "Fine, call Chief Montrose right now. And while you're on the phone, you might want to mention that I showed this to you as well." He handed her the envelope Doug had given him.

She took it, confusion diluting the fury in her gaze for a moment. Then she reached into the envelope and slid out the picture. When she saw it, she started to shake and, for a moment, Burns thought her knees were going to go. Beside him, Susie watched Leonard's reaction with a mixture of savage pleasure and guilt. She knew this moment all too well. Had felt the same mixture of violation and rage and incomprehension when Doug had shown her what was on the flash drive. But, despite that, she couldn't feel any sympathy for Alicia Leonard. Not with what she knew now.

"Tell me, Mrs Leonard," Susie said, "for what possible reason would your ex-husband have an intimate picture of you and Mr Leonard together in his possession? And why does the date stamp on that image go back to 2008, before Mr Leonard said you and he met?"

Alicia Leonard looked down at the picture, shaking her head. It made sense to Susie now, but she knew she couldn't explain to Burns. Redmonds hadn't used her merely as a fucktoy, that was almost incidental. It was revenge. Plain and simple. He had taken the picture of Susie naked and exposed – with a video of Alicia and Michael fucking in the background – not for his own gratification, but as a message.

You can fuck around, I can too, he was saying.

Alicia Leonard looked up, teeth bared white and almost feral behind the crimson smear of lipstick around her mouth as her veneer of composure cracked and crumbled. "How *dare* you? I'll have your job for this, you little prick, I'll –"

"We also found the website, Mrs Leonard," Susie said, cutting her off. "'All the Devils', very colourful. There are several images of you and your ex there, along with the more unsavoury material. Is that why you killed him? Because he had threatened to expose the website and your affair when the questions about his links to the Falcon's Rest and Dessie Banks began after the raid?"

"Wait, what?" Leonard said. "You think I killed Paul? No! No, I couldn't, wouldn't. Yes, okay, we would see each other at that place. And yes, we would sometimes share pictures. But kill him? Why would I, why would you think I…?"

"So you're telling me that if we check the CCTV from your gate system, we won't find a record of Mr Redmonds visiting here the night he died?"

Alicia whirled away, heading for a drinks tray in the corner of the room. Her hand was shaking as she sloshed a large measure of something amber into a crystal glass from an ornate decanter.

For such a desperate action, the sip she took was incongruously elegant.

"No, well, I… Yes, he was here that night. Michael was working late, you see? I was here alone. Paul was hysterical when he arrived. He'd obviously been in a fight, he was black and blue, and he was yammering on about losing a picture and his key to the website. But kill him? No. I wouldn't. Couldn't…" Her voice trailed off and she stared into the glass, looking for an answer.

"So if you didn't kill him, who did?" Susie asked after exchanging a glance with Burns to make sure he was happy with her taking the lead. She wasn't buying this. There was something she wasn't telling them, something – someone? – she was hiding.

"I… I don't know," she said, the fury now absolutely drained from her voice. "Please, that's the truth. Yes, I was seeing Paul – even after the divorce we just couldn't help ourselves. Yes, he was here that night. But he was alive when he left here, I swear."

Susie thought it over. Easy enough to check. If there was a record of him arriving here, then there would be a record of him leaving. But it begged the question, where did he go after he left her?

"Mrs Leonard… the website," she said. "We know that it was administered by a Mark Hayes. We also know that there are images of you, Paul and others on that site. Could he have gone to see one of them after seeing you that night, warn them as well?"

Alicia Leonard looked at Susie as if seeing her for the first time. "Wait," she said. "Who are you? I never got your name."

Susie felt something hot and noxious course through her. She locked her eyes with Leonard, determined to look the bitch in the eyes. "Drummond," she said, her voice low and even. "DS Susie Drummond."

The glass was flying through the air almost before Susie had time to register it. She ducked away, the crystal shattering musically on the wall behind her, the sound quickly drowned out by Leonard's rising scream.

"Fucking bitch," she spat, her lunge forward brought to a sudden halt as Burns grabbed hold of her shoulders and pulled her back into a bear hug. "You fucking whore! You're the reason he's dead! You're the cause of all of this. I'll kill you, I'll fucking kill you!"

Susie straightened up, shot a look at Burns, who was grimacing at the effort of controlling Alicia as she bucked and thrashed in his arms.

"Call it in, will you?" he said over her bobbing head, barely avoiding being butted in the nose. "And for fuck's sake, let Rebecca know what's going on. Someone's going to have to brief the Chief, and it's not going to be me."

55

Doug pulled into the car park at the Omni Centre just down from Princes Street, cutting across Leith Street and up into town. He walked briskly, watching for a small man in a grey suit who might want to finish their earlier conversation. But there was no sign of him, which didn't totally surprise Doug. If he was right, Vic McBride would have bigger problems to deal with now.

It hadn't taken him long to find what he was looking for in the copied files Colin had lifted from the Devils website. It was just a matter of knowing where to look, and who to focus on. He had started searching the moment Burns and Susie had left the flat, feeling only a momentary pang of guilt. He didn't give a fuck about lying to Burns – especially after the way he had treated him and Susie, even though they had effectively connected the dots for him. But it troubled him that he was doing something that could land Susie even further in the shit.

But he had to know. After everything that had happened, everything he had done, the need ached almost as badly as his wounded arm.

The Paradigm offices were based in an imposing Victorian building, the ornate stonework framed by a glass frontage that housed a reception area and what looked like a VIP lounge. In the centre of the atrium was a circular reception desk with a petite woman with hair so blonde it could only have come from a bottle. He asked for Michael Leonard, watched her gaze dance across his face and clothes as she tried to understand what a casually dressed, rumpled man like him wanted in this land of corporate suits and watches that cost more than cars, then she got busy with the keyboard. Doug smiled as he saw the surprise peek through her boredom – yes, Mr Leonard was expecting him.

He was given a pass and told to head for the elevator behind the security doors. After a short ride up, the elevator doors slid open, and Doug was confronted by what could have been a clone for the receptionist downstairs. She had the same bottle-blonde hair, perfect make-up and an expression so bored she could have been anesthetised. She led him down a long, deep-carpeted corridor to a set of dark oak double doors, knocked, then ushered him in.

Michael Leonard stood up from behind his desk, behind which a floor-to-ceiling window gave a spectacular view across the top of George Street and back to the jagged silhouette of the Castle and the Old Town. "Mr McGregor," he said, sticking out his hand for Doug as he closed in on him. "Michael Leonard. Have to say, I was slightly taken aback by your call. You said it was something to do with Alicia and Paul Redmonds?"

Doug returned the handshake, tried to read Leonard's eyes behind his designer glasses. He wasn't giving much away, but Doug could see the set of his jaw, felt the heat in his handshake. All his years of experience at interviewing people told him one thing: Leonard was rattled.

And if Doug was right, it was about to get a lot worse for him.

Leonard nodded towards a chair at the other side of his desk and Doug took a seat. He waited for Leonard to take his own seat, let the silence drag out just long enough for it to feel uncomfortable.

"Thanks for seeing me at such short notice, Mr Leonard," he said. "As I said on the phone, this isn't for publication, it's purely background on the story I'm doing relating to Paul Redmonds' death."

Leonard nodded gravely, glasses catching the light. "Terrible thing," he said, "but I'm not sure what I can tell you, Mr McGregor. I didn't really know Paul Redmonds. Alicia and I have already told the police everything we knew. I'm not sure what else I can –"

"You can start by telling me how long you've been running the Devils site, Michael," Doug said.

Leonard sat back suddenly in his chair, eyes growing wide. He placed his hands on the desk, as though steadying himself. "What?" he whispered. "What do you…?"

Doug reached into his bag and pulled out a loose sheaf of printouts. "It's all here," he said. "See, once I had the access to the site, it was easy enough to find that chat room and pull up the transcripts. Well, easy if you know people who can do that sort of thing. Like a couple of friends of mine, and someone you know. Mark Hayes. You do know him, don't you, Michael?"

"Why yes, of course I do, he worked for the Docking Station, a graphic design company we invested in a few years ago. But why…?"

Doug nodded. He already knew as much; a quick trawl through Paradigm's financial records and a visit to the Companies House website had told him that. Paradigm had loaned start-up capital to the Docking Station and, in return, Paradigm staff had been appointed to the Docking Station board, with a certain Michael James Leonard listed as a non-executive director.

"Is that where you met Mark? Spotted his potential? I've had a wee look through the Devils site – seems you have some rather eclectic tastes, Mr Leonard. Might explain why you were okay with your wife shagging her ex after you two met in Glenview. But then, I suppose it makes sense. You saw a business opportunity, to make perversion pay. So you had Mark set up the site, then got your playmates to sign up." Doug raised his eyebrows. "Talk about screwing cash out of people."

Leonard shook his head, Adam's apple bobbing up and down as he swallowed. He closed his eyes for a second, pushed his glasses up and massaged his eyes. Then he readjusted his glasses and fixed his gaze on Doug, who wondered how many times he had used the move in negotiations. And that, Doug thought, was what this would be to him now. Another negotiation.

"Mr McGregor," he said, "I'm not sure where you get your ideas from, but I must tell you that this is the worst form of fanciful nonsense and, if I may say, utterly slanderous. Yes, I know Mr Hayes, vaguely. But my work here means I'm on the boards of dozens of companies, and your claims that I'm somehow involved in some kind of pornography ring is ludicrous."

Doug did nothing to rein in the smile he felt spread across his lips.

"Who said anything about porn, Mr Leonard?" he asked. "All I said was a site called the Devils. Could be anything. Not that you can really deny it; I've found images there that show you were in it up to your, ah, balls. No wonder you were so keen to keep it quiet. Killing Redmonds would have been your only option, wouldn't it? After he told you that he'd lost his laptop and key, it was all about to come out. His trysts with Alicia, the site, your involvement. Your clients wouldn't have been too happy about that, would they, Michael?"

Leonard leaned across his desk as though he was struggling to hear Doug. "Now hang on, if you think *I* killed Paul –"

"Oh fucking quit it," Doug said. He held up the sheaf of print-outs again. "It's all here. The chat logs. You assuring your clients that the situation would be dealt with. That their details were secure. That you had hired 'outside help' to deal with me and…" – Doug referred to one of the print-outs – 'another example of gross incompetence.'"

He paused. Leonard was glaring at him with enough vehemence to melt stone.

"See, that's the bit that confused me. Having Coulter killed just to send a message to Mark seemed a bit over the top, even for someone with your taste for, ah, discipline. But then I looked at the financials for the Docking Station. Seems Coulter was in for a very big payday when you floated the company. With him gone and the flotation going ahead, you and Paradigm were in line for a very, very good day, weren't you, Michael?"

Leonard was on his feet now, eyes locked on the print-outs in Doug's hands. "You can't, they can't be…" he whispered.

Doug sighed. Denial. He'd seen it so many times before, and yet, no matter how compelling the evidence, some people refused to admit the truth, almost as if they didn't want to believe their own guilt.

"Take a look for yourself," he said, tossing the print-outs across the table to Leonard. "Keep them as a memento if you want, I've got plenty of copies. Bet you thought you were clever, with everyone using your middle name, James. All the messages are in your name, and I've got a friend who can trace the location they were sent from – either here or Inveresk."

Leonard grabbed for the files, shuffling through them rapidly. "No," he murmured. "No, no, no. This isn't right. Yes, I mean, yes, okay, I set up the Devils, but Mark came to me with the idea. He, he…" Leonard looked up, something cracking in his voice. It made Doug want to hit him. "He hacked my browsing history, you see, saw some of the sites I was looking at. Said he could make it so much better, so much more secure and personal. So, yes, we set it up, but I never, never…"

Doug shook his head, pushed himself out of the chair, the anger rising as he stood to his full height. Suddenly, he was back in Portobello, driving his boot into Paul Redmonds again and again and again. The sudden urge to do the same to the man in front of him was almost overwhelming.

"Save it. The police have copies of all this, they'll be asking you the same questions soon enough. But before that, I wanted to give you a message. It's from a friend of mine. Susie Drummond? You know, the woman that sick fuck Redmonds used to send you and your cunt of a wife a message? The one whose image he tried to blackmail me with? Want to hear what the message is?"

Leonard looked up from the print-outs, almost as though he had forgotten Doug was there.

"The message," Doug said slowly, hearing the tremor of rage in his voice and fighting not to release it, "is, 'you are fucked.'"

Leonard stared at Doug then jerked his head back to the print-outs.

He was shaking his head violently now, as though he could ward off the print-outs – as if they were evil spirits. Maybe they were.

"You're fucking pathetic," Doug said, turning to leave. He was halfway to the door when he heard the smooth rasp of a drawer being opened.

"McGregor," Leonard said in a voice that was barely human.

Doug turned, eyes falling on the long, glinting object clamped in Leonard's right hand. Suddenly he could hear Rebecca's voice in his mind, from the morning after Redmonds had died. *There was a stab wound about an inch above the belly button. Something thin and very sharp...*

Something very like the blade that Leonard was now brandishing.

Doug held up his hands, wildly looking around the room. Nothing he could use as a weapon. How far was he from the door? Could he...?

"Now hold on," he said. "This won't..."

Leonard smiled, a horrible baring of the teeth. The facade was gone, the veneer of successful businessman replaced by whatever it was that lived deeper in him – the thing that had driven him to find pleasure in the degradation and abuse of others. There was madness in that smile. And desperation.

"You have no idea, do you, McGregor?" he said, pushing himself away from the desk and standing upright. "You think you're so clever, but you're only seeing what you're being allowed to see. All the devils are here, McGregor, and you'll meet them soon enough. Oh, and tell that little bitch Drummond that she was right, I am fucked. But I'm not the only one."

Leonard took a step to the side, clearing the desk. Doug tensed, ready to dodge, try to hit him and then run for it. Leonard moved forward, bringing the knife up to eye level. It glinted off the lenses of his glasses and Doug tensed, waiting.

And then in one fluid, almost graceful movement, Michael Leonard flipped the knife around and opened his own throat with it.

56

In the chaos that followed, the last pieces of the puzzle started to fit into place for Susie. She ran the checks on the entry gates system at the Leonards' home, the footage showing that Redmonds had visited the night he died, stayed for an hour, then left. Forensic analysis of the property showed nothing conclusive. There were fibres and hairs from Redmonds at the scene, and the remnants of a towel in one of the bins that had traces of his blood, but not enough to indicate he had been stabbed on the scene. And he would have been bleeding anyway, after the beating he had taken earlier in the night. The beating, Susie thought, Doug had given him. For her.

A check of Alicia Leonard's phone records found a brief call made about twenty minutes after Redmonds had left Inveresk. And although they couldn't ask Michael Leonard, who was lying in a coma in the Royal Infirmary, the thinking was that Alicia had phoned him and he had contacted Redmonds, arranged to meet, then stabbed him with the knife that he had threatened Doug with; a wickedly sharpened letter opener with a thin, long blade.

Susie dived into the work, using it as a shield against the abject terror and near-paralysing paranoia that Burns was going to confront her at any moment with the actual picture Redmonds had shown Doug, or some inconsistency in the story they had told him. But he never did. He was too busy trying to nail Doug for whatever he could to look closely at the version of events leading up to what happened in Leonard's office.

Which left Susie to do the legwork.

It didn't take long to verify what Doug had said in his witness statement, that Michael Leonard was connected to the Docking Station and Brian Coulter through Paradigm, which had invested in the company and stood to make a substantial profit when it was floated on the stock market. The problem was, Coulter wanted to keep the company private – and in his control. So killing him served two purposes: it terrified Mark Hayes and ensured Paradigm could cash in. It was, Susie was forced to admit, very efficient.

Hayes gave them the rest of it, almost gleefully enthusiastic when he admitted to setting up the Devils website for Michael Leonard, who went by the name Mr James. He insisted that, although he knew some of the material involved was illegal, he never looked at or "enjoyed that type of thing" himself.

Susie found she didn't care if he was telling the truth or not. Either way, the little shit disgusted her. She saw no flicker of recognition in his eyes when they sat across from each other in an interview room, but still the doubt remained, tormenting the dark corners of her thoughts. Had he seen the picture of her? Were there others? Colin had found no other related images of her, and the master file seemed to have been deleted, but still the question remained. And what made it worse, what would continue to burn her in the quiet moments when sleep wouldn't come, was the knowledge that she would never truly know the answer. The site itself had crashed not long after Hayes was taken into custody, the IT boys saying it was hit by some kind of recursive virus that corrupted the data. When they confronted Hayes, he only gave a small, proud smile and a shrug of the shoulders.

Little bastard.

She felt the urge to call Doug, to talk to him about it all, but knew she couldn't. With Burns on the warpath, going near him at the moment would be suicide. And besides, if she did, what would she say? Thank him for trying to look after her, for keeping the existence of the picture a secret and her out of it, or curse him for making her an accomplice in his lies? She didn't know, but still the urge remained. And she knew she would give in to it sooner or later.

Knew too that it was the reason she was staying away from Rebecca. After all, how would the conversation with her go? "Look, I'm sorry, but I've got a hell of a secret that I can only talk to your boyfriend about. You okay if I do that over a takeaway and a bottle of wine? Just the two of us? Thanks."

No. Maybe not.

So, instead, she fell back on what she knew and hit the gym. She worked out almost frantically, lifting weights heavier than she normally would, letting the burning in her muscles wash through her, blotting out all other thoughts. And at the end of every set, she found herself checking her phone, just to make sure there hadn't been a call.

Finally, sweaty and shaking and unable to do any more, she swiped a numb hand over the screen and unlocked the phone. Accessed the iTunes library and killed the music blaring through her earphones. Then, on an impulse, she tapped out a text message, let her finger hover over the *Send* key then hit it.

Time for one more answer.

57

Janet MacFarlane clamped the cigarette between her lips, fingers trembling as she stabbed at its weaving tip with her lighter. She cursed, took a long, steadying breath and finally managed to get it lit, sucking on the filter greedily, swallowing the smoke and the bitter, acrid taste as she closed her eyes.

She was standing outside the hospital, near the entrance to the A&E department. She considered her options then headed up the hill and onto the path that snaked around the back of the hospital. She knew there was a helicopter pad at the top of the hill, wished suddenly that there was a copter sitting on it, waiting to take her away from here and the pulped mess of a husband she had just stepped away from.

He was stable, the doctors had said. He should have been dead from the injuries he had suffered, the trauma of the beating and the knife wounds that wrapped their way up his arms like bloody tattoos. While there were no guarantees, he was strong, and his vitals were improving.

"Cause for cautious optimism, Mrs MacFarlane," one of the doctors had told her, a thin smear of a man with nervous eyes, a bald head and a smile that made Janet want to cave his face in.

She felt a sudden stab of dark fury lance through her, mixing with something more cancerous than the smoke from the cigarette. She felt heat rise behind her eyes and swallowed down the tears that threatened to overwhelm her. Crying was for the weak. And now, more than ever, she needed to be strong.

She dialled the number and held the phone to her ear. It seemed to ring forever before it was answered.

"Hello?"

The voice was so cool and controlled that Janet had to suppress the urge to throw the phone to the pavement and grind it beneath her foot. She tossed the cigarette instead. "It's me," she said, hearing the raw edge of jagged anger in her voice and doing nothing to hide it.

"Ah, Mrs MacFarlane, what an unexpected pleasure," the voice oozed from the phone, the undercurrent telling her the absolute opposite was true. "Tell me, how is your husband?"

Janet's veneer of control shattered. "How the fuck do you think? You beat him half to death ye fuckin' psycho!" she spat.

"Ah, but I didn't kill him, did I, Mrs MacFarlane? Just as we agreed when you called me to tell me what he was doing."

Janet crushed the bridge of her nose between her thumb and forefinger. "I thought you were going to gie him a skelp, is all! Woulda done him nae harm to know there are things he should-nae be looking into. But this? You crossed a line."

"Oh, did I, Mrs MacFarlane? I apologise if I was over-enthusiastic with your husband, but please, try to remember you came to me. And that, in case you were in any doubt, was the right thing to do. I would caution you not to ruin that choice now by being foolish."

"Foolish?" Janet cried, then bit her lip. Calm. Strong. For Rab. And Douglas. "Ye didnae have to hurt him so badly," she whispered.

There was a pause on the line. When he spoke again, the voice was warmer. Marginally. "I am sorry, Mrs MacFarlane. Truly. You see, I get so few opportunities to express myself, and, as you can imagine, it's been a trying time. So I was a little exuberant. Is there anything I can do to atone?"

Janet bit back the response that seared across her mind, along with images of knives and bolt cutters and power tools.

"Ye can leave us alone for a start," she said. "I saw everything that happened wi' that bastard Leonard on the news. I'll keep quiet, nae one will hear about you from me, but you leave us alone, alright? Me, Rab and Douglas. You call that psycho McBride off, now. Alright?"

"You have nothing to fear on that score, Mrs MacFarlane, I've already seen to it that Mr McBride will not be an issue anymore."

There was a cold amusement in the response that made Janet's skin crawl. "And whit about Douglas?" she asked. "The boy might keep asking questions. If he does, I dinnae want him hurt. Because if he is, I promise I'll gie him and his pals all the answers they want. And I don't gie a fuck who you are, who you know or what you could do to me. You've used up yer favours with what ye did to Rab."

"Mrs MacFarlane, are you threatening me?"

"Naw, son," she said, suddenly craving another cigarette, "ah'm promising. You hurt Douglas or anyone of mine from now on and I'll scream your name from the rooftops. I promise."

The hiss of static filled the line again. When he spoke, his voice was colder than mortuary steel. "Very well, I shall leave Mr McGregor alone. But if he persists in an awkward line of questioning, I trust I can rely on you to deal with him?"

"Aye, I'll watch out for the boy, you can count on that."

"Very well. Goodbye, Mrs MacFarlane. I hope your husband recovers soon. And when he does, I trust you will ensure his silence."

The line went dead before she could reply, leaving her with a mouthful of expletives and a gutful of fury.

She lit another cigarette, held it close to her face, the heat caressing her skin. She had, she told herself, done the right thing. Warning Rab off was better than letting him blunder around and get killed for what he might find. She knew secrets her husband never would, never could, and she had bought her safety through years of favours, blind eyes and payoffs. Sorting problems that needed to be sorted, making sure the Falcon's Rest was watched when it needed to be. Protected when it had to be. It was business.

But it wouldn't have been to Rab. Janet could rationalise it, he would not. If he had found out about the Devils, and what they were interested in, he would have gone to Doug. And then torn the whole thing down around their ears. And he would have died for it.

As it was, he was lying in a hospital bed, bloodied and broken. But he had the chance to recover. To live. The doctors had told her. Cautious optimism.

It was a high price to pay. But then, she thought, deals with the Devil were always costly.

· · ·

He placed the phone on the desk slowly, considered it for a moment. While frustrating, he had been expecting the call, and he had already guessed what she would want.

Yes, he had gone too far with MacFarlane. The price of losing control, allowing himself to vent. It had been a foolish risk to take, but he had been unable to resist, especially with the stupidity of McBride and the incompetence of Hayes adding to his problems.

But, he thought, Mark had done his job in the end: changing the website logs and phone records to point the focus onto Michael Leonard. When – or if – he woke up, he would deny everything, but to no avail. The evidence was overwhelming, cemented by his own desperate bid to take his own life to avoid justice. And Alicia could be trusted to stay quiet. She always had.

He smiled as he pulled the letter opener from his desk drawer, considering it. It was a beautiful item, an elegant and understated sculpture in polished steel, identical to the one he had given to Michael Leonard when he had joined the Devils all those years ago. He remembered plunging it into Redmonds' chest, the look of surprise on his stupid face replaced by a growing terror as he realised something was terribly wrong.

The only small irritation was McGregor. Despite Janet MacFarlane's promise, he would watch the reporter closely. And if he got too close to the truth, he would act.

He placed the letter opener back into the drawer and stood, ready to leave his office. He had a busy day ahead. An interminable meeting of the Justice Committee, speaking in a debate on police funding in the main chamber, then the long, slow torture of constituency business. At least he had the reception in the Garden Lobby of the Parliament to look forward to later. It was, according to the press release, a gathering to celebrate the passing in the last parliament of the Abusive Behaviour and Sexual Harm Bill – or the 'Revenge Porn Bill', as it was more commonly known. It was designed to make the sharing of intimate pictures of former partners a criminal offence. He had voted in favour of it enthusiastically, spoken in support of it during the debate process. And tonight he would celebrate the passing of the Bill.

And no one there, from the catering staff to the First Minister, would give his smile and good humour a second thought. But he would know. And he would remember. If the conversation became tedious, he would smile more widely, nod attentively, secretly feasting on the sweet reminiscences of earlier in the day. Of his last conversation with Vic McBride. Of the look of confused terror in those dull, feral eyes as he drove the letter opener up into the soft, yielding flesh under his jaw. Of the satisfying crunch and meaty shudder as the blade hit the top of McBride's mouth and dug into his upper palate. The glorious warmth of hot blood peppering his face; the feral pleasure of jerking the blade back then burying it in his temple as he fell, the metal passing through the bone and into the pathetic lump of tissue that passed for McBride's brain.

He smiled at the memory. Tonight, he would be a sated predator, prowling amongst his prey. And as he did, he would also think of the Devils, of the images and videos and memories they had shared. He might even nod hello to one or two of them who were attending tonight.

They would be there. In plain sight. Amongst the sheep and cattle. And they would be watching.

58

The key chittered around the lock, tapping out an erratic beat that echoed down the stairwell. He cursed under his breath, flexed his hand and tried again. He got the key into the lock and turned it smoothly, a gentle ripple of cramp running up his arm in protest at the movement.

Better.

Once inside the flat, he paused for a moment to make sure the locks were secured and the cricket bat was close to the door. With Michael Leonard in hospital and the laptop and flash drive in police custody, Doug didn't expect to see Vic McBride any time soon, but it still paid to be cautious. Just in case.

He made his way through to the living room and collapsed onto the couch. Retrieved the bottle of whisky from underneath his seat and placed it on the coffee table. He felt he deserved it, especially after the day he had just had. Another round of interviews at Gayfield Square police station accompanied by a lawyer arranged by Walter. When he heard what had happened at Paradigm, he had made sure Doug had a lawyer with him at all times, sensing a series of articles about an embarrassed police force attempting to flay the brave *Tribune* reporter who uncovered a sex abuse conspiracy and unmasked a murderer.

The Chief Constable – Calamity Cameron as he had come to be known after his live press conference – made grave statements about fully investigating Doug's involvement with the case, and uncovering any procedural errors that officers may have made. "And rest assured," he had said, staring into a camera with all the authority and gravitas he could muster, "if there are charges to be laid, we will lay them."

Doug knew that Burns was on the warpath, looking for an excuse to charge him with everything from perverting the course of justice to the Burke and Hare murders, but he had a feeling he wouldn't get too far. With the links to a high-ranking member of the Police Board, this was a story that had the potential to embarrass Police Scotland for a long time to come. The last thing they needed was a crime reporter trawling over the details in the witness box every day for a month in a trial. No, they would let it go. But Doug would give Burns a wide berth for a while. Just in case.

Unless, of course, Becky spoke to him.

She had grabbed him as he was leaving Gayfield Square. He had known there was trouble the moment he saw her, the stiffness in her walk and the hard, pinched set of her face telegraphing her mood before she even spoke.

"Hi," she said, her eyes refusing to meet his. "Can we talk for a minute?"

"Sure," he said, beckoning for the door. "But not here, okay? How about across the road?" He nodded his head towards Leith Walk, and the row of pubs across from Gayfield Square.

They walked in silence, finding a small booth at the back of the bar. Doug went to get the drinks, ordering Becky a soda and lime, and a Guinness for himself. He set the drinks down and slid in opposite her.

"So," he said, trying to ignore the growing knot of tension in his gut. "What's up? Imagine you're run off your feet with the Chief and the Leonards fallout."

She twitched a smile at him, toyed with the straw in her glass. "You could say," she said then fell into a silence that Doug felt compelled to fill.

"Look, Becky, I'm sorry for all the shit I've caused with this. Really I am. I just had to see him, you know, after everything that happened…"

She jerked her head up, tears in her eyes. "Tell me about that, Doug. What has been happening? From the morning that Susie turned up at your flat after hearing Redmonds died to you confronting Leonard, what the fuck has been going on? 'Cause there's a hell of a lot I don't seem to know."

He took a gulp of his Guinness without tasting it. "Becky, what do you mean? Susie came to me because I knew about her and Redmonds. I helped her out the best I could. Then I got sent the laptop and the flash drive, and you know the rest from there."

"Ah, but do I Doug?" she asked, rummaging around in her bag. "You told Burns and Susie that the laptop was sent to you. Tell me, was that before or after you went to London to see Colin and Hal? And was it after you'd taken a wee night-time drive to Portobello the night Redmonds died?"

Doug felt his mouth go dry. "What?" he said, his voice a coarse whisper. "What do you…?"

"This," she said, handing him a print-out. "It came back the other day. Taken on a CCTV camera at Lauder Road on the junction down to Portobello High Street."

Doug studied the image. It was a grainy black-and-white shot of the junction with a time and date stamp in the bottom right corner. Just to the left of centre, heading towards the traffic lights and the camera there was a three-quarter shot of a sleek, grey car, a shape hunched over the steering wheel. Doug couldn't make out the details, but he didn't need to. He knew his own car when he saw it.

"Don't worry," Becky said, easing the image out of his hand, "Burns hasn't seen it. Nothing conclusive anyway, just another vehicle in the approximate area we were able to track Redmonds to before he died. But it got me thinking, Doug. How come you were up when Susie called on you? She said you were, felt guilty about disturbing you. And when did you get that laptop?"

Doug felt his mouth drop open. "Becky, I… I…"

She slammed her hand down on the table, the drinks jostling

precariously. Doug felt the collective gaze from the bar fall on them. "For fuck's sake, Doug," she hissed, leaning into him, "please, tell me what the fuck is going on. I know there's more to this than you and Susie are saying. I want to help. But I need to know. So, please," –an edge of pleading quivered in her voice and eyes – "just tell me."

Doug looked at her dark eyes and the slightly crooked set of her mouth that he always liked. Tell her, he thought. Tell her the truth. Tell her everything.

But if he did, it wouldn't just be his secret and guilt he would be exposing, it would be Colin and Hal's. And Susie's. After everything, could he do that to her? Leave her exposed and vulnerable again, when he had already given so much to try and keep her safe?

He pushed away from the table. "I'm sorry, Becky," he said, finding he couldn't hold her gaze now. "But I don't know what you mean. Yeah, I was out for a drive that night before Susie arrived – you know I don't sleep well with my arm being the way it is. But that's it. The laptop was sent to me, I don't know by who, and as soon as I found the website, I called in Susie. I went to see Colin and Hal to collect my thoughts after everything that's happened. I know I've been a bit all over the place. And I want to fix that."

Doug leaned forward, trying to give her his best reassuring smile. She studied his face for a moment, her skin pale, eyes magnified by tears, and then she shook her head slowly.

"No, Doug, no. I know you're lying to me, keeping something from me. And you're not the only one. I've put up with a lot of shit from you, Doug – the drinking, the late nights, the times you've asked me to pull a few strings, or get you a step ahead of everyone else in an inquiry – but this is too much. You've crossed a line."

"Becky, I…"

She shook her head again as she stood up, pulling on her jacket and turning away from him. The sound of her heels on the bar floor were like gunshots as he watched her go. He thought of following her, of trying to catch her up and explain.

But he knew he wouldn't. There were some things he just couldn't tell her. For both their sakes.

Now, sitting alone in his flat, he felt a prickling in his eyes, wiped angrily at the tears that were forming there. She was right, he had put her through a lot of shit, expecting her to be there. He had taken advantage and used her, fallen into the comfortable illusion that she was getting as much out of their relationship as he was.

He grabbed his phone as he reached for the whisky bottle, unthreading the cap. Noticed a text message from Susie, unlocked the phone and left it unread. He flicked through his contacts, got to Becky's number. Hit *Dial*. Listened as it rang and went straight to voicemail. Hung up without leaving a message.

He flicked over to the text message Susie had sent him. He must have missed it earlier, the phone on silent when he was in the police interview room. He read it slowly, as though it was in a language he had never seen before. In a way, he supposed it was. He sat for a moment, listening to the quiet of the flat around him. The gentle swish of the traffic outside, the tick of the clock in the hall. He laid the phone on the arm of the chair, then replaced the cap on the whisky bottle and tossed it onto the opposite couch.

Despite himself, Doug gave a coughing laugh. Then he picked up the phone and slowly, ignoring the pins and needles that crawled up his arm as he moved his hand, he keyed in an answer.

59

Rebecca looked at the phone on the coffee table in front of her, the screen glowing gently as it told her of the missed call from Doug. Not that she had really missed it, she had sat on the couch watching the phone buzz gently on the table, resisting the urge to pick it up and talk to him.

But she couldn't. Not when he was lying to her. Not now. Especially not now.

Rebecca felt her stomach give a sudden watery lurch and launched herself from the sofa for the bathroom, making it just in time. She heaved up the contents of her stomach, gasping for breath as she spat out the last viscous wads of saliva. She closed her eyes for a moment, then flushed, watching as the half-digested remains of dinner swirled down the toilet.

She turned to the sink, grabbed the bottle of mouthwash and took a slug. As she rinsed, her eyes were pulled to the small shelf that sat below the mirror. As well as her toothbrush, toothpaste and floss, it held another item, not much bigger then a pen.

She picked it up, looked at it again with a sense of numb disbelief and wonder. *You've crossed a line*, she had told Doug. Was she trying to tell him then, to drop a hint? The truth was, they both had. Not just one line, but two. She looked again at the small window in the pen, at the two clear pink lines that sat there and the printed word *Pregnant* that seemed to scream out at her.

Rebecca took a deep shuddering breath, placed the test back on the shelf, stared at it. She thought of telling Doug. Would he be excited, terrified, overwhelmed? Would he want to be a father or would he run a mile? And would this bring them back together, compel him to tell her the truth about what really happened that night, or would it drive them further apart?

And was that, ultimately, what she wanted? She loved him, but was she – were *they*, she thought, the sudden realisation that she was no longer a single entity giving her gut another bilious squeeze – better off without him? Would a baby make him a better man, or merely deepen the problems he had with his drinking and secrecy and the obsessive streak that drove him on in pursuit of the next exclusive?

He wasn't a bad man, but she was realistic enough to know he was a flawed one. And brittle after everything that had happened. And now there was this. She remembered the night it happened; they had been out, come back here and, in their semi-drunken fumbling, got lost enough not to bother with a condom. She thought back, remembering the sensation of him coming inside her, the terror and sudden panic swept away by the crashing waves of her orgasm. It seemed so long ago now.

She picked up the test again, her hand shaking slightly. She felt the tears slide down her face as she focused on the window and that one, simple word: *Pregnant*. She rubbed at it gently with her thumb, again stunned by the enormity of it and what it meant. A new life. A new start.

Maybe.

She wiped away her tears, straightened her back and headed for the living room. Picked up the phone and scrolled to the selfie they had taken in St Andrews, her leaning into him, both of them smiling at the camera. What, she thought, would their child look like? Would they have his nose, her eyes? Would he – or she – have Doug's unruly hair and crooked smile, or her dimples and chin? What else would he or she get from them? She found herself excited and terrified by the thought. So many possibilities. So many questions.

And all of them would be answered.

In time.

Acknowledgements

They say writing is a lonely occupation but, if you're lucky, you never write a book alone: there are always friendly faces waiting when you pull your head from the glare of the screen. To Bob McDevitt, Sara, Craig, Laura and everyone at Contraband, Douglas Skelton, James Oswald, Craig Russell, everyone at the scene of the crime and, of course, Alasdair Sim and Elaine Cropley, thanks for keeping me company on the journey.

Special thanks to Michael Nicolson for the technical pointers and the patient answering of my incessant questions about laptops and security – I owe you a fine death, sir, and I promise to deliver.

And, lastly, to my wife, Fiona, who kept me on the path and kept me going, every step of the way. You and the kids are the only company I ever need.

Love you, B. Always.

Neil Broadfoot's high-octane debut, *Falling Fast*, introduced readers to the world of Edinburgh-based investigative journalist Doug McGregor and DS Susie Drummond. Widely praised by critics, crime fiction authors and readers alike, it was shortlisted for both the Dundee International Prize and the prestigious Deanston Scottish Crime Book of the Year Award, immediately establishing Neil as a fixture on the Tartan Noir scene.

Before writing fiction, Neil worked as a journalist for fifteen years at national and local newspapers, covering some of the biggest stories of the day. A poacher turned gamekeeper, Neil moved into communications, providing media relations advice for a variety of organisations, from public bodies and government to a range of private clients.

Neil is married to Fiona and has two daughters. An adopted Fifer, he lives in Dunfermline, where he started his career as a local reporter.